F
R27   Reich, Tova.
            Master of the return.

MASTER
OF THE
RETURN

MASTER OF THE RETURN

Tova Reich

A Helen and Kurt Wolff Book
Harcourt Brace Jovanovich, Publishers
San Diego   New York   London

HBJ

This is a work of fiction.
All the events and characters of this book are
products of the author's imagination, and
any resemblance to actual persons, living or dead,
is unintended.

Parts of this book were written with the generous support of a Fellowship for
Creative Writers from the National Endowment for the Arts, and some of the
writing was done in the tranquil setting of Mishkenot Sha'ananim in Jerusalem.
The first chapter, "Bring Us to Uman," appeared in *Moment* magazine.

Library of Congress Cataloging-in-Publication Data
Reich, Tova.
Master of the return.
"A Helen and Kurt Wolff book."
I. Title.
PS3568.E4763M37   1988   813'.54   87–19246

ISBN 0-15-157880-X

Designed by Beth Tondreau Design

Printed in the United States of America

First edition

A B C D E

*In memory of
my mother,
Miriam Weiss*

Contents

MASTER
OF THE
RETURN

BRING US
TO UMAN

The pages from the journal of Samuel Himmelhoch were
found under a jerrycan in the tomb of Hannah and her seven
sons. Abba Nissim, the caretaker of this and other holy graves
in the old cemetery of Safad, noticed the jerrycan when he
entered to light some candles for a tour group of Hadassah
ladies. In his interesting English, which he had polished during
his imprisonment by the British, Nissim recited a spare version
of the story of the martyr Hannah, whose seven boys had been
slain, each in turn, after they refused to bow to the pagan idol
of Antiochus Epiphanes. "Sevenfold woe to smithereen a
mother's heart," Nissim said. His eyes roamed from somewhere above the pastel hairdos of the grandmothers, which

1

were covered with glossy white skullcaps provided by the keepers of the cemetery, to the Styrofoam jerrycan beyond. He led the women in a brief prayer and instructed them in the custom of placing a stone on the graves as a token of their visit. Then he stooped out through the low passageway and, with a sorrowful nod of his head, acknowledged the coins that the ladies dropped into his cupped palm as they filed out. A white pigeon perched on Nissim's shoulder and pecked at the bread crumbs that could always be found in the web of his white beard. Without asking permission, the ladies raised their cameras and shot. For the sake of earning a living, Abba Nissim had long since resigned himself to being a graven image.

As the women trudged up the hill to their waiting bus, Abba Nissim returned to the tomb and lit another candle. Under ordinary circumstances, the jerrycan, which he recognized at once as belonging to Himmelhoch, would have made no impression at all on Nissim. Himmelhoch had often spent the night in this crypt, sleeping for brief intervals but mostly rising to pray in midnight solitude and to break his heart under the stars at the grave of the daughter of Rabbi Nahman of Bratslav. As for Abba Nissim, he had done more than simply allow Himmelhoch to squat in Hannah's sepulcher; he had given Samuel Himmelhoch his blessings. For Himmelhoch was a penitent and, before his return to the true path, had strewn many horrible sins all across the Americas, Europe, Africa, and Asia, not to mention his specialization in Israel. It was almost as if Himmelhoch had exhausted all the varieties of transgressions when he finally saw the light, and, from the point of view of Nissim, himself a pious descendant of ten generations of inhabitants of the mystical city of Safad, Himmelhoch's devotions were to be encouraged. What was different now was that, by all accounts, no one had seen Samuel Himmelhoch for nearly a year, and this included his young son, Akiva, and his wife, Ivriya, whom people were beginning to call Ivriya the Agunah, Ivriya the Abandoned Wife, and who was herself already seeking confirmation of her husband's death so that she could be released into widowhood.

Abba Nissim unscrewed the cap of the jerrycan and raised his candle to investigate what was inside. There was a little water left, and it had sprouted life, green and brown: the Lord is wondrous in His ways. The can must have been there for a long time, maybe even longer than twelve months. How could Nissim have failed to notice it? Perhaps it was because he himself had made no attempt to search for marks of Himmelhoch's passage, trusting that the penitent was wandering in expiation from grave to grave somewhere on this planet.

Yet, more and more, the general belief was that Himmelhoch was dead. Himmelhoch's attachment to his son, Akiva, was famous, and it was well known, too, that he had taken upon himself the solemn task of educating the boy in righteousness. Never, except on one occasion, had he separated himself from the child for more than three days, and now almost a year had passed and Akiva was already forgetting what his father had meant. But what was more significant was that Samuel Himmelhoch had acquired the aura of a memory or a legend, for the attainment of which one must be properly dead. Even reports of sightings had the quality of vision or hallucination. For example, a hiker in the Wadi Amud between Meron and Safad claimed that he had seen Samuel Himmelhoch crouching in the niche of a cave above a fresh-water spring, chewing on a sprig of anise. A woman swore that, while she was immersing herself in the ritual bath of the Ari on the fringe of the old

3

cemetery of Safad, Himmelhoch had risen from the water. Reports also came from the south: that he was seen floating with his beard absolutely perpendicular in the pool of a cave in Liftah, outside Jerusalem. And even from Europe: that he was running the lighting effects at the Crazy Horse Saloon in Paris; that he was managing the *son et lumière* extravaganza on the Acropolis. These last two reports were false without question. But the curious thing was that, though all these accounts were blatantly outrageous, each one contained a reference to water or to light, which compelled the knowledgeable listener to consider for a moment before rejecting it. As a penitent, Himmelhoch was known for his almost fanatic attention to the cleanliness of his body and his attire (Ivriya had often had to wash his robes again and again before he was satisfied that not a single stain was visible), and, in his former life, while he was still a conscious sinner, he had traveled widely and made fortunes inventing spectacular lighting effects for some of the most notorious rock groups. Now, as Abba Nissim peered into the jerrycan, he read the contents as a sign from heaven that Samuel Himmelhoch's body had been translated into worms and maggots.

But what about Himmelhoch's soul? When Abba Nissim lifted the jerrycan and discovered the journal underneath, green and sodden, his brief pang of mourning turned into rejoicing. For here in these pages was the reflection of Himmelhoch's soul, a witness to its total emigration to the next life. Nissim transported the damp manuscript into the sunlight and spread the pages out on the tombstones to dry. The words of Samuel Himmelhoch emerged, like clarity and understanding after long confusion. Those words were read by Abba Nissim. Afterward they were copied and studied by many others, even

4

disseminated as a sort of underground pamphlet among the more zealous and extreme converts to the Hassidism of Rabbi Nahman of Bratslav. For several years after its discovery, the original manuscript was preserved and displayed in a lucite case at Uman House in Jerusalem's Old City. Every morning a fresh bouquet of rosemary and myrtle was placed beside it. "Each blade of grass has a melody of its own," Rabbi Nahman used to say, and the children of Uman House were taught to listen closely for the song that the flowers sang to Himmelhoch's journal. On the day the Israel Defense Forces moved in with their bulldozers and leveled Uman House, as well as several of the adjacent Arab structures in the Moslem Quarter of the Old City of Jerusalem, Himmelhoch's journal was pulverized. Thereafter it became know in certain circles as "The Other Burned Book." All of it reverted to rubble and vapor, a circular, aesthetic culmination that would certainly have pleased Samuel Himmelhoch himself had he been around to enjoy it. Fortunately, copies of the manuscript still exist for the enlightenment of anyone engaged in a quest like Himmelhoch's, and even those not similarly involved might find in its pages something of interest.

From
The Journal of Samuel Himmelhoch

It is for you, Akiva, that I put this down. I am sitting now at a table in the same room in Meron, above the tomb of Rabbi Simeon bar Yohai, where I once fasted for six consecutive days, shunning food as well as all speech except prayer, awaiting an answer from the Creator of the Universe to the question that vexed me then—whether or not to marry your mother and give you life. The thirty-third day of the Omer has just ended. You are asleep on the very bed I rested upon during my ordeal, your mouth open, your shaven head strange and raw, your fine sidelocks, all that remains of your first hair, moist against your cheeks. You are having a dream that I shall never know. I have just risen to remove your hands from your private parts. You are three years old. This midnight hour, instead of lamenting the destruction of the Temple and the loss of everything holy, I have decided to write for you.

Akiva, today I have wrested you from your mother, from your babyhood, and made you my own. For the next ten years, until you are a bar mitzvah, all your sins will fall on my head. Be a good boy, Akiva. My wretched head is weighed down with more than enough sins of my own patent. Ambition, and all the corruption that springs from desire, from wanting and wanting, has always been my greatest sin, and still is, God have mercy. I watch you sleep and think how satisfying it would be for me if you grew up to become the holy man of your generation, maybe even the harbinger of the Messiah. I want to rear you for hideous suffering.

Do you remember how it was this morning, Akiva? Already that seems centuries ago. We stepped off the bus in Meron, you and I. You were exploding with mischief and adventure, your long curls bouncing as you danced along to keep up with me. How crowded it was—do you remember?—as we made the slow, short ascent to the sacred tomb, the bonfire blazing on its roof. But a path was somehow cleared for us as we advanced; you have a magical quality, a glow, that compels people to give way—they don't understand why themselves—as before a special personage. I recognize this aura in you, Akiva. It is a gift

6

you must use wisely. Singing all the way you were, "Praises to You, Bar Yohai, Praises!," a little bow and a quiver of arrows strapped to your back. We passed the lovers, brazen in their open embraces. We passed the prostitutes, the dandies, the card players, the smokers, the families slaughtering and roasting sheep, grease illuminating their faces. We passed the tourists, the idlers, the soldiers, the artists, the intellectuals, the souvenir hawkers, the food vendors, the journalists, the photographers, the teen-agers chained to their guitars, the bandits, the hustlers, the beggars. All these deluded souls we passed. Through this grotesque carnival we made our way, you and I, and for me it was like a synopsis of my profane career. Closer to the tomb, near the pinnacle, the secular world was at our backs. Here were men and boys swaying in prayer, chanting, pleading for a hint to the enigma. Farther up, at the very entrance at last, the holy men sat, immersed in the subtleties of the Zohar. We moved from one to the next, you and I, Akiva, like other fathers and sons gathered there, and each holy man in turn raised his shears, blessed your head, and cut off a lock of your hair, until your blessed head, except for your *payot*, was completely shorn. Akiva, I saw your reflection in the eyes of the holy men, and I could sense that they instantly recognized you to be exceptional; they knew you, Akiva, to be someone apart from the other three-year-old boys receiving their first haircuts this Lag BaOmer day. Dutifully I collected every precious hair that fell to the ground and stuffed it all in the little brown velvet pouch your mother gave me. I shall carry this back to her as an offering. Your mother, like all women, is nothing but a sentimental materialist, she should be healthy.

Inside, I prayed as I had never prayed before, poured out my soul, first at the grave of the incomparable cabalist Rabbi

7

Simeon, and then at the tomb of his son Eleazar, in the center of the chamber. You, Akiva, circulated in the crowd, receiving gifts of sweets from everyone, as if they were your due. When we stepped outside again it was bright noon, and there you stood under the spring sun, dazzling in your white silk robe, your *tzitzit* with the dark horizontal stripe and the long fringes, the bow and arrow on your back, and, on your freshly shaven head, a skullcap of embossed gold velvet. Whose eyes were not drawn to you? You, an aristocrat, a revelation. Everyone stopped you. "Little prince, where are you from?" they asked. And upon each one you bestowed the same reply: "I am from Uman," you said.

All I can do now is to ponder this strange answer that came spontaneously out of your sweet mouth, as if a spirit were speaking in your voice. I am convinced that it is this answer of yours that has moved me to sit down and write for you tonight. How am I, your father, your teacher, your mentor and guide, to respond to your response? For on the simplest level it is a lie. Am I to chastise or punish you for it, then? For you know as well as I that you pushed your way into this life through the mortal screams and unclean blood of your mother, not in Uman, but on a stainless-steel delivery table in the Hadassah Hospital in Jerusalem. I saw it with my own eyes above a mask, and there are documents to prove it. Officially, my Akiva, you are a native of Israel, and in eighteen years from the date inscribed on your birth certificate the earthly powers will summon you to battle and bloodshed. I pray to God that you will refuse this earthly call in favor of heaven's service. Your physical being, as far as I know, has never been in Uman. You live—eat, sleep, play, cry—in our apartment in the Bokharan Quarter of Jerusalem. You climb the pomegranate tree in

8

the courtyard; you build with your blocks on the stone floor; your diapers hang from the clothesline on the porch. Yet, as I continue to meditate on your answer, I believe, more and more, that there is a truth and depth to it that at first, in my blindness, were hidden from me. For you, Akiva, have grasped that in your pure essence you have already come from and dwelt within the very place that I myself have struggled to reach for so many years, a place where, black sinner that I am, I have failed and failed again to arrive. When were you in Uman? Perhaps before you were born, when all knowledge was yours. Forty days before your descent to this earth, the angel Gabriel tapped you between your nose and your upper lip, causing you to forget all you knew, but he tapped lightly, Akiva. I have often observed a divine smoothness in that part of your face. I have often been struck by the residues of heavenly knowledge coming from your mouth.

How many times have you heard me imploring the Almighty: "You have brought us up to here, bring us to Uman"? How many times, Akiva? Yet you sat there calmly, listening to me sing myself into a frenzy of longing. All the while you must surely have pitied me, knowing, as you do, that He had already brought you to the very place where He has deemed me unworthy to be taken. Uman: I can see it in my mind's eye. The holy grave of Rav Nahman, now, alas, in the backyard of a Ukrainian peasant woman whom the devout must stuff with chocolates in exchange for the privilege of praying there for an hour. One hour is all we ask, yet how difficult it is to attain— and for me, so far, impossible. One pathetic hour among all the hours in a lifetime to recite the ten specific psalms that Rav Nahman had designated, a simple quest on the surface, but, miserable sinner that I am, beyond my powers. Yet I have persevered. The reward is incalculable: an end to nocturnal emissions. This is the specific reward, priceless in itself, but to my mind it is a mystical metaphor for the more general rewards—a cessation of the cravings for food, money, fame, sleep, desire, the whole corrupt baggage. These, truly, are the benefits that Rav Nahman implied would accrue to all those who took the trouble to come and say the ten powerful psalms at his holy grave in Uman. In this manner he would repair and remedy their souls. Others have deserved it. Why not I? I have tried so many times, Akiva, more times than I have paper to write you about it. Yet Rav Nahman said that it is all the more worthwhile to persevere toward a goal that has been thwarted again and again. "No one was ever given an obstacle that he is unable to overcome," Rav Nahman said. And in his tales, which you love to hear so much, Akiva, he describes many arduous quests packed with terrible obstacles. The obstacles were placed there for a purpose. The message is for me: I must never give up. But what a paradox it is, living as I do in Jerusalem, the summit of the earth, to be unable to make this descent to the heights. Akiva, you are blessed for having come from there. You must never forget your source. That is why I want you to pay attention as I record for you only a few of my attempts to be brought to Uman, sorry as they were, and I am doing this at the risk that you will judge your own father to be nothing but a ridiculous and pathetic creature, of no consequence whatever.

Where to begin? You, Akiva, were born in the month of Iyar, on the thirty-third day of the Omer. Upon this day, almost two millennia ago, there was a respite in the devastating plague that had begun on Pesach and lasted until Shavuot. This was the plague that wiped out twenty-four thousand of Rabbi Akiva's students for the sin of not sufficiently honoring one another. For Rabbi Akiva, a man who knew how to laugh, the thirty-third of the Omer was a day of rejoicing, and therefore I called you Akiva. I hoped—indeed, I truly believe—that you are the *gilgul*, the reincarnation, of the happy soul of the sublime Rabbi Akiva. It was in the month of Av, less than a year before your birth, that I had carried out my decision to marry your mother.

My decision to marry your mother came, as I have said to you, after rigorous contemplation and grave, self-imposed abstinence. It was not because of your mother's invalidism that I hesitated. Rather, it was the memory of Ivriya riding her horses bare-breasted in Rosh Pinna before her fall. The lust in her eyes as she galloped, to which I myself can testify—could such bold and profane passion ever truly be dispelled, or, at the very least, deflected in the service of the sacred? And her turn to religion—was it genuine, or was it the consequence of her accident, or was it, even more basely, her scheming for marriage? So I fasted and prayed, and afterward I walked with a stick through Wadi Amud from Meron to Safad, dipped my body into the clear and cold rainwater of the *mikvah* of the Ari, and consulted with Abba Nissim beside the grave of Rabbi Yosef Karo. Abba Nissim is a holy man. He converses with the birds. "It would be an act of great *hesed,*" Abba Nissim said. I myself insisted upon pushing your mother's wheelchair under the canopy, her withered legs modestly arranged beneath her off-white dress. Ultimate kindness and charity, as Abba Nissim had counseled.

All this happened, Akiva, only a short while after my return from one of my journeys toward Uman. You understand the problem. I cannot simply buy a ticket and board a plane to Moscow or Kiev. No visas are granted to Israeli citizens. We lost that privilege in the year 1967 of the Common Era, as a result of one of our state's hollow victories in its stubborn campaign to pre-empt the work of the Messiah. But it's just as well: the Russians, despite themselves, are agents of the divine, for the difficulty they created is but another *meniah,* only one more obstacle, of the sort that Rav Nahman, may his memory be a blessing, considered desirable and enriching. In that trip before my wedding I sought to emulate, in my minor and limited way, the great journey that Rav Nahman had taken, though his was in the other direction, from Medvedevka in the Ukraine to the port of Haifa in Eretz Israel. My plan was to go to Istanbul, Rav Nahman's stopping place and the very city in which his great-grandfather, the sainted Baal Shem-Tov himself, had received the vision that warned him to turn back from his own journey to the Holy Land. Akiva, how can I be so bold as to continue to describe my own puny trek in the same breath with the pilgrimages of these great *tzaddikim?* I flew from Tel Aviv to Istanbul. It was as effortless as holding your breath. My plan was to remain in Istanbul as long as was necessary to devise some mode of making my way across the Black Sea to Odessa.

Istanbul is a corrupt city. I had passed through once before, for a short spell only, and to its corruption I had given my donation. Corruption has weight, Akiva. It sinks to the bottom and becomes the stratum upon which everything else is built. I have observed this phenomenon in West Germany, too, where I spent lost time with the electroshock musicians I used to consort with, and none of the quantities of health food that

were consumed there, none of the Hindu asceticism they dab-
bled in there, none of the clean steel-and-glass structures they
erected there, none of the beefy fists beating breasts there,
none of the fine social causes they took up with Teutonic
efficiency there—none of these could disguise the bed of poison on which all of it rested. Akiva, I ask myself if the same
is not true in my own case. Have I, Shmuel Himmelhoch, your
father, succeeded in expunging every remnant of the defile-
ment that was in me before going about the task of creating
this new self? The fact that I have not yet been deemed worthy
of making the passage to Uman speaks for itself.

The last apparition I wanted to meet on my first visit to
Istanbul was another of my kind. This time, however, I headed
directly for the synagogue in the Galata section, hoping to find
a fellow Jew who would offer me hospitality. But because I was
determined to conduct myself as Rav Nahman had done during his stay in the city, no door was opened to me. Like
Nahman, I went about without a top hat, barefoot, no belt to
hold my gabardine together. My hair was still as long and wild
as it had been in the old, bad days, for at that stage in my
penance I had taken the vows of a Nazarite, and I was barred
from cutting my hair. In the eyes of the Jewish establishment
there, I was a lunatic, a menace, an Israeli dropout. I told the
rabbi that my name was Shmulik Onion, and to a leader of the
community I introduced myself as Moshe Dayan. The beadle
inquired if I was a *kohain,* and I informed him that I was an
Essene, but to another I claimed to be a fossil from the ten lost
tribes, and to a fourth yet I said I was a descendant of Sabbatai
Zvi. That last claim truly alarmed them: they are very sensitive
on the subject of false messiahs in Turkey. I played war games
in the marketplace, just as Rav Nahman had, only his were

between the enemy and the French forces of Napoleon, whereas my battles, fought with sticks and savage howls, were between the Moslems and the Zionists. I did all these mad and infantile things, and others even less inspired, variations on the holy Rav Nahman's behavior in Istanbul in the year 1797 of the Common Era, but not a single Turkish Jew remembered or recognized the connection. Rav Nahman subsequently explained his actions as his program to be cursed and reviled by reaching the depths of *katnut*, smallness or degradation, a necessary step in circumventing the obstacles on the road to ascent. But I, dust that I am, was not even worthy of aspiring to degradation. No one invited me to his table for the Sabbath. I was forced to take a room in a hotel and eat alone.

In the hotel I ran into Mohammed, a Libyan I had known in Tangier in the days when I had made a career of a brand of dead-end degradation that Rav Nahman would have associated only with Sodom and Gehenna. What I used to do with Mohammed in those days I would never describe to you, Akiva. Why give you ideas? What purpose would it serve to load your head with such filth? Mohammed had a friend with him, Moustafa. "Sam, you old freak!" Mohammed kissed me on the mouth. "What are you up to these days?" I explained to him that I was trying to get to Uman in the Ukraine to worship at the shrine of an old guru. "Far out, man!" He was scheduled to board a ship for Odessa in two days, and from there to travel overland to a terrorist training camp somewhere off-limits in the belly of Russia. "I'll get you a ride, you son of a whore!" I recalled the story of the young Ishmaelite who had been attracted to Rav Nahman in Haifa, alternating in his attachment between extreme affection and belligerence, promising in the end to arrange a caravan that would bring the holy

14

man to the graves of Tiberias. I interpreted Mohammed's offer as a favorable sign. That Rav Nahman later said he had suffered more from the love of the Ishmaelite than from his hatred was the wisdom I had not absorbed.

Akiva, in order to obtain my heart's desire I was obliged to play along with Mohammed and his pal Moustafa. I had to flatter their notion that my present guise was merely another stage in my development as the ultimate freak; it was tolerable to be so misconstrued, I concluded, for he, Mohammed, had the power to grant, and I, Shmuel, was the abject petitioner. How treacherously easy it is to slip back into the old, despicable mode! Arabs are very convivial on the surface, but beware, Akiva. The real world for them is not what you see; it exists, rather, in the innermost inner courtyard of the house, in the lowest and most hidden chamber of the heart. Ten portions of prostitution were granted to mankind, our sages teach us, of which nine were given to the Arabs.

I pretended to be akin with Mohammed—a fellow Semite. I laughed at what amused him; I shared my bread and fruit with him; I nodded automatically when he reminisced about our days and nights in Tangier, and even offered some rotting memories of my own. It was not the first time in history that a Jew had had to soil his tongue to get what he wanted. The night before we were planning to embark, Mohammed insisted that I smoke hashish with him. I could not risk refusing. Once upon a time, I was never not stoned, not for a single hour of the twenty-four. But since my great change, I am high on the One Above. Only on the festival of Purim do I now allow myself the pleasure of the pipe, for on that day it is actually a *mitzvah* and I do it in the name of heaven. Holy visions float through my head in shades of amber and blue. I am transported. Do you remember how it was last Purim, Akiva? We even gave you a few drags. And what a dance you danced then! A wine cup in your fist, on your head the gilded crown of King Ahashverosh that your mother fashioned for you, every muscle of your strong young body in harmony. You are a splendid dancer, Akiva, just as Ivriya once was. The Bolshoi would grab you, but you will perform for the Lord alone.

So I smoked with Mohammed and Moustafa. I even consumed a cake of pure hashish that Mohammed pressed on me. It is dangerous to refuse an Arab's hospitality. Perhaps it was because I was no longer accustomed to it, perhaps it was because I took in more than I realized, but soon I was staggering to the bed, and then a void sucked me in. I do not even remember getting undressed, but when I awoke late the next morning, all I was wearing were my *tzitzit*. Moustafa was squatting in a corner, lapping a milk porridge from a bowl. "Where is Mohammed?" "On the Black Sea, *habibi.*" "Why didn't he wake me?" "He tried, old man. He whacked you with a stick. He poured a bucket of water on your head. He bit you in a place only others can see. He cursed your mother and your sister. You wouldn't budge. Here, he left you this note: *Auf Wiedersehen,* you Zionist pig. See you in Tel Aviv. *Insh'Al-lah.*" For the record, I no longer consider myself, strictly speaking, a Zionist. The son of Hagar!

Akiva, you know the elusive tale of Rav Nahman's about the king's minister who went out to search for the lost princess? You remember how he found her a captive in the empire of the Evil One, and she told him that, in order to obtain her release, he must go away and yearn for her—long for her totally, pass a full year in pining for her. And on the last day of the year he must fast and not sleep. So he did all this, but then, on the final day, he was tempted by a pretty apple, Akiva, and he put it in his mouth and fell into a deep sleep. When he awoke he asked, "Where am I in the world?" Still he continued on his quest. I, on the other hand, flew home the day I awoke. Why? It became clear to me that I was not ready. I was not yet the king's minister, not deserving to be dispatched on a mission. I was not even the king's most inferior slave. I was at the bottommost level. I had not yet truly succeeded in casting off any of the old shells. Rav Nahman chose Uman as his burial place in order to repair the souls of those Jews who had been killed suddenly in a pogrom in that city, without being given a chance to repent. He, of blessed memory, has the power to remedy the souls of the dead as well as the living. My soul, I understood, was not even primed for correction. From Tel Aviv I took the bus to Meron, where I entered into the period of fasting and prayer I told you about. Akiva, I was not even fulfilling the most basic commandment to be fruitful and multiply. My own seed was decaying inside me, poisoning me. In my pride I had aimed directly for the heights, presumed to leap over even the first and most elementary steps. Where I was in the world, even Nahman couldn't bend down to help me.

This failure to reach Uman, Akiva, was not my first, but for me, up until that time, it was the most painful, and so I describe this one to you in its sordid details and not all the others that preceded it. When I flew to Istanbul I had deluded myself into believing that I had acquired merit. I was wrong. Twice before the disaster in Istanbul I had stood at the Soviet border, a supplicant, once in Finland and the second time in Iran. I was turned away. I had used fake passports. I had worn disguises. The Russians, instructed by heaven, were not deceived. Another time I crossed the Sinai in a Reo, hoping to enter Egypt and stow away on one of the Soviet naval vessels that were still docked, in those days, in the port of Alexandria. A preposterous scheme. It was the Israeli border guards who barred me on that occasion. They, too, were guided by powers they could not name. And those attempts do not include the numerous times I had started walking from wherever I stood— Jaffa Road, Strauss Street, Dizengoff Circle, wherever—and simply put one foot ahead of the other and said to myself, I am going to Uman. It was clear that I dared to walk without having learned to crawl. Even if, on the surface, my behavior seemed impeccable, inside I was tormented by my secret weaknesses and my evil inclinations. Alone in the fields between midnight and dawn, I would confess to God, like a son to his father; I would conceal nothing from Him, I would beg Him to call me when He judged me ready. "Aren't there enough graves for you here in Israel?" your mother, Ivriya, asks. "The whole country is a cemetery." Keep this in mind, Akiva: Our sages, in their wisdom, have cautioned us against indulging in too many conversations with women. Ten portions of speech were allotted to the world, our wise men teach us, of which nine were appropriated by woman.

They used to call her Ivriya the Beauty, and some of the old charm still hovers over her face. All vanity. When she would race, her rich hair blended into the chestnut mane of her favorite stallion. Now it is losing its thickness and shine. What does it matter? She obeys me and conceals every strand under a kerchief, even in bed. I remind her of the righteous married woman who, despite her exemplary charity and virtue, once

18

inadvertently allowed a single hair to show, and though at her death she was admitted to the Garden of Eden, she was condemned to be stuck to the door for eternity by that rebellious strand of hair. Though Ivriya is still as lean as a young boy, her breasts, once her pride and her flag, have been pulled down toward the earth by time and by your suckling, Akiva. You know, not much more than a month has passed since you ceased climbing into her lap and tugging at her blouse. She had sinned with her breasts, and she has been judged. Her legs are wasted—pitiful, really—but still I must fight with her to put on socks. The ground of Jerusalem is holy and one may not tread upon it with naked legs. "But my feet aren't feet any longer, and anyway they sit like stones on the ledge of my wheelchair." Thus she argues. A technicality, I say; everything must be covered. At night I lift her into bed, and in the morning I lift her out. We are together in the way of a married couple only on Friday night, as befits a student of Torah, provided she is in her period of cleanliness. This is your mother, Akiva, to whom I was wed on the fifteenth day of Av, Tu BeAv. She conceived soon after, and for the next nine months at least there was no obligation or excuse for conjugality. During that time all my energies were once again obsessed with reaching Uman.

"Good-bye, Ivriya," I said on the day her pregnancy was confirmed, "I'm going to Uman." Not in any way different from the masses of tamed husbands who peck their little wives' cheeks in the morning and shuffle forth to fulfill the curse of Adam. "Oh, Shmuel, what will become of me—pregnant and in a wheelchair?" But I turned a deaf ear. "You are like a pot with a seed in it," I said. "Sit out in the sun and in the rain. God will help." "But will God carry me in and out of bed,

Shmuel? Tell me that!" Have you ever seen your mother mop the floors, Akiva? Pure dynamite! One hand spins the wheel and the other pushes that squeegie around faster than lightning. She will survive us all. "Invite one of your girlfriends to stay with you while I'm gone—Sora or Bruriah or Golda or Tikva. Let her sleep in my bed. When I return, we can burn the mattress." There are times when a high spiritual purpose requires what the uninitiated might perceive as cruelty. "I won't wear socks while you're gone, Shmuel, not for a single minute; God is my witness." "Do not take the Lord's name in vain." With this severe admonition I parted from your mother that morning. "Shmuel, please, Shmuel!" Her wail haunted me all that day, like a slight and common tune you can't push out of your mind.

Carrying a large satchel in which my few essential belongings rattled (a single change of clothes, my prayer book, my Bible, my prayer shawl and phylacteries), I walked up Yehezkel Street to Barclay's Bank, where I kept a decent account filled with tainted money earned in wickedness. I closed this account. The paper inflated my suitcase but added little worth. Having accomplished this, I made my way along Mea Shearim Street toward the Old City, entering through the din of the Damascus Gate. In the marketplace I purchased several bolts of cheap fabric, a pair of scissors, candles, matches, a jerrycan, some sheets of cardboard, and a felt-tipped pen. You see how quickly we human beings accumulate possessions. By then it was already late afternoon, and I stopped at the Western Wall for the evening prayer. From there I climbed the Mount of Olives and entered the cave where the prophets Haggai and Malachi are buried. The Cyrillic inscription on the gate, from the days when the Russian Orthodox Church supervised this tomb, buoyed me with the feeling that I was already halfway to Uman. Here I set up housekeeping. The caretaker knew me from my many visits, and he did not protest. What did I eat? Carobs, figs, and olives, so that I could earn the privilege of reciting the blessing over the fruit of the trees. Each evening I filled my jerrycan at the Intercontinental Hotel, and thus I was able not only to quench my thirst, but also to rinse my hands upon awaking, as is required. Every day I went to the ritual bath, and in that fashion I maintained the cleanliness of my body. Friday at noon I collected my food for the Sabbath from the garbage that was cast out by the supermarket on Agron Street. While my money lasted—for it was necessary to replenish the fabric constantly—I bought my bread, and that was the sole item I purchased for myself. What does a person need for the maintenance of his body? I lacked for nothing in that department. Toward the end, my money ran out and I was not ashamed to beg in the streets the American tourists frequented: "Give to the schnorrer! Give to the schnorrer!" I cried in my fetching imitation of Yankee English. To the unknowing I was a buffoon, but never judge hastily, Akiva: the ragged clown at the side of the road might well be one of the hidden righteous thirty-six upon whom the survival of the world depends. Bread I had to buy to carry out the obligation of partaking in the three Sabbath meals, and on a profitable day I sometimes collected enough to purchase more fabric as well. Akiva, except for the Passover holiday, when I went to Safad and celebrated our liberation from slavery at the modest table of Abba Nissim, I spent almost the entire period of your gestation in Jerusalem. I was not far away from you; I was pregnant with your soul. Though physically I never left Israel, I consider this to have been one of my more successful attempts to reach Uman, one of the times I came closest.

At first my methods were crude, Akiva, and disturbing even to me, not because of their impact on others but, rather, because of what they reflected about my own passions. Everyone must learn, and your father is no exception. In time I refined my technique. But in the beginning I ignored the cloth I had bought, leaving it stacked in one of the alcoves of the sepulcher, sometimes, in my weakness, unrolling a few meters of a bolt to cover myself on our cold Jerusalem nights. With my felt-tipped pen I made a sign, in Hebrew and in English, which I attached to a stick and carried around in the streets: "Daughters of Israel, Dress Modestly in Accordance with the Precepts of Our Torah." Whenever I spotted a woman with bare arms or legs, or worse, Akiva (you are old enough to guess my meaning—I won't go into particulars), I followed her in the street, like a gray and irksome shadow, embarrassing her, I suppose; but the laws of decency, I felt, superseded the injunction against humiliating your friend in public. Besides, these women were not and never will be my friends, God forbid. Akiva, if only they understood the extent of their transgression. For it is not simply the issue of exposing the flesh that is so reprehensible. Even more serious, to my mind, is the distraction they cause to those who wish to concentrate their thoughts exclusively on holy matters. And simply from the aspect of vanity: some good friend ought to advise them that their vulgar style of undress is just not becoming. The body that is revealed arouses little more than thoughts of death and decay. But is that my role? I'm not a fashion consultant, merely a wayfarer to Uman.

The task was not easy, Akiva. How to pick out these women while averting one's glance? Often I walked for many kilometers without having any woman squirming under the shadow of my sign. At those times my sign and I were like the shadows in Hiroshima that remained after the blast disintegrated the bodies that had cast them. At other times I hovered over the sinner, the words on my sign her caption and blurb. I was inescapable, tenacious, an appendage that could not be lopped off. There were many incidents of confrontation that I shall not go into, for your sake as well as my own, Akiva. Only one I'll tell you about, because after that I altered my approach. At Sabbath Square it happened, just a few blocks from where you were germinating, and it involved an American woman, bareheaded and barelegged, holding a child's hand. It was her child, she admitted. "A married woman must cover her hair," I said. She was not married, she answered. Where to begin in such a case, Akiva? I spat three times on the ground, on the spot in front of her lacquered toenails, where my gaze was fixed. She began to scream at the top of her lungs, drawing a hot and jubilant crowd. "This is not a stable!" I shouted. "He spat at me! He spat! He dared to spit! At me!" She would not put an end to her screeching; like a creature attacked by a swarm of bats she was, and I, for my part, began to circle her, calling her tart, harlot, wanton, *pritzka, pritzka!* I was out of control. Akiva, I wanted to see her dance.

This was a negative approach, I realized. Moreover, as much as I disapproved of this woman, I was even more troubled by the response she elicited from me. I returned to my tomb and spent the night in tortured prayer. Sleep was out of the question, for whenever I dozed off I would see her on the screen on the underside of my eyelids, her face invaded by one huge mouth frozen in the shape of her endless scream, her crimson toenails lengthening into shrieking tongues, her hair lashing. The next day I spent like an industrious little tailor, cutting the material I had bought into lengths of about two meters each. From then on, until my mission was ended, I walked the streets, my satchel filled with the pieces, and whenever I noticed a woman dressed in an unseemly way, especially at a holy site, I would plead with her, for the sake of my soul, to do me the kindness to wrap herself in one of my shawls. "Help me earn my passage to Uman," I would implore. Most of the time they were beguiled, and they would oblige. In general, women like to oblige—for good or for ill, it matters little to them. How they preened! How they draped themselves! God have mercy. And how covetous they are. Even the rags I forced on them became a thing to possess. Yet, despite the financial loss it represented to me when they walked off with one of my cloths, I often preferred that they do so, for the ones that were returned to me had absorbed the wearers' smell so thoroughly, in warp and in weft, that I could not possibly bring them with me back into the closeness of the tomb. In this way, Akiva, I passed most of the forty weeks that you passed in the womb. I returned three days before your birth. "I thought you'd be here by Pesach," Ivriya said. And after that she treated me exactly as she always had, as if I had gone nowhere at all.

Akiva, how can I describe to you the rapture that overwhelmed me the moment I raised my eyes from the Book of Psalms and witnessed your squashed little red face emerging from between your mother's inert legs, your hair matted, your torso smeared with blood and a cheesy substance, your arms flailing, and then your manhood. My son, I said to myself, this is my son. I vowed then and there to devote myself to you, to give all my energies to your proper upbringing. Eight days later, I took the knife in my own right hand and performed the covenant of your circumcision, your *b'rit milah*, as our forefather Abraham had done for his son, Ishmael. With my own mouth I performed the *metzitzah*, suctioning off the blood from your wound. And I wept when I recited the benediction welcoming you into the covenant of Abraham our father. "So may he enter into the Torah, the nuptial canopy, and into good deeds," the congregation replied. Amen. My heart soared. And from then on, Akiva, as you know, we have always referred to that part of your body as your covenant, your *b'rit*, a place of holiness, not a plaything or a joke. A symbol, Akiva, a symbol of our contract with the Lord. Remember that, my son: you must treat it symbolically.

But, in the way of all infants, you were attached at first to your mother. Nevertheless, I observed you closely, watching for signs of development and recognition, looking for hints to your nature. I would leave you for two or three days at a time, but not longer, seeking my solitude in the hills of the north or in the deserts of the south. Each time I would go away I would pray for you, wonder about you, yearn for you, pine for you. When I would return, I would examine you for changes. To me you were always remarkable, Akiva. I was condemned to entrust you to Ivriya, but I will admit, to her credit, that she cared for you well, in the limited way of a mother. The mother attends the body, the father the spirit. A father's love is unique. Who can describe the depths of sorrow to which Rav Nahman must have been plunged when his only son, Shlomo Ephraim, died at fifteen months? Four years later the father, too, was dead. Akiva, when you reached the age of Shlomo Ephraim at his passing, I felt it to be an especially precarious time for you. How best to protect you? This was the question I posed to myself. It was just about then that an opportunity arose to reach Uman. I interpreted this opportunity as a sign. Rather than stationing myself at your cradle to guard you day and night, I would journey for your sake to Uman, though it would mean a long separation for you. "How can you do this to Akiva?" Ivriya cried. No longer was she demanding for herself. "Not *to* Akiva, but *for* Akiva. You are incapable of understanding, Ivriya." "Oh, what will become of us?" she whimpered. I replied with a harshness like Rav Nahman's when he was preparing to depart for Israel and his own daughter sought to prevent him with a similar lament. This daughter would go to her in-laws, Rav Nahman had said. Her older sister would become a servant. Her younger sister would be taken in by someone out of pity. Their mother could find work as a cook. Everything would be sold to pay the expenses for the trip. Rav Nahman understood how domestic cares bind and cripple a man, cutting off every opportunity for achievement and greatness. I spoke similarly: "You, Ivriya, can use your talents as a floor-scrubber to support yourself. The baby can be sent to a religious friend or to an orphanage." Out of my love for you, Akiva, I spoke this way. You deserved a father who had been brought to Uman.

Can you imagine, Akiva? The streets of our land are now filling up with gloomy and discontented émigrés from Russia. Occasionally, perhaps out of perverse curiosity, I stop one and inquire if he had ever taken the trouble to make the pilgrimage to Uman. Not a single one I have spoken to has ever done so. To me this is a waste beyond belief. So near at hand it was for them, so possible, so approachable, yet they had never bothered. To the spas of Sochi and Sukhumi on the Black Sea they pinched their kopecks to go, but never to Uman, to take the ultimate spiritual cure. Why not? I posed this question to Reb Lev Lurie, the leader of our group of Bratslavers. "Precisely because there were no obstacles," he replied. Reb Lev is a charismatic and forceful interpreter of the teachings of Rav Nahman. The absence of obstacles never stood in Reb Lev's way. He is a Russian from Kiev and for two years lived in Uman, beside the sacred grave. Reb Lev is the one on whom I rely. Other followers of Rav Nahman go by different teachers. For us there is no single leader, no heir apparent, no "rebbe," as is the case with the more common Hassidic sects. For us there is only Nahman, Nahman, Nahman—unparalleled, unduplicated, inimitable. For our faction of Bratslavers under Reb Lev Lurie, the pilgrimage to Uman is paramount. The others may regard it to be of lesser importance. "This worshipping at a grave, is it not a form of idolatry?" I once asked Reb Lev. For we know from the Book of Deuteronomy that when Moses our teacher died by the kiss of God, he was buried, some say by the Almighty Himself, yet no one knows the whereabouts of his grave, and the reason for this, our sages tell us, is so that no one would take it into his head to make a cult of deifying him, with pilgrimages to his grave as to a shrine. "Those were in the days of pure faith," Reb Lev explained. "In our impoverished times, we require the intervention of the righteous." In our impoverished times, Akiva, I am the most impoverished. You were not yet a year and a half on this earth when three comrades from Reb Lev's class invited me to join them on the road to Uman. Akiva, I jumped.

In addition to myself, the group included Rami Marom, Roman Unger, and Shimon Breslau. Each one came with a past. Rami is a Moroccan, handsome and bowlegged like a cowboy, an innocent artist who was once a member of the Rosh Pinna group to which your mother also belonged. He painted your mother and her horse, Akiva, but it is a picture you are strictly forbidden to look upon. The horse was wearing a blanket. Rami still paints, although his subject matter is now the sacred; he closes his eyes and praises God with each brushstroke, like Enoch the simple cobbler, who sang a hymn to God with each stitch; when Rami's prayers are answered, he signs the images, "With Heaven's Help." Roman is the child of Polish refugees who married in a DP camp. He used to be an electric guitarist, empty-headed and frivolous. Now he scurries up and down our land, from Metulla to Eilat, searching for a suitable wife. With the help of God, he will one day find his match. Shimon, the son of a Haifa policeman, took his first acid trip at the age of nine; Shimon the Demon, he was called. Before he joined our group, in the early days of his penance, Shimon wandered in the hills of Judea and Samaria with a flock of sheep, trying to emulate our forefathers. It was Roman, the wife-seeker, who by good fortune managed to get hold of some stolen Mexican passports. He had expected to get four, but when, in the end, only three became available, Rami, Roman, and I met, and we decided to exclude Shimon. The decision was a necessary but painful one. Shimon is an appealing young man. There is no one who does not wish him well. Yet, despite the great and deep changes that had taken place in him, we concluded that for a trip of such delicacy Shimon would be a liability. We, of all people, were certainly not in a position to criticize another struggling soul, but the consensus was that he was still unstable. As tactfully as we could, we explained the circumstances to him. He was downcast, but resigned. "You're right," he said. "I'm not ready for Uman."

Rami became Carlos Flores, Roman, Miguel Gonzales, and I was Manuel Domingo. We practiced addressing one another by our new names, but in every other respect we did nothing at all. We took no pains to adjust our dress or our appearance. In uncanny ways, each of us resembled the tense and brooding men in the photographs—or at least Rami, with his artist's eye, thought so. They were solid, well-used passports, perfectly valid but close to expiration, and so the changes in our outward appearance could be justified by the changes in our lives since the dates the documents were issued. My man, Domingo, was bald with compensatory baroque sideburns and an impressive bandit's mustache. Well, my own head was shaven, and, anyway, who could tell?

For this trip to the airport, a momentous occasion, after all, I wore my most magnificent mink *streimel* on top of my black velvet yarmulke. My sidelocks, hanging loose and unkempt to my shoulders, could be tolerantly viewed as the logical extension of Domingo's sideburns. My beard, which grazed the third button of my gold-striped satin caftan, was merely the culmination—a fanciful elaboration, as it were—of Domingo's mustache. We felt absolutely confident, Flores, Gonzales, and I, as we marched up to the first control at the airport, accompanied by two comrades from Reb Lev Lurie's class who had come along to see us off. A small herd of Orthodox men is most disarming. Officials tend not to suspect them of duplicity. It occurred to me, as I watched a female hand stamp the passports of Rami and Roman and motion them on to security, that a terrorist—my buddy Mohammed, for instance—could get himself decked out as one of us—beard, fur hat, black caftan, the works—infiltrate arrivals without a hitch, and proceed to mow down an entire charter flight from the Bronx. Mohammed could do this if he thought of it, but, God be blessed, he doesn't have a Jewish head.

With my eyes lowered, for it is forbidden to gaze upon a strange woman's face, I watched the ink-stained female hand flip through Manuel Domingo's worn passport. She flattened the booklet out on the page with the photograph. Her arm jerked. "Shmulik!" she cried. "Shmulik Himmelhoch!" My heart stopped. Reflexively, my eyes rose to the face. This was no strange woman. This was Dorit, whom I had known only too well in our wild army days together. Here she was, the coarseness that had once been latent in her face now in full bloom. "What's new, *motek?*" I was reminded of how her loud and vulgar voice had always mortified me. I shrugged. Give me a break, I said to her in my heart, you owe me for what you claimed were your best times. She raised her soiled hand and rumpled my beard. This is what I had to endure, Akiva. "Shmulik, you old scoundrel!" she said. "Manuel Domingo, indeed!" She put down her hand, took up the seal, and stamped. In our tiny Israel, as it turns out, it's better to know somebody than not to know; *protectzia,* we call it. "Get going, you *mamzer!*" She gave me a familiar shove toward the security zone. "*Ciao,* Shmulik," she hollered. She pronounced it "keeow," somewhat like the English word for the animal that moos. "Shmulik" came out something like "shmuck."

Thus it was that when I joined my comrades at the second control, which was presided over by Nurit, whom I had known from the beaches of Sharm al-Sheikh, I was not a bit alarmed. "Shmulik Himmelhoch!" Nurit squealed. Rami and Roman turned to flee. I grabbed them by their *gartel*s. "Don't worry, it's okay," I calmed them. Nurit sneered. "The Mexican delegation, ha! Shmulik, you were always a case." Very deliberately, she inked her stamper. Nurit, for her part, was always a tease. But just as she was about to bring the seal down on my passport and release me from her cruel power, there was a great commotion in the hall. "Here comes Pancho Villa!" Nurit declared. Charging straight for us was Shimon Breslau. His beard was in motion, his caftan flapping; his face was a glistening red; one hand was occupied in keeping his black felt hat from falling, while the other was jabbing and pointing, like a knife thrust. "False passports! False passports!" he was yelling. *"Gevalt!"* Rav Nahman used to say. "Never give up hope!" Who can predict the unpredictable ways of our Lord? When Rami, Roman, and I were ready to surrender in despair, our two friends who had come along to bid us a peaceful departure rescued us from calamity. Each one grabbed Shimon by an arm. With the second fingers of their free hands they tapped the veins bulging on Shimon's temples. "He's crazy," they announced to the grim bystanders. "One hundred percent! Deranged! Certified! A basket case! Cuckoo! Nuts!" And they hustled poor Shimon away, demented and raving over the loss of Uman.

All this happened even before we stepped off Israeli soil, Akiva. What could we anticipate as we continued our journey? "It's time to *bentsh gomel,*" Roman said. So right there in the airport lounge we opened our prayer books and recited the benediction upon being saved from a disaster. Then, with profound fervor, we went on to chant the traveler's prayer. Our sages have supplied us with a blessing or a prayer for everything, Akiva: upon hearing thunder, upon seeing the great

31

ocean, a rainbow, a tree blossoming in spring, a hideous deformity of nature, a crowned sovereign, a Jewish learned man, a distinguished philosopher; upon smelling fragrant woods, spices, oils; after going to the toilet, upon learning of a death, upon rising in the morning, and before falling asleep at night. For everything we thank God—for the fruit of the trees, for the bread of the earth, for not having created us women, for allowing us to survive—there is not an object or an event, good or bad, actual or potential, for which we do not express our gratitude to the One Above. "Save us from the hand of enemies and ambushers and robbers and wild beasts on the road, and from every catastrophe that menaces and befalls the world." Thus we beseeched God with our full hearts and souls, and He heard our prayer. From then on our journey was unremarkable. We flew to Vienna like any normal passengers, concentrating our efforts during this segment of the trip on collecting enough chocolate for the Ukrainian babushka, with her obscene appetite for sweets and with the holy grave in her backyard. We refused the food presented to us by the menial disguised as a stewardess, on religious grounds. Only chocolates we requested. She found this entertaining, and every once in a while would pass by and, without glancing at us or slowing her pace up and down the cramped aisle, would lower her fist, open it, and drop a chocolate bar into one or another of our laps, as if she were joined with us in a conspiracy against the authorities who parcel out the candies—a coquette. In Vienna we had no difficulty at all passing through the controls. To the Austrian officials we were dark and strange foreigners: Mexicans, Jews, Africans, Orientals—all the same, all other, all undesirables. The sooner we were dispatched the better, especially in the opinion of those who recognized our subspecies—

ghosts of their own festering heyday. If by our own free will we elected to enter the dungeons of Russia, so much the better; we were doing their dirty work for them. With drums and fanfares they would lead us to our doom. Good-bye and good riddance. We boarded the plane to Kiev. So overwhelmed were we by our good fortune that we hardly spoke a word to one another during that flight, as if we were caught in a magic spell that any sound could shatter.

It was morning as we approached our destination. The city stretched below us. We wrapped our phylacteries around our arms and heads, stood up in the aisle, and began our prayers. Just as we commenced the recitation of the Amidah, the seat-belt sign flashed. As you know, Akiva, during this prayer it is forbidden to talk or to respond to any distraction, no matter how urgent. All available crew on that plane massed upon us and struggled to shove us back into our seats. Nothing would make us budge. In the end they left us to our fates, scurrying to their own places to fasten themselves in for their personal safety. Let the Jews smash their stubborn heads against the ceiling, they figured, we'll clean up the mess later. The wheels slammed down on the runway of "Holy Russia," and we, bumping and crashing and soaring within, approached ever nearer to our heart's desire. Blessed is He who kept us alive, and sustained us, and permitted us to reach this day.

Oh, how close we were, Akiva, close enough to break your heart. Had it been up to us, we would have started running the two hundred kilometers from the airport in Kiev straight to Uman. But the apparatchiks couldn't figure us out. What were we really after? There was something sinister behind this, surely. Our Mexican passports were useless to us at this juncture. Israel was the point of embarkation, stamped in indelible

ink. Besides, we had no visas. Were we spies? Potential insti-
gators among the disaffected Jews clamoring to emigrate?
Weren't we headed in the wrong direction? They went
through our suitcases piece by piece, lifting each item and
shaking it out, ripping the seams of our garments, flaunting our
strange artifacts for one another's amusement. "Hey, Pavel,"
Masha cried, waving a pair of Rami's *tzitzit*, "get a load of
this!" She set them on top of her bleached hair, the tassels
dangling flirtatiously over her face. She kept them on throughout the inspection, blowing the fringes away to stuff into her
mouth the precious chocolates we had collected. What were
our real names? they demanded to know. We had no choice
but to tell them. Roman did all the translating and the talking,
in a mixture of Polish and Russian. Truly, truly, all we desire
is an hour's prayer beside this grave in an old lady's backyard.
To cure us of our nocturnal emissions and other vices. You can
accompany us if you care to—escort us there, remain with us
throughout, maybe even put in a little prayer in your own
behalf, it can't hurt, bring us back to the airport, and send us
off yourselves. This is all we want. Nothing more. Either they
could not understand or they could not believe, and even if
they could both understand and believe, they were not prepared to risk taking the sole credit for letting us through. They
summoned higher officials, and yet higher, and, strange to say,
Akiva, the more elevated in rank the official was, the smaller
he was physically. We were in a den of Russian bears. They
inspected our persons; I'll spare you the intimate details, Akiva.
Then they left us overnight in a sealed chamber somewhere in
the airport. We prayed and did not sleep. Though we had not
eaten for nearly three days, not one of us would touch what
remained of the chocolate, our ticket to salvation and bliss.

In the morning they returned in all their varied sizes, and with them was a new one we had never seen, a veritable midget. He was carrying a folder. Without even bothering to look up at us, with hopeless impartiality, he opened the folder and proceeded to read in flawless Hebrew: "Rami Marom, Moroccan, Third World, you may proceed to Uman if you wish. Roman Unger, misguided but harmless and impotent Pole, you may go and carry out your foolish business at the grave. Samuel Himmelhoch, former lighting engineer for decadent musicians, corrupter of youth, hooligan, deviant, misfit, you will be put on a plane immediately, and shipped, collect, back to the nonexistent Zionist state where you belong."

Blessed is the True Judge—the benediction upon failing to be brought to Uman. I ask you, Akiva: how can I renew myself? My pure child, tell me what I must do to change. I shall begin at once.

HOW THEY
BROUGHT HIM
FROM MERON
TO SAFAD

Not long after Samuel Himmelhoch's journal was found by
Abba Nissim in Safad's old cemetery, the body itself was discovered, about ten kilometers away, in Meron, close by the
tomb of Rabbi Yochanan the Shoemaker. As a matter of fact,
it was an old comrade of Nissim's, the retired bandit Shyke
Pfeffer, who came upon the corpse when the metal fig-picker
he used for a walking stick gave off a hollow ring as it struck
bare bone. Pfeffer crouched down and, like the forest creature
he now resembled, glanced sharply in all four directions, scout-
ing for intruders. With his callused hands and curling amber
fingernails, he quickly swept away the sodden leaves and dirt
that blanketed the body. The exposed face had already been

sampled by the creatures of the earth, Shyke Pfeffer could not help noting. Nevertheless, it was unmistakable. "Well, a good morning to you, Shmuel Himmelhoch," Pfeffer spoke out loud. "And how goes the Jew?"

The next thing Pfeffer said, since Himmelhoch did not answer (and this is one of the more exasperating aspects of being in the company of a corpse—the way it haughtily, spite-fully ignores you), was "I didn't do it!" These words came out of his mouth quite involuntarily, because in his mind he had already begun considering what steps to take about his discov-ery, and when the common idea arose of contacting the au-thorities and he pictured all that would ensue, his mouth reacted automatically. So: "I didn't do it," he flatly stated. Shyke Pfeffer was an expert on the police—their tactics and their mentality. In his prime he had been Israel's most notori-ous criminal, a specialist in highway robberies and burglaries, although he had never killed a person, man, woman, or child, and in this respect he estimated he might be unique in a land where every man was a soldier. But he, for his part, had refused military service, on the grounds of his pacifist convictions, and after a short period in jail, from which he escaped—as he had escaped from every single subsequent imprisonment—he took up his life's work. In the villages and kibbutzim of the north, Pfeffer's primary sphere of operation, children would terrorize one another at night by whispering hauntingly, "Shyke Pfeffer's outside! Shyke Pfeffer's going to get you!"

Of course, had Shyke Pfeffer gone to the police with the body, and had they solemnly determined that it was the victim of a murder, they would never have risked accusing the old bandit in any case, even if—a truly remote possibility—even if they actually suspected him. This was because Pfeffer had

38

acquired the status of legend, of folk hero, and, moreover, the authorities could not bear to suffer the added humiliation of his inevitable escape were they obliged to lock him up. In addition, it was the firm opinion of the police that Shyke Pfeffer was now quite harmless—a lunatic, even—his brain having been pickled in hashish and other assorted drugs for nearly half a century, and the final proof of his dementia was that he had become religious. Shyke Pfeffer, embroidered skullcap on his flowing gray locks, blue fringes dangling from his loose trousers, could station himself on the floor of the Israeli Knesset, lean against the speaker's podium, and slowly, leisurely, puff his fragrant pipe of hashish. Nobody would bother him, and he knew it.

The thing to do now, Pfeffer decided, was to run and fetch his wise friend Abba Nissim of Safad and proudly show him the find. Maybe it wasn't so spectacular a discovery as the already famous journal—without question it wasn't as lasting—but it was certainly not a thing to be despised. Shyke Pfeffer took measures to conceal the corpse once again, as best he could, and then he set off down toward the wadi for the half-day walk to the mystical city of Safad, beckoning in its blue light. On second thought, Pfeffer concluded that this was an occasion for expediency, so he placed himself at the side of the road, waved his stick, and soon enough, a Harley-Davidson gunned by a Christian Arab from Bethlehem screeched to a stop and picked him up. "We have nothing against you Jews," the driver shouted convivially; "Jesus was also a Jew." "One hundred percent," Pfeffer shouted back, "on both sides."

Shyke Pfeffer sat on the low stone retaining wall overlooking the old Safad graveyard. Sammy the Arab sat beside him, for

39

he had agreed to give Pfeffer and his friend a lift back to Meron. Why not? It was in the nature of an international good-will gesture; the old man had said it was an emergency. Besides, it was thrilling to take the sharp mountain curves on his new bike at top speed. If they cracked up, it would be two old Jews for one young Arab, so we'd still balance out in the end, Sammy calculated. Pfeffer and Sammy shared a pipe as they sat side by side, watching Abba Nissim shepherd a group of Japanese tourists from tomb to tomb. "Please, do not bow! Do not bow!" they could hear Nissim exhorting his charges. The Japanese shot their last shots, satisfied themselves that they had completed a thorough tour, and went on their way. Then Shyke Pfeffer leaped down the slope and, with animated punctuation, passed the news to Abba Nissim. Without hesitating, Abba Nissim climbed up the pathway and took his place on the motorcycle. He was about fifteen years older than Shyke Pfeffer—over seventy, in fact—but he was tall and stately, whereas Pfeffer was as gnarled and wind-twisted as the trunk of an ancient olive tree. With great dignity, Abba Nissim hitched up the skirt of his striped satin robe and mounted the vehicle. One arm encircled the muscular belly of his friend Shyke Pfeffer, and the other rested on his own head, to hold in place his black velvet turban. As they roared back to Meron, two streamers of white birds flew in their wake, anticipating the repast of bread crumbs that was arrayed for them in Abba Nissim's beard.

"Jesus was a rabbi!" Sammy cried out, halting only barely long enough for the two old Jews to stumble down. Shyke Pfeffer could hardly suppress his excitement. He seized Abba Nissim's hand and practically dragged him up the hill. Vultures circled overhead. "Here," he said, brushing the last clumps of earth off the partly decomposed face. "Do you have any doubts? It's Shmuel Himmelhoch, all right. You found his jerrycan in Safad, and I found him himself, in all his glory, here in Meron. He must have died of thirst."

"Spiritual thirst, perhaps," Abba Nissim said quietly. And he quoted from the prophet Amos: "Behold, the day is come, saith the Lord God, that I will send a famine in the land, not a famine for bread and not a thirst for water, but to hear the word of God."

Abba Nissim bent over the corpse and examined it more closely. "Is that you, Shmuel?" he inquired confidentially. The subject offered no confirmation, but neither was there a denial. One thing was sure: Samuel Himmelhoch was in the air, if not, strictly speaking, on the ground. He was "in," as he would have said in his sinning, polluted days; he was "hot," he would have said, were it not for the fact that he was so cold. First the jerrycan and the journal, and now a personal appearance by the author himself. It was natural for people to associate the body in question with him. Probably it was his. Certainly he would claim it. "There's no question that this can very well be the vessel that contained the soul of the dear Jew Shmuel Himmelhoch," Abba Nissim said, straightening out. "What could have happened to him? Noble soul, may he intercede in our behalf. But now it is our obligation to inform the family. For them it will be the end of hope, but, on the other hand, the certainty will come as a blessing and relief. And his *agunah*, his chained wife, will be cut loose for marriage."

The laws pertaining to the dead are many and complex, eliciting strenuous disputations on numerous points, but on the necessity of getting the body into the ground as quickly as possible there is universal agreement. Even the body of a criminal who has been hanged must be taken down and buried on the same day; how much more so the remains of one who has escaped execution! In Jerusalem, if you draw your last breath in the afternoon, the earth already weighs heavily on your chest by sunset. In the less elevated cities, though the urgency may not be so strong, it is nevertheless palpable. Of course, the case of the remains of Samuel Himmelhoch was unique. In the first place, it was more an issue of reburial than of burial. Second, there was the matter of positive identification, problematic in itself, since viewing is generally frowned upon out of respect for the dead, who is in the unfair position of not being able to make the best possible appearance. Even Himmelhoch's closest living relative—his wife, Ivriya, that is—might have had trouble recognizing him in his present condition; in kindness, perhaps she should be spared. More invasive forms of identification, such as autopsies, are, as everyone knows, in violation of the Torah's laws. Yet the black birds did not cease to spread their broad wings over the body, and the white birds that had escorted Abba Nissim from Safad fluttered forward and then yielded into the shrubs. Like a reflection of the forces that battled for Shmuel's soul, Abba Nissim thought. And when Nissim closed his eyes for a moment, he heard Himmelhoch calling to him in a tormented voice from a dark, narrow place: "Abba! Abba!" Himmelhoch wailed. "It will soon be all right, Shmuel," Abba Nissim said, stroking the body. "Don't worry, Shmuel. We'll take care of you."

From the yeshiva atop the sepulcher of Rabbi Simeon bar Yohai, Abba Nissim telephoned Ivriya Himmelhoch, as well as Reb Lev Lurie, at Uman House. Now, as he waited for the family and friends to make their way up to Meron, he sat on his haunches beside Shyke Pfeffer, rocking back and forth, chanting psalms over the body of Samuel Himmelhoch. The unburied dead must never be left unattended. "Have you noticed the birds?" Pfeffer inquired. "They're working up an appetite." It was almost noon, lunchtime. "There's also a stink," Pfeffer added. "Even out here it's strong." "Shmuel was always so fastidious," Abba Nissim reminisced. " 'A student of Torah with even a single stain on his garment is deserving of death,' he would say. In my view, Shmuel Himmelhoch would not have taken pleasure in being seen like this." "Maybe we should fix him up a little," Pfeffer suggested. "It would hinder the identification," Nissim pointed out. In this fashion, pausing between stanzas in the psalms, they discussed and argued the matter, until at last they made the decision to bring Himmelhoch into the yeshiva and perform the rites of purification in preparation for the burial. "It will save time to do it now rather than after they arrive," Abba Nissim said, and that was the determining factor.

Shyke Pfeffer convinced the lady at the kiosk to donate a large black plastic garbage bag, and into this they inserted the rigid corpse of Samuel Himmelhoch. At first they tried to carry him, but the body, although partly consumed, was bloated with gases and other foreign elements, and it was a heavy load for two aged men. So they dragged it the distance, reasoning that no one would know what was inside anyhow, and the dead would not thereby be dishonored. And even if some clever bystanders figured out *what* was within, they could certainly not know *who*. "Suppose someone tries to steal it," Shyke Pfeffer said. As an ex-professional he was always alert to the possibility. "I mean, should we resist in such a case?" And he told his friend Abba Nissim how he had once held up a lady on the Afula highway, had relieved her of a suitcase—a very elegant piece of leather luggage, by the way, with brass fittings—and when he had opened it had found inside a dead dog, not even pedigreed. The suitcase, too, was worthless after that, so intrinsically did it reek. But, as it happened, on this occasion no one coveted their package, for by the time they reached the building at least two stiff limbs were protruding and the stench was like a royal carpet unrolling a corridor just for them.

Abba Nissim and Shyke Pfeffer toiled over the corpse. It rested on a board on the floor, naked, its feet pointed toward the door to allow for the exit of the impurities. As they washed the body in warm water, plunged out the orifices, cut the fingernails and the toenails, combed the hair, they did not cease singing the verses from the Bible. "His head is like the finest gold; His locks are curly, black as the raven." They stood the corpse up on its feet and poured nine measures of water over it, allowing the water to run off onto the floor. "Then I will sprinkle clean water on you, and you will be clean; from all your filthiness and all your idols I will clean you." They dried him thoroughly; they placed sand under his eyelids to signify the dust that he was and the dust to which he was already returning. They dressed him in white leggings and smock, wrapped him in shrouds, and, when they were through, draped a large prayer shawl over him, washed their own hands in salt water, and sat down again on the floor to chant the psalms. "Remember not the sins of my youth, my transgressions, O Lord."

"Shmuel," Abba Nissim addressed the neatly swaddled package on the floor. "Shmuel, thank you so much for giving

44

me the opportunity to perform the *mitzvah* of preparing you for burial. Of all the great deeds a person can do for his fellow man, this is the highest, for the recipient cannot say thank you."

"Thank you."

"Who said that?"

"Who said what?" Shyke Pfeffer asked.

But before the puzzle could be solved, the attention of the two living men in the room was distracted by a violent screeching of tires, like a siren. Abba Nissim kissed the psalm book soundlessly, closed it, and set it down sadly on a study table, as if, in parting from it, he already missed it. He rose and looked out the barred window. In brazen violation of all the rules, a scarlet Mercedes had driven right up the footpath and come to a full and grinding stop directly in front of the entrance to bar Yohai's tomb. Students and teachers were running out of the building, dashing about like black insects whose nest had been disturbed, screaming and shaking their fists at the driver. The driver, for her part, was ignoring them significantly as she briskly strode to the rear of her car, clicked open the trunk, and extracted a wheelchair. She was a large, handsome woman with well-groomed hair colored like a confection. She was dressed in a stylish sleeveless shift and high heels, and she did not bother to acknowledge the agitated protests that boiled around her. But when she spotted a young boy taking aim at the windshield of her car, she efficiently startled the stone out of his hand. "I warn you, fanatic!" she said in her husky voice. Obviously, she had them keenly under her surveillance, even as she seemed to be oblivious to their presence. She was, as Samuel Himmelhoch used to say, "one mean mama"—not his, but his wife's, Ivriya's. "It's a steel womb you've come from," Samuel

45

Himmelhoch used to tell Ivriya. "Beware you don't become your mother." Himmelhoch had refused to set foot in his mother-in-law's house, and he had forbidden Akiva to do so as well. He would not enter her "Nazi car" if his life depended on it, he had asserted. He had informed his mother-in-law well in advance not to expect him at her funeral. "I wouldn't miss yours for all the money in the world," she had responded. "You can bet your life I'll be there—knife in hand." She was Frieda Mendelssohn, M.D., the pathologist, and one of the most outspoken combatants against the Orthodox opposition to autopsies.

All the way up to Meron, as she palmed the steering wheel, her left arm triangulated out the window, Frieda Mendelssohn rambled on, in fond anticipation of what she planned to do. "I'll slice him up, Ivriya darling. Believe me, it'll be the biggest thrill of my life—that bastard! He brainwashed you, the no-good freak, that's what he did. He seduced you into his medieval cult. He was a con man—nothing more, nothing less. He got what he deserved. He stole you away from me, and my adorable little grandchild, too, he kidnapped. I'm speaking as a parent, you know; alienation of affection, it's called. I think I could have sued. He has it coming to him, your charming husband. I don't suppose he ever took out a life-insurance policy. Name one decent, responsible thing he ever did in his entire rotten career. But, speaking as a professional, sweetheart, you know, I've got the law on my side this time, one hundred percent. Because of the possibility of foul play. Sorry, gentlemen, we have no choice in this case: the autopsy is mandatory. It's out of my hands, so to speak. Just let those crazy zealots, those religious maniacs, try to stop me! Just let them try! I'll summon the body-snatchers. I'll call out the

46

paratroopers. And then, of course, there's the whole issue of positive identification. Oh, Ivriya baby, I just can't wait to get my hands on what's left of him."

Ivriya Mendelssohn Himmelhoch was strapped in the seat beside her mother, her face turned away, her eyes fixed upon but not absorbing the receding landscape of early autumn. Whenever Frieda Mendelssohn glanced toward her daughter—to assess a reaction, say—what she saw was a narrow skull wrapped in a dark kerchief, like a bandage, and shoulders so frail they broke her heart, and two legs—props, nothing more—that jutted straight forward and ended in a pair of childish black cotton shoes from China, buckled with single straps and having rubber soles that would always be an alarming, untrodden new pink. What's the point of answering? Ivriya thought. Let her just get it out of her system. Her mother's words buzzed at her left ear and became only another abstract element in the background noise, and the daughter would be reminded that the bitter flow had been going on during the entire journey only when there was the contrast of a pause. Over and over, Ivriya reviewed in her own mind her decision to leave her son, Akiva, at home, in the care of Sora Katz, the friend who had moved in soon after Shmuel had disappeared. How long ago was that now? Nearly two years. That's right: Akiva just turned five last spring, and he was already three when Shmuel vanished. It wasn't that she was concerned about the care Akiva would be receiving. Sora was perfectly competent, better with the boy, in many ways, than was Ivriya herself. Oh, she was always losing her temper with Akiva, screaming and yelling at him—but that wasn't the worst. Sometimes she beat him so hard, she knew it wasn't for his own good. It didn't do her much good, either, only made

47

her despise herself, as if she needed an extra portion of self-hatred. Then she would kiss him a thousand times and hug him till he nearly suffocated, and explain to him that he should try to understand how hard it was on her, with Shmuel gone and no one to say whether he was dead or alive. Oh, it was too much to ask of such a young child, far too much. No wonder he was always squirming out of her reach, squeezing into corners where her wheelchair couldn't maneuver, and now, even when she moved forward intending to kiss him, he flinched, jerked away, as if he were expecting a blow. He was so difficult, so very difficult—like Shmuel—powerful, strong-willed, irresistible. He broke her down, like Shmuel. "You're killing me! You're killing me!" she'd shriek at the poor kid. What a guilt trip she was laying on him! Maybe she should have brought him along, after all. Maybe it was this uncertainty that was driving him wild. Had he come along, he would have seen the body, he would have experienced the funeral, he would have watched them lower his father into the ground, and maybe all that would have given him a sense of reality, of finality. He would have known exactly where he stood in this world: an orphan, in the secret and exclusive society of orphans. Maybe it would have calmed him down. Oh, she didn't know what to do. Some people said, Yes, take the kid, definitely. Others said, Leave him home; it's too great an ordeal for one so young. She thought maybe she'd take him with her just so she'd have an excuse to avoid dealing directly with her mother—because of the necessity of attending to the baby, you know. Then she thought, better to leave him at home, because there'd be more than enough for her to cope with, without having to worry about his needs. He was an extremely demanding child, Akiva, and the more tense and strained the situation, the more demanding he became. Well, she should face up to it—the real reason she hadn't brought him with her was that she was exploiting the opportunity to take a little vacation from him. Sometimes she simply could not stand to be near him, he irritated her so profoundly. And yet she loved him. She had never known there were such reserves of ferocious love inside her until she had had him. She loved him; oh, she loved him. He was so bewitching—so dark-skinned and bright-eyed—and his smile: it was electric. And how he could enjoy himself! And how clever he was, and how pure, how honest. He'd take one look at the corpse: "That's not my father," he'd say in his ringing young voice, and what would they do then?

"You know, Ima," Ivriya said to her mother as Mount Meron grew higher before them, "an autopsy is not particularly useful in determining identity anyhow."

"That's what you think, darling." Frieda Mendelssohn was delighted to have at last provoked an exchange from her daughter. "Never underestimate the powers of science."

"But, Ima, suppose you do perform the autopsy. And suppose that, on the basis of your examination, you make a conclusive determination about the identity of the body. Ima, suppose, for argument's sake, you discover, without a shadow of a doubt, that the body is *not* Shmuel's—what then, Ima?"

So the Frieda Mendelssohn that Abba Nissim was observing through his window, the powerful Frieda Mendelssohn who had thoroughly disarrayed the yeshiva students, was actually a far more subdued Frieda Mendelssohn than the one who had set out from Jerusalem earlier that day, for all her delicious prospects and plans had shriveled up the instant her daughter, the cadaver's wife, so sensibly stated the case.

Abba Nissim watched as Frieda Mendelssohn set up the

wheelchair, lifted Ivriya out of the car, deposited her in the seat, and arranged her legs. The mother had a strong back, but the daughter was delicate and fine-boned. Perhaps she took after the father, Abba Nissim reflected, for often it happened that large women deliberately chose fragile men, and when such a man performed his duty and died young, as was decent and expected of him, the great wife became the grand widow that had been her destined vocation all along. Abba Nissim gently wriggled the enshrouded corpse of Samuel Himmelhoch off the board it had been resting upon. He carried the board out the door and set it down on the steps, to serve as a ramp for the wheelchair. The yeshiva students retreated in bewilderment. What could this mean? Abba Nissim was well known among them, and by many he was regarded as a *nistar*, a hidden holy man, one of the rare members of an elite network of cabalists who worked miracles and communicated with one another in a sacred, enigmatic language, through thoughts and dreams. What could it mean that Abba Nissim should perform this humble service for so vulgar and corrupt a woman? "Well," Frieda Mendelssohn declared, "I never expected to find a Sir Walter Raleigh out here, of all places!" She smiled at Nissim, displaying expensive teeth; she was an attractive woman and accustomed to the courtesies of men. She placed her broad, competent hands on the bars of Ivriya's wheelchair and pushed her daughter up the makeshift ramp, Abba Nissim directing the way to the chamber where Samuel Himmelhoch lay, waiting patiently on the floor. Nissim had spoken not a single word—neither to the mother, whom he had never had the pleasure of meeting before, nor to the daughter, whose food he had tasted and whose hospitality he had enjoyed on more than one occasion, nor to the yeshiva students, whose dark forms, as they stood back to make way for this odd procession, were bowed and rounded, like question marks.

When they entered the morgue they found Shyke Pfeffer dancing ecstatically, his hands beating and plucking invisible musical instruments. He was singing Psalm 150, the last of the book and also the final one of the ten that Rav Nahman guaranteed would serve as a general remedy for all spiritual blemishes if recited at his grave in Uman. Alas, poor Samuel Himmelhoch had tried—God knows he had tried—but he had never been worthy of making it to Uman. "Praise Him with drums and dance . . . with cymbals . . . with bells. . . . All things with breath will praise the Lord. . . ." Pfeffer stopped short when Ivriya Himmelhoch materialized at the door, piloted by her formidable mother. Frieda Mendelssohn glared at Shyke Pfeffer. "Is this what you people consider appropriate behavior?" she asked Abba Nissim; her tone implied that she and Nissim were already old and intimate collaborators, in on the private joke together. Then Dr. Frieda Mendelssohn proceeded to appraise the corpse. "Well, it certainly smells like Shmuel," she pronounced at last. "Ivriya, honey, why don't we just run him over?" "Ima, please," Ivriya said softly. She rolled her own wheelchair closer to the body and took her place silently beside it. "Blessed is the True Judge," she said, and she lowered her face into the palms of her hands.

She remained in this position, not looking up even as Reb Lev Lurie, the leader of Uman House, entered the room, flanked by Roman Unger and Rami Marom, inseparable since their attainment, together, of Uman. They brought a khaki-colored canvas army stretcher with them, the "bed," and onto this they lifted the remains of their comrade Samuel Himmelhoch, the third passenger on the trip to Uman, the unfortunate one who had not made it—may his poor, wandering soul arrive at last. Ivriya felt the weight of a consoling arm across her shoulders and breathed in a kitchen smell that was not her mother's. She raised her head. She saw Reb Lev, Roman, and Rami, conferring with Abba Nissim and Shyke Pfeffer in the corner of the room opposite her. Her mother hovered over this group, a bold girl struggling in vain to penetrate the boys' huddle. "I want some say in the plans," Frieda Mendelssohn kept interjecting. "I have some rights. As the only member of the family who hasn't completely lost her mind, I demand some input!" But the five men ignored her—she was a distraction that did not even merit the acknowledgment of annoyance—and for her mother's sake Ivriya was embarrassed. Ivriya placed her hand on top of the one that was draped over her shoulder and looked up into the dark, ardent face of Bruriah Lurie, Reb Lev's wife. "Be comforted, Ivriya," Bruriah said in her flat American accent.

Ivriya nodded. "How did you get here?" she asked.

"In Roman's van." Ah, Roman's van! In which he used to transport her and Akiva around the city and into the country, although, in truth, since his marriage to Tikva, far less often, lately almost never. But what a relief it had been to get out of their dismal, gloomy apartment in those days after Shmuel had vanished, when Roman had still been single and free, and how Akiva used to love their excursions, for both doors of the van were brightly painted with the words "Uman Boys Band," and the letters seemed to skip and hop like musical notes—it was as if they were traveling in a gypsy wagon—and inside there were always instruments strewn about—drums, tambourines, cymbals, fiddles, flutes, guitars—and Roman lounging back in the driver's seat singing at the top of his voice: "You have brought us up to here, bring us to Uman! Bring us to Uman!"

"Maybe we can use the van to bring Shmuel to the cemetery," Ivriya said.

"I don't know," Bruriah replied. "The men are deciding." Poor Bruriah, no matter how deeply she immersed herself in the mission of her husband, Reb Lev Lurie, no matter how totally she sacrificed herself for the ideals of Uman House, she could never completely shake off the bland shadow of the American girl she had been, which lingered in her voice and her gestures, trivializing the personage she had become, rendering her slightly synthetic. Oh, what were those cynical forces that prevented a person from changing, changing utterly? "You weren't the only woman in the van?" Ivriya asked.

"God forbid. Tikva's here, too."

"Ah, Tikva," said Ivriya. "How could I miss you?" And Roman Unger's wife stepped forward, preceded by the fanfare of her taut, pregnant belly. She must be in her seventh or eighth month, Ivriya figured. "How good of you to come, Tikva," Ivriya said. She took Tikva's hand and rubbed its rough back against her cheek. She truly cared for Tikva, and was moved by the sight of her standing there in the background, deferring to Bruriah, her severe black scarf pulled tightly over her shaven skull, the ends dangling modestly over her swollen breasts. In the Rosh Pinna days, before they had returned to the faith, she and Tikva had been as close as sisters. They had even shared the same pair of eyeglasses; their vision was distorted in exactly the same way. She certainly did not hold it against Tikva that Roman Unger no longer took her and Akiva out in the "Uman Boys Band" van. Far from it. She was personally delighted that the two of them, Roman and Tikva, were so absorbed in each other, for hadn't it been she, Ivriya

53

herself, who had cooked up the match in the first place? And hadn't she, Ivriya, been the one to arrange for their first three meetings—in her own living room, as a matter of fact? And hadn't it been she to whom Roman had come to announce that he certainly liked Tikva well enough to proceed with the marriage, but why hadn't Tikva spoken a single word, not a single word? Was she dumb? Not that he had any prejudices against mutes—on the contrary, in a wife he thought it might be a definite asset—but he felt he had a right to know in advance: was Ivriya keeping something from him? And hadn't it been she, Ivriya, who had taken Tikva aside: "If you want this good man, Tikva, you'd better say something fast"? "I am testing him," Tikva had solemnly stated, and she burst into tears. It was a celestial match, and Ivriya had been the agent. She was proud of her achievement. She understood Tikva's anxious nature, how Tikva invested in worrying about each and every dreadful possibility, as if whatever she anticipated and endured through worrying could therefore not happen in actuality. Ivriya appreciated what it must have meant to Tikva to make this difficult journey up to Meron at such an advanced state of pregnancy: imagine all the calamities Tikva must have felt herself obliged to anticipate with her worrying. And this wasn't Tikva's first pregnancy, either, Ivriya knew.

"You know, Shyke Pfeffer's here," Ivriya told Tikva.

"It's all right, Ivriya. I feel strong. God will help." Tikva Unger took Ivriya's delicate face between her two big hands and kissed the widowed brow.

"Did Goldie come, too?" Ivriya wanted to know. Golda was Rami Marom's wife, an American, like Bruriah.

"She couldn't make it," Tikva said. "It's a long story. This is not the time or place." Now Ivriya really had something to look forward to, for no one could tell a story the way Tikva could. Perhaps that was the reason Tikva had feigned muteness with Roman Unger, for a person's most splendid treasure and gift should be concealed in order that it be found by the one who cares enough to search for it.

Reb Lev Lurie separated himself from the group of men. Even in this dark chamber he gave off a light; indeed, there were those who claimed that Reb Lev Lurie suffered from too much light. Did this light emanate from some source within, or did it come from the nearly transparent green eyes in the pale face framed by the burning red beard and sidelocks? None could say, but neither could anyone deny the existence of the light that encased Reb Lev like a veil, from head to foot, drawing people to him and preventing them from coming too close, attracting and repelling at one and the same time. His disciples attributed the light to the years Reb Lev had spent praying and studying in Uman, beside the holy grave of Rav Nahman. His detractors, on the other hand, considered this light the demonic glow of an ensnarer and twister of souls. But even Reb Lev's most passionate enemies were obliged to acknowledge his power. As Roman Unger used to say (on Purim, when a little good-natured mockery is permissible): "If two such great powers as Reb Lev Lurie from Kiev, Russia, and the Rebbetzin Bruriah Lurie, formerly Barbara Horowitz from Brooklyn, New York, could live together in peace, how much more so can such lesser powers as the Soviet Union and the United States of America? How to do it? Reb Lev and the Rebbetzin Bruriah provide the example: total commitment to a single cause. And what should that cause be? Fear of heaven, love of Torah, and wholehearted devotion to the teachings of Rav Nahman of Bratslav."

Obviously, the men had made some decisions with regard to the funeral arrangements for Samuel Himmelhoch, and it was now Reb Lev's duty to announce them. But since the men already knew the plans, and since it was unseemly for Reb Lev to take the time and trouble to make the announcement solely for the women's sake, he approached the corpse to inform it directly: "Ah, Shmuel, Shmuel, how you must be struggling, lying here exposed, on display, unsettled—neither here nor there—your soul unable to appear before the King of Kings, the Holy One Blessed Be He, for final judgment until your worldly shell is properly hidden. We have decided to carry you, Shmuel, on your bed, from Meron to Safad, through the Wadi Amud that you loved so well. We shall recruit some yeshiva students to help us. Luckily for you, Shmuel, the rainy season has not yet begun and the wadi is still dry. And on the way we shall eulogize and remember you, Shmuel, for it will be impossible to do so in Safad, since, for financial reasons, you'll be sharing a plot there, thanks to the gracious good offices of Abba Nissim, the caretaker of the cemetery. So, Shmuel, if it's all right with you, we shall be obliged to expedite the burial in haste—*chik chok*—put you in, say a quick Kaddish, and that's about all we'll have time for in Safad if we wish to remain undetected. The privilege of resting in Safad is very great, and therefore we have waived the requirement of burying you before sunset, for we cannot afford a private grave, and the night will conceal our activities. We ask your forgiveness, Shmuel, if in any way these arrangements do not please you. We know that you have never, in life, objected to sharing living quarters. We have taken the liberty of assuming that your attitude has not changed in death."

"Always the squatter, always the trespasser. That's Shmuel

in a nutshell," said Frieda Mendelssohn. She rolled her eyes toward the ceiling. "And how in heaven's name do you expect me to walk through that wretched wadi in my high heels?"

"The women can travel in your car, or in the van. As you wish."

"I would like to accompany Shmuel," Ivriya said.

"That's ridiculous, honey," said her mother. "You can't even walk on your own two feet. What will they do? Put you on the stretcher with the stiff? It'll kill them. There's going to be a hernia epidemic in this place. Believe me, I know what I'm talking about—I'm a doctor. If you want my opinion, the whole idea is moronic. Ivriya, you come with me in my car. For your sake, darling, I'm even prepared to transport the deceased. You can ride in style together. We'll put him in the trunk. He'll be very comfortable there. I'm sure he won't complain."

"We'll find a mule for the widow," Abba Nissim said, "and she can ride through the wadi stately upon it."

"I'm coming, too," said Tikva. Of course Roman Unger objected to this idea, pointing out that even if Tikva had no regard at all for her own health and safety, she had the well-being of the baby in her womb to consider. What if she tripped? What if she fell? What if she was too tired to continue? How could they carry her? Even for the mule she would be too heavy a burden, especially with Ivriya already riding upon it. And besides, how would the van get to Safad? "Bruriah will drive the van," Tikva said. All Roman's protests were in vain, as he knew they were destined to be even before he started his litany, for Tikva, his stubborn wife, had made up her mind.

It was close to dusk when they descended into the wadi, accompanied by five students who claimed to have known Samuel Himmelhoch from his sojourns at Meron. "That gives us exactly ten men," Roman Unger said. "Now we won't have to go running around to find a *minyan* in the middle of the night." He was pleased that at least that detail had been cleared away. Roman Unger was Reb Lev Lurie's beadle, his right-hand man, and his instinctive approach to any situation was administrative. Now he was the one to organize the pallbearers, hastily scribbling down a rotating schedule—one man to an end of a pole, for a total of four (although there was one yeshiva student who carried the whole way—"It's my load," he had insisted—so Roman had only three men to juggle). Roman, for his part, did not once touch the litter; he considered himself to be a partner in a joint pregnancy with his wife, and contact with the dead would be plainly unlucky. Nevertheless, Roman did not shirk; he did his share. He spent his time running back and forth, checking on the two lantern-bearers who preceded the body and the two who came after it, and looking after his wife, Tikva, who walked heavily alongside the mule upon which Ivriya rode. A fifth lantern-bearer lit the way for the women at the end of the procession. This was usually either Shyke Pfeffer or Abba Nissim, because they were the two oldest men in the group and were consequently excused from prolonged periods of carrying the bier. The lanterns themselves were makeshift affairs, really, nothing more than short sticks to which glass jars had been taped; each jar was half filled with olive oil, and in the oil a wick floated. The wicks were always tipping over and flickering out, and so they required constant maintenance by Roman Unger, who scurried about rekindling the torches as they were extinguished. From above, it was a somber and mysterious procession, silent except for the steady droning song of the yeshiva student who had refused to relinquish his end of the pole: "The pangs of the Messiah—here they come, here they come today." This was the young man's song, and Reb Lev ruled that it was not, strictly speaking, music, but in this case a prayer, a dirge, and therefore permissible in mourning.

"Reb Lev is doing a lot of carrying," Ivriya noted. She had a fine view from her perch atop the mule.

"It's to honor Shmuel," said Tikva. "He really thought very highly of him."

"It must be very heavy, though."

"Oh, it's as heavy as a millstone," put in Shyke Pfeffer, who was now holding the lantern for the women. "As heavy as a ball and chain. As heavy as wedlock. As heavy as exile. As heavy as dinner on Shabbat afternoon. I'm beginning to regret I ever found your Shmuel."

"Could this be the same Shyke Pfeffer I once knew in Rosh Pinna?" Ivriya wondered out loud. "Is this the magnificent, the legendary Shyke Pfeffer who used to leap over the mountains and skip on the peaks?"

"It's the same poison-tongued Ivriya Mendelssohn, that's for sure," said Shyke Pfeffer. "If you want my humble opinion, we should not proceed a step farther. We should stop right here in the wadi, dig a hole, and stick Shmuel in. He wouldn't mind a bit. He loved the wadi."

"But it's a tribute to be buried in Safad," Tikva said, "among all the holy men."

"You should be ashamed of yourself, Shyke Pfeffer," said Ivriya, "complaining about carrying a quarter of a corpse that's already fifty percent rotted away. Look at Tikva here. Look at

59

the load she's carrying, and not a murmur, not a little peep."

Shyke Pfeffer turned to look at Tikva. He lowered his lantern to illuminate her great belly. "And how is it for you this time, Tikva?" he asked.

Tikva's eyes were on the rocky ground in front of her that would receive her next step. She was wearing Ivriya's glasses. "In some ways easier, in some ways harder," she answered Shyke.

"Do you remember how we went through this wadi together, Tikva? Once, long ago. It was night then, too, and you didn't have your glasses, and you weren't squinting at the world through Ivriya's, either, and you held on to me the whole way, and I led you like a dog leads a blind man, and it was raining, too, and I taught you how to walk between the raindrops, and when we came out at Safad you were perfectly dry."

"Do you think it's going to rain?" Reb Lev asked Roman Unger.

"That's all we need." Roman had just made his way to the head of the cortège, where Reb Lev Lurie and a yeshiva student were now carrying the lanterns.

"Is it time for us to relieve the pallbearers?" the student wanted to know.

"In a few minutes," said Roman Unger.

Reb Lev drew Roman away from the student. "Have you gotten any material on that new computer, Roman?" he inquired.

"I saw something in the mail before we left, but I didn't have time to really look at it."

"I suppose we'd be safest with the IBM," Reb Lev mused.

"Maybe so," said Roman, "but then, once we've made our decision, our biggest problem will be to find someone who'd be willing to bring such a machine into the country. We could never afford it if we had to buy it here and pay the taxes. Double, that's what it'd cost—double, minimum! And I'm not even beginning to calculate the cost of the software, or the problem of getting it to operate properly on two hundred and twenty volts, or the matter of warranties, parts, and repairs here in Israel for such a sophisticated piece of equipment—without a receipt, even! There are plenty of details that will have to be worked out, Reb Lev, believe me."

"God will help," Reb Lev said. "Bruriah's mother is supposed to be coming from the States in a few months. She always brings a few cases of diapers. Who'd ever think a computer would be nestled in an innocent case of Pampers? And the diapers would make excellent cushioning. What do you think?"

"It would be suspiciously heavy," Roman said.

"The machine could be taken apart. Something can be worked out. You're such a worrier, Roman; that's why you and Tikva make such a perfect couple. You can sit all day and worry together, like two old ladies discussing their operations. If I were like you, Roman, I'd still be stored away in Russia chewing frozen potatoes, God forbid. Faith, Roman, faith. 'If you have faith, you are truly alive,' Rav Nahman used to say. Of course, he was referring to faith in the Creator of the Universe, but it also applies to faith in the optimistic outcome of daily affairs, which derives from faith in the Almighty. Can you imagine, Roman, what a blessing a computer would be at Uman House? All the Gematria work that I now do by hand, referencing and cross-referencing the numerical values of the letters and words in the Torah, could be programmed into the computer. This labor of mine is truly in the name of heaven, for no letter in the Torah is superfluous, and if I can demonstrate the perfection of the Torah mathematically, through Gematria, then who in his right mind could deny the existence of its divine author? It would no longer be a matter of faith, but of reason—black and white. I do believe that the computer's inventor was a holy man, and that the computer itself is a divine gift, which we must use to honor His name. Did you know, Roman, that the numerical value of the word 'computer,' *mehashev*, is three hundred and fifty, which is only eight less than the numerical value of the word *mashiah*, 'messiah'? Is it too presumptuous to suggest that the *mehashev* of Uman House will lead, say, in eight years' time, to the coming of the *mashiah?*"

"The numerical value of 'Shmuel' is three hundred and seventy-seven," said Rami Marom.

"*Nu*, so? What about it?" Abba Nissim asked.

"I don't know," Rami Marom answered. "I just figured it out. Maybe it means something." They were the lead bearers of the stretcher at this time, walking directly behind Reb Lev Lurie and Roman Unger, and so fragments of the conversation about Gematria were wafting toward them.

"What do you think 'Himmelhoch' would come out to?" Rami speculated idly.

"I don't know," Abba Nissim said. "Not that much, despite the string of letters. But if you translate it, it means 'high heaven,' and that is also the meaning of your name—Marom."

"You think I'm related to Shmuel?" Rami took some time to assimilate this new possibility. "Who knows? Maybe I'm from the Sephardi branch of the family. But I don't know why, I can't feel any connection at all to this fellow we're carting."

"All Jews are brothers," said Abba Nissim.

"Well, I sincerely hope that this guy getting a free ride on this stretcher here is a Jew at least, for all the trouble he's putting us through. What if it's an Arab? What if it's not even a man? What if it's a woman?"

"Of course it's a man. It's a man in the image of God, and a Jew who struggled with his passions every day of his life. Only such a one could have suffered such a fate, Rami. Who else could it be?"

The walking was slow and hazardous, even after the moon appeared. Except for brief conversations here and there between people who found themselves to be temporary partners, and but for the droning song about the pangs of the Messiah sung by the one full-time pallbearer, there was only a silence deepened by the night rustlings of the Galilee. Those who could spare a thought from the concentrated attention mandated by carrying and by treading safely in the dark, were urged by Reb Lev to reflect on Samuel Himmelhoch. "The secondary benefit of thinking about Shmuel and his fate will be that you will also be simultaneously thinking about yourself," Reb Lev explained. "For all men are like a withering bloom, a passing shade, a broken pot, like a dream that flies by. Think, also, about the ways in which you might have offended Shmuel, and in your hearts ask him now to forgive you."

The memories of Samuel Himmelhoch were traded, not as they walked, but during the rest periods, which became more and more frequent as the night advanced.

Accordingly, as befitted his position in the group, Reb Lev Lurie of Uman House was the first to speak: "How well I remember the day our beloved Shmuel Himmelhoch first walked into my chambers. Never mind how he was dressed. Never mind the length of his hair, the gold ring in his nostril, the chains encircling his neck, the shirt that was open to display chest curls dyed with henna, not to mention a shameful tattoo. Never mind the trousers that squeezed and accentuated the groin, placing constant pressure on that department and thereby serving to give prominence and priority to the insatiable demands of that department. Never mind all that. I could discern at once that beneath this lurid exterior there was a distinguished soul—a distinguished but deeply mired and troubled soul that had been to places and partaken in acts that I had no desire to even begin contemplating. And I could also see that this was no small-time hippie, yippie, beatnik, or what have you, but a hard-core bohemian from the major leagues who had sampled everything, who had taken in and given out all the dirt, all the *shmutz* and *dreck,* from the lowest of the lowest depths. And now he was turning to me. 'One must always look for the good points in every Jew,' Rav Nahman said, and in our Shmuel Himmelhoch's eyes I could detect not only the superficial corruption and decadence, not only the pain and anguish, but the inner nobility of character, as well as a genuine yearning to change, to repent, to return. My task was awesome, for here was a precious soul indeed, well worth the saving, but my task was also delicate, for this was also a rare and dignified soul that, with one false move, could be lost

64

forever. On that day, my friends, Shmuel Himmelhoch related to me that he had been in India, where he had gone with one of his rock groups for whom he provided the lighting. He had been sitting half naked in the lotus position at the feet of a guru somewhere in the vastness of India, when suddenly he had been overcome by a question. The question was: What does all this have to do with me? And now he had found his way to my door, in quest of the very things that *had* to do with him.

"I will not violate the confidences that Shmuel honored me with on that day or later—I will not break Shmuel's trust—but I am certain he would forgive me if I imparted to you that he felt that, after all the sins he had committed, God would certainly reject him. 'You must conquer God,' I advised him, as Rav Nahman has taught us, because in His feminine emanation, in His *shehina*, God, like a woman, desires and longs to be overcome, but God, for His part, loves to be vanquished not through flattery and wiles, but through supplication, through meditation and prayer. 'But I cannot pray,' Shmuel said. It was then that I instructed Shmuel to go out into the meadows and the fields to converse with God. It is not necessary to make an appointment, for God can be everywhere at once. Go out and complain to Him. Break your heart before Him. Tell Him all your regrets, your woes, your vexations and aggravations, no matter how petty or base. Don't be ashamed. Speak to Him in your own language. Sing to Him. Cry out to Him. Pour out your heart like water before Him. Only through meditation can you improve and perfect yourself. If you have difficulty expressing yourself before God at first, then repeat a single word over and over again. Eventually, God will take pity and open your mouth. Shmuel then told me that he already had a word—a 'mantra,' he called it. He had paid a guru ten thousand dollars for this mantra. He opened the embossed leather pocketbook he wore over his shoulder, took out a receipt, and showed it to me. The mantra was 'feh.' Feh, feh, feh! To tell you the truth, I don't exactly remember what the mantra was. What does it matter? All I know is that it was a solid-gold mantra. This is what I said to Shmuel Himmelhoch on that day: 'Shmuel,' I said, 'I will give you a mantra free of charge. But it is not a cheap mantra, for it cannot be bought.' The word I gave him was *gevalt*. '*Gevalt! Gevalt! Gevalt!*' Incidentally, I might add that on that same occasion Shmuel remarked to me, as others have remarked before, about the glow that emanates from my person. It may not be bright enough to light our way through this wadi tonight, but it exists; enough people have noticed it, and Shmuel among them. As an expert in the field of lighting, Shmuel was curious to know its source. This is not 'Lighting by Samuel Himmelhoch,' I told him. My friends, he understood.

"Oh, our cherished Shmuel Himmelhoch was such a perfectionist, as we all know, and as the journal found by my dear friend and colleague Abba Nissim has confirmed. Never was he satisfied with himself. Even as he progressed and mastered the techniques of prayer and meditation, he was still not totally satisfied. Shmuel, I beg your forgiveness if in any way I have failed you as a teacher. If only you could come back from the dead now, Shmuel Himmelhoch, how well and how mightily you would be able to pray!"

Abba Nissim also spoke: "Tonight, by this sweet spring in the wadi that Shmuel Himmelhoch loved, among the date and almond trees, the anise and the mint, surrounded by trusted friends, all of us together for the last time, I don't think it would be improper to remember Shmuel in the most intimate of ways. On the contrary: Shmuel would have desired—indeed, insisted—that we recount and, above all, learn from his struggle to overcome the temptation that plagued him and impeded his advance toward spiritual perfection. I am referring, of course, to the universal appetite for sex, which in Shmuel Himmelhoch's case was far stronger than common, as it was for Rav Nahman of Bratslav himself. Perhaps the measure of the temptation is also the measure of the essence of the man. In the early months of Shmuel's return to the faith, we spent many hours together, he and I, walking to the holy graves of Tiberias, Meron, Safad, Hebron, Jerusalem, praying and crying out, and although our beloved Shmuel honored me with a multitude of confidences, it was a long, long time before he could bring up the subject that tormented him most acutely. And when he did, it was with the force of a volcano erupting, equally pent up and equally fiery, for Shmuel's blood literally burned. Then he poured out to me, in merciless detail, all that he had done, in all its foulness and carnality, and it was a loathsome confession indeed—loathsome and terrifying. It would be a grave sin to even attempt to imagine the ways in which Shmuel indiscriminately violated his own body, as well as those of an astonishing variety of God's creatures on earth, living and dead. Yet he said to me—and this was perhaps the most tragic admission of all—he said that nothing he had done, however sordid, had ever matched the acts he committed in his own imagination. And Shmuel also said to me that never, not once, had he ever been totally satisfied. Through four full weeks, in all our waking hours and sometimes also as he or I slept, Shmuel talked, and when at last he had emptied himself out, the relief he felt was enormous. Not for nothing did Rav Nahman stress the value of confession. However, I cannot deny that at the end of those four intense weeks, I, for my part, felt quite sick.

"The first comfort was the emptying of his heart. The second comfort came to Shmuel when I described to him how our revered Rav Nahman suffered as keenly from the same temptation, and that much of Rav Nahman's energies were devoted—in the years of his youth, when he was in the greatest danger—to subduing this desire. With respect to this failing, I told Shmuel, he was in the best of company. Rav Nahman said that he was absolutely determined to surmount the sexual temptation, that, if necessary, he would yield to the Evil One on everything else, but never on this. What did Rav Nahman do? At first he indulged his other appetites—eating, for instance, much more than the ordinary man eats—as he concentrated on annihilating every vestige of his sexual cravings. He prayed and wept to God for many years, imploring to be rescued from this grave peril. In the end, he subjugated this appetite totally, and he reached a level of indescribable purity. So removed did he become from this desire that he could no longer imagine how it could be a source of temptation to anyone else. He said that any man with even an ounce of intelligence who considers anatomy and bodily functions would find the sexual act intrinsically repulsive and disgusting. Rav Nahman also said—and this affected Shmuel deeply—that sexual temptation comes from depression; therefore, we must always make every effort to be joyful. Shmuel was truly struck by this insight. The corrupt Western culture, Shmuel said, claims exactly the opposite: that depression leads to the suppression of the sexual drive. But the truth was Rav Nahman's, and Shmuel now realized how depressed he had always been.

"It is painful to conjure up the degree of comfort and hope that our dear Shmuel Himmelhoch took from the possibility of reaching Uman. For Shmuel, Uman represented the cure for all his most intimate afflictions. Perhaps it can be said that he placed too much hope in the powers of Uman. For Rav Nahman never promised the complete and everlasting cessation of all the lower drives. There are those, indeed, who find it necessary to make the pilgrimage to Uman each year. Around Rosh Hashanah is the best time. And as for the promise of an end to nocturnal emissions, that is primarily directed at young boys, who should recite the ten psalms and give a penny to charity by the grave in Uman, preferably before the age of seven; Akiva Himmelhoch, for example, Shmuel's own beloved son, would benefit enormously. But in the mind and heart of our valiant Shmuel Himmelhoch, Uman was the ultimate goal. It was the ideal. He made many attempts to reach it, as we know, and though he failed in his lifetime, I maintain that we should not view his attempts as merely heartbreaking; they were noble—indeed, heroic—and for those attempts alone he will be judged among the righteous. After one such attempt—during which he stumbled into the old trap, this time with a couple of sons of Ishmael in Istanbul—he came, in utter dejection and anguish, to seek my advice at the old cemetery of Safad, where I am the caretaker, and where we are now, alas, returning him. At that time he threw himself across the tombstone of Rav Nahman's daughter and wept in such bitterness and despair, it cannot be imagined. It was during this period that he made the decision, with my guidance and full approval, to take for a wife the woman who is now his widow. He needed the proper traditional outlet that marriage would provide to control his appetites. That is what we concluded. In his free life Shmuel had known the woman under consideration, and he had wronged her, used her. Now she was a cripple, and through this marriage he could absolve himself of his previous wrongdoings, he could earn extra credit with the One Above, and he could save both himself and the woman. And she would serve him as a constant reminder of the futility and pitifulness of passion, for when he would be compelled by his husbandly duty to gaze on the parts of her body that were now wasted—those very parts that, in the past, had inflamed him—he would be struck anew with the knowledge of what a sorry and pathetic thing it was that had tempted and intoxicated and driven him crazy for so many years. His wife, for her part, would earn the great deed of easing her husband's passage to the spiritual, if not the physical, Uman. Shmuel Himmelhoch, your earthly journey is now almost ended. May you reach your destination at last."

Roman Unger: "With all due respect to Abba Nissim—may he continue to live many long, good days, may his candle shed light—I would like to say, on behalf of the widow of our beloved Shmuel Himmelhoch, that his marriage to Ivriya Mendelssohn represented far more than an act of expiation or of benevolence on Shmuel's part. For, inasmuch as it was possible for Shmuel to divert his attention from the pursuit of his own perfection in whatever realm, and to love a woman, he loved his wife. Except for myself, of all the people assembled here tonight, Ivriya knew Shmuel the longest. And although for many years they each traveled on separate paths and sampled many things, Ivriya, I believe, had always been Shmuel's destined one. She was the one to whom he always returned. She was, so to speak, the bride of his youth, although, as many of us know, Shmuel had been married once before. I would venture to suggest that if our venerable Abba Nissim had had the opportunity to know Shmuel Himmelhoch's former wife, he would genuinely appreciate the present one.

"Perhaps it was wrong of me to mention Shmuel's first marriage on this occasion, for it was a brief, fruitless union, and in the final summation of Shmuel Himmelhoch's life and career it is scarcely worthy of mention. Yet something about this trek through this wadi tonight to convey Shmuel to his final resting place reminds me of that time. For I feel Shmuel's presence very strongly here and now, just as I felt it after his first marriage, when his mother and father sat for seven days, mourning him as if he were dead. Not that Shmuel's parents—peace be unto them—were especially devout or observant people, but when their son took a Negro woman as his bride, they felt impelled to follow the traditional course of Jewish parents whose offspring marries out of the faith. As for myself, at that time I, too, was a veteran, full-time sinner, and for my part, I'm ashamed to say, I had no objection to Shmuel's marrying a *shiksa,* even a green one. Nor did it bother me at that time that the woman was a certified schizophrenic; her madness only made her more interesting to us in those mad days. The only thing that troubled me then was that this particular black schizophrenic *shiksa* was a stewardess for the German airlines, and, to tell you the truth, even that didn't bother me enough to make me say something to Shmuel. God help us, we were bad.

"But all this is past history, and I'm wandering away from the point. What I really wanted to tell you was that when Shmuel's parents sat *shiva*—in stockinged feet, on top of crates or directly on the floor, their garments torn and soiled, the door flung open to comforters and strangers alike—Shmuel's presence, the presence of the son they were mourning, was felt very powerfully indeed, just as I feel it now. But now, on this journey to Safad, it is his spiritual presence I feel. Then, while his parents mourned him as if he were dead on account of his marriage to a black Gentile schizophrenic who flew Lufthansa, it was his physical presence I felt, for the fact of the matter was, Shmuel was actually there. He had come in on the first day, sat down on the couch, and refused to budge for the full seven days of mourning over him. There he sat, even as friends and relatives came in to console his bereaved parents and took their places on the sofa beside the deceased. The truth was, nobody could throw him out, especially his parents, for to do so would be to acknowledge his existence, and since he had been officially declared dead, the recognition implied by dislodging him would be a contradiction in terms. So Shmuel sat on for seven days, eating, yawning, smoking, scratching, blowing his nose, popping his blackheads, examining his fingernails, checking for lice in his long, tangled hair, and in general pretending to be alive. He was in his early twenties then, I think, and this was probably the longest period of time he had spent with his parents since he ran away from home at age fourteen. Shmuel was always such a startling, such an astonishing person. He was a natural original, both as a sinner and as a penitent. To me he was always a loyal friend, and he never forsook or disdained me, even in the days when his material fortunes rose. I shall miss him deeply. May the Merciful One protect him under His wings forever, and keep his soul alive."

Shyke Pfeffer: "It's true what Roman Unger says, about Shmuel Himmelhoch being the most faithful of friends. It seems, after all, that Roman and I agree on many points, including our taste in women. Tikva will also tell you how it was with Shmuel: no matter how rich and famous Shmuel became, no matter what distances he had traveled—to the four corners of the earth, to outer space, even, I wouldn't put it past him—when he came back home to the Land of Israel, he never failed to stop by and visit his old friend, the poor robber, Shyke Pfeffer. This is the truth. Shmuel always found time for me, even when my exploits ceased to be celebrated on every tongue from Metulla to Eilat. Never once did I find out that Shmuel had been in the country without coming by. If someone would say to me, 'Did you know, Shyke, that Shmuel Himmelhoch is back?' I would answer, 'Certainly, I've already seen him,' or I'd say, 'He'll be popping in any day, then'—as the case may be. I was never disappointed.

"And when he came for a visit, what a holiday it was! Always he would bring the finest of presents—I couldn't begin to describe to you what treasures he laid before me—but best of all was the dope: the most exquisite hashish, the strongest marijuana, the purest cocaine on the market. For the old has-been Shyke Pfeffer, Shmuel Himmelhoch spared no expense. This was a friend the likes of which never was and never will be again. I'll miss him, believe me. And always Shmuel would greet me like this: 'How's business, Shyke?' he'd say, because he respected my line of work and took it seriously, you see, and he'd embrace me and kiss me on each cheek. And sometimes he'd say, 'Enough already with the daily aggravations of petty burglaries and stickups in the Galil, Shyke. You deserve a vacation.' And he'd carry me off somewhere restful, all expenses paid. A few times he took Tikva and our son, Einstein, along, too. And once Ivriya came also. It was to Dahab we went that time—excuse me, Roman, if such memories hurt you, but I bring them up only to praise the generosity of our mutual friend Shmuel Himmelhoch. Every day in Dahab we swam among the luminous red and blue and gold fishes in the crystal-clear waters of the Red Sea, wove in and out among coral and sponge, and for one full, shimmering week not a stitch of clothing touched our bodies. It was paradise, better even than the Garden of Eden, for we enjoyed all the benefits of Before the Fall, plus all the post-Fall pleasures as well. Where can you find such a friend as Shmuel Himmelhoch? I ask you.

"And what about the time Shmuel visited me after Tikva took Einstein and left for good? You can imagine how low I was feeling. But Shmuel said, 'Enough with this senseless moping over a woman, Shyke.' And he flew me, first-class, to Cairo. All day long we slept on the freshest linen in our air-conditioned, five-star luxury hotel, and every night we went to the opium dens. The waiters in these opium dens were chimpanzees. At first I thought they were merely hairy dwarfs dressed in tuxedos and bow ties—so dark and smoky were these opium dens. But no, they were monkeys—our first cousins, according to the wisdom of the goyim—and they served us very smartly. They brought us our opium on little trays and they brought us whatever else we asked for, and they themselves, these monkeys, were always stoned, and when the police came and raided the place, they arrested the monkeys and left us, the patrons, in peace. It was a very civilized system. Why do I tell you all this? Why do I remind you now of how sinful Shmuel was, and, moreover, of how he also led astray such innocent bandits as myself? Only so that you will appreciate what he had to overcome, for the pleasures of his former life, while wicked, were nevertheless pleasures. Yet he gave them all up. 'In a place where a penitent stands, even a *tzaddik* may not stand.' These

74

are the words of our sages. Shmuel, when he repented, displaced many of the most righteous.

"Yet even when Shmuel Himmelhoch forsook his bad old ways and began his return, he did not neglect his senile friend the outlaw Shyke Pfeffer. Absolutely not. He came to see me many times in the course of his early wanderings with Abba Nissim, and not for a moment did he consider me hopeless or a lost cause or unworthy of his efforts. For hours he sat and talked to me, seeking to persuade me to embark on the road he had taken. 'But you don't understand,' I tried to explain to him: 'I have a reputation to maintain. What about my fans? What will they think when they hear that the cool and unflinching Shyke Pfeffer has gone holy and soft?' But Shmuel convinced me that I could return in penance in my own unique style, that there was also room for the likes of me, that my admirers would come to admire me even more. It was as if this faith he was offering me was another gift he was bringing from the world he had just visited. So far, at least, I haven't regretted accepting his gift. He was not a tolerant person, Shmuel Himmelhoch, but of me he was tolerant. It was my honor and my privilege to find him today. When I saw you lying there, Shmuel, I said to myself, The Creator of the Universe has put the opportunity in my path to repay you for all the acts of loving-kindness you have done for me in the past. We've made many trips together, Shmuel. This one looks like our last. I won't forget you, Shmuel, and I know that when you appear before the Supreme Judge in the seventh heaven to give an account and a reckoning, you'll remember how your old friend Shyke Pfeffer found you in the mud and slime in Meron, cleaned you up, and went to all this trouble to arrange a dignified burial for you. You won't forget your old friend Shyke Pfeffer, I'm sure. Put in a good word for me with the Chief Constable up above. Don't forget, Shmuel. I'll need it."

Rami Marom: "We all know that in Shmuel Himmelhoch the nomadic spirit was strong. Even after his return to the Torah path, when he settled down here in Israel, he did not end his restless traveling. He wandered the length and breadth of our Holy Land, and he knew her shape and face intimately, in the way an artist knows his model, or a lover his beloved. He was in motion from the day he left home, not long after his bar mitzvah, and even tonight, in death, he's still on the go. If ever there was a wandering Jew, it was Shmuel Himmelhoch. If ever there was a true son of Cain, a fugitive and a vagabond on this earth, it was Shmuel Himmelhoch. Yet, though he had been almost everywhere in the world, there was one place he could never reach, and it was to this place that he longed to be brought above all. I mean, of course, Uman.

"In the journal that our revered teacher Abba Nissim found in Safad, we read about the trip to Uman that Shmuel took with Roman Unger and myself, with the help of some Mexican passports that suddenly became available, a miracle from above. As you know from the journal, the high privilege that was granted to Roman and to me was arbitrarily denied to Shmuel Himmelhoch. We were allowed to proceed, but Shmuel was not. What Shmuel does not go on to tell you in those pages, however, is that the Soviet authorities modified their plans and didn't ship Shmuel home right away. Instead they held him hostage in the airport, pending Roman's and my return from the blessed grave in Uman. This is not the time or the place to describe to you the peaks of ecstasy that Roman and I reached during our three days of praying and meditating

76

and pouring out our souls and breaking our hearts by the modest grave of Rav Nahman of Bratslav, may the memory of the righteous be a blessing. But you can hardly imagine our surprise when we came back to Kiev and were greeted, right there in the airport, by Shmuel Himmelhoch himself. We weren't expecting it. What was the point of keeping Shmuel hostage, we wondered, if nobody had even bothered to inform Roman and me, the very persons whose conduct Shmuel's confinement was meant to control? And the truth of the matter was that we felt terribly ashamed and guilty with respect to Shmuel, but Shmuel, peace be unto him, relieved us at once. Not a single word of reproach left his mouth. On the contrary, he was delirious with joy. He had been with us in Uman every minute, he said. In our prayers, in our songs he was with us, in our bliss and in our rapture he was by our side. He was, he said, like the astronaut who had been obliged to remain in the spaceship circling the moon while his two comrades landed and walked on the surface. The exploit of the two would have been impossible without the orbiting of the third. So, too, Shmuel said, Roman's and my time in Uman would have been impossible were it not for his time locked up as a hostage, without food or companionship, in the airport of Kiev. Just as the astronaut who had kept the spaceship in motion had been, it can be said, to the moon, so, too, he, Shmuel Himmelhoch, had been to Uman. 'I, too, have been brought to Uman,' Shmuel said, and Roman and I were delighted that he felt that way about the outcome of the expedition, that he didn't hold any grudges against us personally. What could we have done, anyway? It wasn't our fault. Had Shmuel been in our position, he would have grabbed the opportunity, exactly as we had. He would not have declared to the authorities that if his companion couldn't

77

come, he wouldn't go, either. What would have been the point? What would it matter to those atheists if any of us went? We had come so far. It would have been a pity to turn back.

"And now I, too, believe that Shmuel Himmelhoch was with us in Uman. I truly believe this, with all my heart and with all my soul. So don't pity our dear Shmuel Himmelhoch because of his failure to reach Uman. He was there. He said so himself. And the final proof is that Shmuel would never have allowed himself the luxury of dying before getting to Uman. And now he has passed on. I am sorry for you, my brother, Shmuel, you were very pleasant to me. Your love was more wonderful to me than the love of women. How the mighty have fallen."

Ivriya Himmelhoch began: "I want to talk about some of the sides of Shmuel's character that none of you could have possibly known."

"Only the males may speak!" cried the yeshiva student who had been carrying throughout the march and singing of the pangs of the Messiah.

The group was now resting on rocks along the banks of a narrow stream, but Ivriya was still mounted high atop her mule, with no place to hide, for Tikva, in her condition, was not able to stretch and lift her down and there was no other woman present to handle a sister. This was to be absolutely the final rest period, Reb Lev Lurie had decreed. The midnight hour was drawing close, and suddenly it seemed imperative to get Samuel Himmelhoch into the ground on that day and not on the next. As it was, the decision to carry out the burial after sunset was questionable enough. Himmelhoch's remains had lingered far too long; the situation was intolerable. There were two paths they could now take to reach the old cemetery of Safad, Shyke Pfeffer explained: the long and straight one, almost a proper road, or the steep, craggy, shorter route. To save time, they chose the second.

Roman Unger said, "Reb Lev, can you make some sort of exception in this case? I think Ivriya should be allowed to say a few words."

"We certainly have precedents for women addressing the congregation at large," Reb Lev said. "There's the Song of Miriam, for example, and also Devora's Song. Those were sung in moments of triumph, it's true, but since ecstasy and joy, according to Rav Nahman, are holy, exalted states, if a woman is permitted to relieve herself on those occasions, then how much more so in the pits of sorrow? What is your opinion, Abba Nissim?"

"It would be acceptable for the widow to speak, in my view, if she is a minimum of four feet distant from the men, and if, as she speaks, the men sit with their heads lowered and do not gaze upon her. Also, as an extra precaution, we might erect some sort of makeshift barrier to separate the males from the females, or perhaps the women can cross the stream and the widow can speak from the opposite side."

"All excellent suggestions, Abba Nissim," said Reb Lev. "Had we known in advance that the widow would desire to speak, we might have required that she purify herself beforehand by immersion in the ritual bath. But Shmuel, peace be unto him, let himself be found only this morning, and there hasn't been time for any preparations."

"The men can immerse themselves immediately after the burial," Abba Nissim suggested, "in the *mikvah* of the Ari, right above the graveyard. Thus will we cleanse ourselves not only of the impurities of the dead, but also of the frivolity of female thought and discourse."

"Oh, but the water will be so cold," Rami Maron heard himself say.

"At the very least we can take comfort in the almost certain knowledge that the widow has not been rendered unclean by conjugal relations for a period of at least two years," Abba Nissim added.

"Good point," Reb Lev said. "And by my calculations, the numerical value of *nekayva,* 'female,' is one hundred and fifty-seven, which is eight more than *hesped,* 'eulogy,' and eight less than *kina,* 'dirge.' Thus, the female is sandwiched between eulogy and dirge. These two forms of expression are her proper domain and borders. They are the wings with which she reaches out to the world. They are her conduit and outlet. They are her natural territory, and therefore I believe we can proceed. So, then, we're all in agreement. The widow may speak."

"The role of woman is to wail at funerals," Shyke Pfeffer objected, "not to blab. And by the way, I haven't noticed a single drop of moisture in the widow's eye. Are her tears precious gems? What is she saving them for?"

"Forgive me, Reb Lev," said the yeshiva student who sang of the Messiah's pangs, the one who had protested in the first place; "I cannot hold by your ruling in this instance. In general, it seems to me that you tend to the side of leniency. I for one cannot permit myself to listen to the voice of the woman, nor, for that matter, can I allow Shmuel to do so. So, if you'll give me leave, I shall move on, and take the body with me. Who, in the name of piety, will follow?"

"I'm with you," said Shyke Pfeffer.

"Good. The two of us will go ahead. Our progress will be slow, but we'll manage. Shmuel seems to be getting lighter and more insubstantial. When this interlude of idle chatter is over, the rest of you can catch up." The yeshiva student turned to face the hills, thrust his arms down behind him, squatted, and lifted the front end of the stretcher by its two poles. Shyke Pfeffer raised the litter by the two rear poles, but because he was considerably lighter and weaker than the younger man, the stretcher slanted and the body began to fold up and slide downward. The two men put the stretcher on the ground again while the yeshiva student collected the rope belts of his comrades, tied them together, and used them to strap the body to the bier in two places—under the arms, and in the depression where the thighs meet the groin. Then the student and Pfeffer hoisted the stretcher for a second time and mined slowly into the darkness. The student's song about the pangs of the Messiah—here they come, here they come today—drifted back to the others more and more faintly.

"I didn't mean to cause so much trouble," Ivriya said. "Maybe they're right. Maybe I shouldn't speak at all. Maybe Shmuel wouldn't have wanted me to."

"You may speak or not, as you wish," said Reb Lev.

Ivriya crossed the shallow stream on her mule, and Tikva Unger waded beside her. The men turned their backs, sank their heads, and shielded their eyes. Ivriya Himmelhoch spoke: "I'll try not to embarrass Shmuel with my words. He was the first man I ever knew, and, judging by the way things look now, he'll probably be the last. I met him when I was fifteen, a wild and rebellious daughter—may we be spared such anguish from our own children. He was three years older than I, and already he had about him the air of a man sated by the pleasures of this world. He seemed like an orphan. It was, all in all, an extremely attractive pose. We met at a discotheque called Brain Damage. It's not important. That was nearly twenty years ago. Really, we grew up together, Shmuel and I. We passed through many things, together and apart. Always he came back to me, as Roman was kind enough to say in my defense, sometimes for longer periods, sometimes for shorter. Even when Shmuel was married to his first wife, he visited me. Is adultery a transgression under those circumstances? Anyway, that's beside the point. All the while I was leading my own life, don't forget, parallel to Shmuel's or joined, as the case may be. I had my horses and my friends in Rosh Pinna, my poetry, my travels—the years I spent in Amsterdam, Ibiza, New York. But you don't want to hear about me. I'm not the guest of honor here tonight. Even the guest of honor is no longer here tonight.

"When I had my accident at the age of twenty-five, Shmuel was out of the country. He was on that very same pilgrimage to India that Reb Lev told you about. It has always seemed uncanny to me that the turning points in both our lives came at about the same time. But that's how it has always been between Shmuel and me: what we had was not an ordinary marriage; it was blood. We were kin, Shmuel and I, brother and sister, not physically—God forbid—but in the spiritual sense, soulmates. I was already an outpatient at the rehabilitation center—I was back home, at my mother's, that is—when Shmuel came to see me for the first time after my fall. He stormed in like a prophet, blazing with the fires of revelation and discovery. He had been reborn into a dazzling new world, the intoxicating and rarefied world of faith, and he wanted to drag me there, too, never mind my doubts and my resistance. But at that time I had had enough of people pushing me

82

around, forcing me against my will, always for my own good. I gave Shmuel a hard time, I admit. I was depressed. 'Depression is not permitted,' he said to me like a good Bratslaver. 'I can't help it,' I told him. 'I'd be crazy if I weren't depressed. Who'd ever want a woman who's out of commission from the waist down? Who'd ever consider marrying someone like me? Would you marry me, Shmuel?" I asked him point-blank. How could I doubt it? Of course he would marry me, he insisted, but first he would have to be released from the vows of asceticism he had taken, and this was a serious, maybe insurmountable obstacle, since there was no longer a Temple where the requisite sacrifices could be brought; but soon the Messiah would come, he assured me, and the Temple would be rebuilt, and he could be absolved from his Nazarite vows and we could get married. Those of you who knew Shmuel in the early days of his penitence will remember that he was a Nazarite then: he never cut his hair, he drank no wine, he did not touch a corpse, and, because Shmuel was always an extremist, he also took upon himself the added vow of sexual abstinence, which, as far as I know, is not required of the Nazarite and by some sages is actually regarded as sinful. Yet, despite my cynicism about what I called his 'latest high,' Shmuel came to visit me often, and often, when he left, I would hear myself singing.

"It was Abba Nissim who released Shmuel from his Nazarite vows. This was after Shmuel had come back from one of his trips to Uman, where he got into a mess in Turkey. You can read about it in his journal. With all due respect to the majestic Abba Nissim, I'd like to give my version of what happened then between Shmuel and me. Shmuel came to see me with a freshly shaven head. All that was left of his hair were two tame sidelocks. He was now ready to proceed with the marriage, he informed me. It was I who demurred this time. 'So, has the Messiah already come?' I said to Shmuel. 'And I didn't even hear the shofar blast.' I'm sorry, but I was a little sarcastic. My main reservation, I told him, was religious. This faith of his—I didn't know if I could subscribe to it as whole-heartedly as he did; it seemed to me, at least the way he practiced it, to be a mania of some sort, a madness, and also a straitjacket, an intolerable restraint. Shmuel argued by telling me that parable of Rav Nahman's, about the king's minister who informed his master that all the wheat in the land had been contaminated: whoever would eat of it would become crazy. What to do? Import wheat from another source. But they could never bring in enough wheat for the entire popula-tion. Then bring in enough uncontaminated wheat just to feed the king and his minister. But what was the value of being sane in a land where everyone else was crazy? In such a situation, *they* would be the ones who'd be considered mad. The solu-tion: the king and his minister would also eat of the con-taminated wheat, but they would make a sign on their fore-heads so that when they gazed at each other they would be reminded that they were actually crazy. This was the story Shmuel told me. I don't know why, but it affected me very much. Somehow it reassured me about Shmuel's fundamental balance. If he acted strangely, he was at least aware of it. Also, it seemed to me that he was saying that we, the two of us, Shmuel and I, were conspirators of a sort, that we shared a secret knowledge, and that even if on the surface we resembled everyone else, we at least understood what was going on. Even so, it took Shmuel nearly a year to convince me to marry him.

"I won't deny the existence of the Shmuel Himmelhoch you knew. He was that way: uncompromising, eccentric, tenacious, zealous, extreme, loyal. And I won't deny the harsh, tormented, possessed Shmuel Himmelhoch of the journal fragments, either. Shmuel was all that and more. I know you don't want me to talk about his messianic stirrings, just as every mention of Rav Nahman's identification with the Messiah ben Joseph and the Messiah ben David is censored out of the literature. I'll keep my mouth shut, don't worry. Shmuel was all the things you thought he was, but above all he was a stylist, and he was constantly polishing and perfecting his chief work of art—namely, himself. But there were, I want to tell you, other sides to Shmuel Himmelhoch that you will never be privileged to know. It's not true what Shmuel writes in his journal—that he gave me only minimal assistance with my personal needs. It's simply not true. He did far, far more for me than merely helping me into and out of bed. I'm not required to give you the intimate details. He liked to say that his fate in this world was to search for my eyeglasses. And he said this tenderly. It was a loving complaint. And do I need to remind you of what a gentle father Shmuel was to Akiva? It was Shmuel who paced with Akiva in the night. It was to Shmuel's lap that Akiva ran when he hurt himself at play. It was Shmuel who picked out the lice eggs from Akiva's hair, patiently, strand by strand, and it was a great tangled web of fine baby hair before it was cut at Meron when Akiva turned three. I don't understand why Shmuel refuses to allow the softer side of his nature to be known. Perhaps I'm embarrassing him by exposing it. Shmuel, am I embarrassing you? Wherever you are, Shmuel, give me a sign and I'll stop."

Roman Unger stood up on the opposite bank of the stream, his hands cupping his mouth. "Tikva," he called, "is she through?"

85

"What do you mean, 'Is she through'?" Tikva yelled back.

"I thought I heard her say 'stop.' We really must get going."

"You mean you couldn't hear me the whole time?" Ivriya cried.

"I heard every word, Ivriya. Don't worry. Some of the men had their fingers stuffed in their ears, but I listened to every syllable."

"What did I say, then?" Ivriya demanded.

"Come on, Ivriya, another time. We're in a rush."

"I'm not budging from this spot until you repeat at least one thing I said!"

"Okay. You said that you and Shmuel were both crazy: 'brain damaged' were your words—right? You said you were crazy because you were actually blood relations, and relatives should never get married, as everyone knows, for the sake of the mental and physical health of their children. And you also said that that's the reason Akiva now needs glasses. Okay, Ivriya? Now do you believe I was paying attention? Now are you happy?"

The last segment of the journey was taken in clenched, resolute silence broken only by the stumbling of the marchers. Even the men staggered on the stones, snapping branches and crackling dry grass, but they quickly righted themselves. It was cold and dark, and the news of the discovery of Samuel Himmelhoch's body that had reached them only that morning now seemed like well-rubbed history. When Tikva Unger's ankle turned in her Old Testament sandals and she collapsed, Roman rushed frantically to her side and insisted that she ride the mule with Ivriya. Then, when the mule's legs buckled under the great

86

weight, Tikva was gently shimmied down and supported, for the rest of the trek, by her husband on one side and by Rami Marom on the other. Reb Lev Lurie stated that there was no doubt in this emergency that the husband and wife might appear in public arm-in-arm. And as for Rami Marom's physical contact with the person of another man's pregnant wife, there was the twofold consolation that Tikva was certainly not in her menstrual phase, and, second, since the gender of the fetus was still unknown, the optimistic supposition was that Rami might actually be touching a male. Do not gaze at the vessel but at what is inside it, our fathers instructed us. The main thing was that Rami not touch more than was absolutely necessary.

When the marchers rose out of the wadi, they still had not caught up with the remains of Samuel Himmelhoch. They came out of the wadi into a broad meadow, which, in that darkness, seemed like a still lake. Ahead was a small, glowing crescent, and the group advanced toward this as if pulled. Black goats moved like their own shadows. Beyond the goats sat their Bedouin master, on an old wooden closet that had once been a toilet tank. The chain was still attached, and the Bedouin played with it, as with a rein or a leash. Patiently he awaited the approach of the mourners. He knew they would arrive, for it was he who was drawing them with his riches, with his radiant, gold-toothed smile. "Lighting by Samuel Himmelhoch," Ivriya mumbled when she was close enough to discern what that gleaming crescent was that had attracted them like a mirage. The Bedouin snapped his fingers, breaking the spell he had cast. His youngest wife emerged from the black tent, bearing a heap of tart apples in a copper bowl.

Rami Marom stepped forward to serve as spokesman and

interpreter. Regrettably, they must decline their host's generous invitation to sit down and slice the apples and sip some Turkish coffee. If the master of the tent would not thereby be insulted, they would prefer to take the apples along with them. By the way, had the esteemed son of Ishmael perhaps noticed a bier passing by in the night, conveyed by two men, one young and wild, the other old and wild? And wasn't the old Jewish cemetery not far from here? The foot of the cemetery, the Bedouin said, was directly across the wide field beyond, but the field was so overgrown with brambles and thorns it would make treacherous hiking indeed, for the ladies in particular. There was also a road that bordered the field and led to the top of the cemetery, but that was a longer route by far. If the men elected to traverse the field, he, their cousin in the lineage of Abraham, would be willing to transport the two women in his very fine pickup truck. They could return for the mule later. The Bedouin flashed his golden grin. This offer provoked a huddle of the four men. Reb Lev said, "It's late, and the women will only slow us down." "In any case, women are forbidden to enter a cemetery," Abba Nissim pointed out; "it brings misfortune to the world," he added cabalistically. "And it's no longer a matter of escorting the dead," Reb Lev put in. "So I'll accept his offer?" Rami Marom concluded. "Not on my life!" said Roman Unger. "You're out of your minds if you think I'm going to let my wife get into a car with an Arab. They all have one thing on their minds, and you know what it is." So it was decided that Roman would take his place in the cab of the pickup truck beside the Bedouin driver, and the two women would be loaded in the back. Once the women were safely deposited on the outskirts of the cemetery, Roman would run down the hill to meet his companions, and since he was traveling by car and they by foot, they would probably arrive at approximately the same time.

When the men came out of the field, their caftans were in shreds; burrs and thorns sequined their garments. The grave-yard fanned out along the mountain slope before them. At the pinnacle they could see Roman Unger's van, its headlights shining. They entered the cemetery, climbing the hill past the fresh graves of children murdered by terrorists, and, as they ascended into the ancient burial grounds, a deep weariness overcame them, a sure sign that they were trampling upon the bodies of the dead. They found Shyke Pfeffer and the yeshiva student in front of the cave where Hannah and her seven sons are said to lie. Frieda Mendelssohn was sitting on a rock beside the opening, like a sentry. The empty stretcher was lying at her feet.

The yeshiva student addressed Abba Nissim: "Please inform this daughter of Lilith that she must remove her person from these holy grounds at once." He indicated Ivriya's mother without looking at her directly.

"I'll be damned if I'm going to miss the grand finale after all the trouble I've gone through!" Frieda Mendelssohn locked her arms across her chest.

"She'll be damned indeed," said the student.

"How did you get here so fast?" Roman Unger inquired.

"Oh, we flew," said Shyke Pfeffer. "Suddenly, without the whole congregation, including everyone and his cousin, not to mention the ass, Shmuel made himself as light as a feather. It was as if his body weight had turned to vapor and all we were bearing was his ethereal soul. Suddenly he was as light as a cloud. As light as a balloon. As light as air. As light as a beloved child. As light as a matzoh ball."

"And where is he now, may his memory be a blessing?"

"In there." Shyke Pfeffer pointed to Hannah's crypt. "Is that where you were planning to put him anyway, Abba Nissim?"

"In fact, I had in mind Hosea's tomb. For God had commanded Hosea to take a wife of whoredom and children of whoredom. For some reason, I thought Hosea would be a more congenial companion for Shmuel. But it is forbidden to disturb the dead, and I suppose Shmuel will be just as comfortable at Hannah's."

"We thought you'd want Shmuel placed where you found his journal," Shyke Pfeffer said petulantly.

"Maybe so. But the great virtue of Hannah and her seven sons was their complete rejection of false images. They refused to bow down before idols, and for that they were slain. And Shmuel Himmelhoch, if I may say so without speaking ill of the dead, was compelled to struggle every minute against his idolatrous inclinations. Well, maybe Hannah and her boys will be a good influence on Shmuel."

"No one's even sure that Hannah and her seven sons are in there anyway," said Shyke Pfeffer.

"Yes, that's a fact," Abba Nissim confirmed.

"You did well, Shyke Pfeffer," said Reb Lev Lurie of Uman House. "In all your actions with respect to Shmuel Himmelhoch, you deserve to be praised. Alone you found Shmuel, and alone you buried him. You were right not to await our coming. You were right to place him with Hannah, for the Hannah of the Bible is the mother of Samuel the prophet. Thanks to you, the mortal remains of Shmuel Himmelhoch were hidden away on the day they were uncovered and were not allowed to linger until the morrow, which is now upon us."

Reb Lev picked up the empty stretcher. "The numerical value of *mitta,* 'bed,' is fifty-four," he said, displaying the bier, "which is three times eighteen or *chai,* 'life.' " He turned the bed over thrice. "The numerical value of *din,* 'judgment,' is also exactly fifty-four. May the judgment of him who has just been removed from this bed be turned to mercy. May the Almighty turn our mourning to dancing, our sackcloth to joy."

Reb Lev continued: "Shmuel Himmelhoch, it's so hard for me to believe you're truly dead, you who were so quick and vibrant. It's so hard for me to believe you're lying on the ground in there with your feet toward the door. Yet, through these thick stones of the sepulcher of the righteous and modest Hannah, I feel you easing into your niche. Shmuel, now at last you understand everything clearly. Now you understand the utter foolishness of all your mortal concerns and apprehensions, the vanity and triviality of all the desires and temptations that plagued you. Forgive us, Shmuel, if we have bothered you unnecessarily on this, your last earthly journey. We meant to please you. From Meron to Safad we bore you through the wadi, with honor and without contempt. Your material parts are now in place. Now your soul is unencumbered, free to seek entry into the kingdom of heaven. We have brought you up to here, Shmuel Himmelhoch; may you now be taken there."

THE DEAD
HASSIDIM

"It's beginning," Tikva Unger said to her husband, Roman. She held her breath, precisely in violation of everything she had been taught; it was as if she were silencing all of her body's machinery in order to attend more closely to the exquisitely high-pitched vibrato of the spasms. Her gaze turned inward and private; a no-trespassing warning dropped like a screen in front of her face, excluding Roman cruelly. "I told you not to walk through that wadi!" he blurted. Hardly a week had passed since their return to Uman House from the funeral of Samuel Himmelhoch, but Roman instantly made the connection between his wife's fall during that bleak march and these alarming contractions, which, according to his calculations, were

93

arriving a month too early. Roman and Tikva faced each other like combatants across the orange formica table in their room at Uman House. Taped on the wall between them was a large aerial photograph of the city of Jerusalem, with a representation of the Holy Temple superimposed on the denuded plateau of Mount Moriah, the Dome of the Rock and the Mosque of al-Aksa having been wishfully, magically swept away. From down the hall came the shrieks of one of Reb Lev and Bruriah's brood, soon joined, in the spirit of fraternal solidarity and just plain sociability, by the howling of two more. "I want you to go to the hospital," Roman said.

That was absolutely out of the question. Tikva knew exactly what happened in hospitals; she had had Einstein in a hospital, and under no circumstances would she repeat the experience. It was lodged as a sour memory in her heart, an obsessively ruminated regret. Simply put, she had been robbed of the experience of childbirth; that is exactly what she had told Roman many times. In the hospital you were transformed into a patient, an invalid, a case, a specimen, a disease. They shaved you and purged you and weighed you and strapped you and punctured you and probed you and drugged you and hung you up like a side of beef for anyone to glance at indifferently, men included. No hospital would ruin it for her this time, Tikva vowed. But it might very possibly be a premature baby, Roman insisted. What if something went wrong that could be swiftly corrected in a hospital but that at home would mean everlasting disaster and calamity? What if, as a result of her stubbornness, her childishness, their son were an imbecile, a vegetable? Would she ever be able to forgive herself? "Would you, Tikva?" "God will help," said Tikva. She squeezed her eyes shut and laced her fingers across her belly, like a closing gate.

"I'm having another one," she said. Roman put out his hand to stroke her lightly. "Don't touch me!" Tikva screamed.

She wanted him to go at once to fetch the old Bokharan midwife, Shifra-Puah. And, also, to bring Ivriya Himmelhoch. Tikva needed a woman at her side now, a close friend. Bruriah Lurie would not do. Tikva wanted someone who would not judge her, who would forgive her, someone in whose presence she could scream at the top of her lungs and collapse into weakness. Tikva had witnessed four of Bruriah's seven deliveries so far, and Bruriah had spat them out soundlessly—pop, like missiles; the women caught the babies in mid-air. But even the formidably exemplary Bruriah Lurie would be a better companion at this time than her pants-wetting husband, Roman. As soon as Roman brought Shifra-Puah and Ivriya to her side, he must leave her in peace. He could go and make himself useful by reciting a few psalms in the study hall. He could learn a tractate of Talmud with Reb Lev Lurie or with Rami Marom or with Shimon Breslau, or with anyone he chose—she didn't care. Abba Nissim was visiting at Uman House now, too; Roman could go and unravel a mystery of the cabalah with Abba Nissim, if that suited him. He could unravel or ravel to his heart's delight. He could jam with the Uman Boys Band, he could pray at the Wall and stuff a petition into a chink, he could fly a kite. Only don't bother me. She didn't want him now. She wanted Shifra-Puah, she wanted Ivriya Himmelhoch, she wanted her mother.

Her mother, during this startling early phase of Tikva's labor, was on mess duty in the communal dining room of the northern kibbutz where Tikva had grown up; the mother was scraping pork and sour cream off the plates and stacking them in the dishwasher. Years ago, when this troublesome daughter,

Tikva, had taken up with the gangster Shyke Pfeffer, the mother had rationalized it as a developmental stage and had even, let it be said, taken a perverse secret pride in the arrangement, for Shyke Pfeffer, though degenerate, was at least a figure of renown, and colorful. The mother had even offered to keep Einstein Pfeffer, the product of that lustrous union, but Tikva, contrary as always, chose a fanatic boarding school in Bnei Brak over the wholesome children's paradise of the kibbutz. When Tikva became a religious maniac, the mother had retreated, bewildered by the suspicion that her daughter was a mental case, and then, overcome by the scope of Tikva's ingratitude and lack of consideration, the mother had drawn away entirely, in cold wrath. As she performed the automatic kitchen tasks, Tikva's mother was wondering if there was any halfway-decent man left on this earth who would still take the slightest notice of a fifty-year-old woman with callused hands, who had toiled too long in the sun. No one had even bothered to inform her that Tikva was pregnant.

Shifra-Puah, the old Bokharan midwife, lived in one of the narrow side streets that honeycombed off the Mahane Yehuda marketplace in central Jerusalem. Her height was four feet eight inches; the hennaed braids that descended from her flowered kerchief were just as long (or as short); her face was as lined as an old leather tobacco pouch that had been folded into the back pocket of a pair of pants and sat upon for decades; always there was a cigarette drooping from her dry lips. No one, herself included, knew her exact age, but it was well established that, at the very least, she was not a day younger than eighty. She was also reputed to be astoundingly wealthy, the owner of priceless estates scattered throughout Jerusalem, properties for which whole armies had exterminated one another. Where did this wealth come from? No one could say. Shifra-Puah told fortunes, and was highly regarded as a midwife; it was commonly said of her that whoever had not seen Shifra-Puah in action had never experienced birth. Shifra-Puah also traded in jewelry, silk dresses, satin and velvet robes, cashmere shawls, laces, tapestries, and carpets from Bokhara, which had been in her family for generations. The walls of her two rooms off Mahane Yehuda were piled—floor to ceiling, as well as under the tables, the beds, under anything that had an under—with cartons and bundles and suitcases of these treasures. In the middle of all this stood Roman Unger, pleading with Shifra-Puah to come to Tikva at once. "It's still too early, dumbbell," said Shifra-Puah, her cigarette bobbing hypnotically. "How do you know?" "How do I know? How does anyone know anything, little faker?" "Come now anyway, Shifra-Puah. Please. For the sake of my peace of mind. You'll ride in my van like a queen. Come as my guest. Come for a glass of tea and a piece of cake."

Ivriya Himmelhoch was also reluctant to go, and Roman was obliged to entreat her just as strenuously. "For Tikva's sake, please. She needs you now. She wants you, Ivriya, she asked especially. Have you already forgotten how Tikva traipsed through the wadi for you last week? I'm not blaming you, Ivriya—don't think I'm blaming you—but because of her fall it's coming too soon. And do you remember how I defended you that night against the words of Abba Nissim? And do you remember how I demanded that you be allowed to speak? Ivriya, your character is being tested. Only don't come for my sake. Don't come for Tikva, even. Come for the sake of your future peace of mind. You'll never forgive yourself if you don't come now."

97

First of all, Ivriya pointed out, she had just risen from *shiva,* from the seven days of mourning over her husband, Shmuel Himmelhoch, may his memory be a blessing, and she needed some time to clear her head and get herself organized. Akiva was tired, too. She would have to bring him along, of course. What about his routine? What about school? And her companion, Sora Katz: she, too, would have to come, to assist Ivriya at Uman House. And if Sora Katz came, so, naturally, would Sora's son, Shneour Zalman. It really was too complicated. Tikva was reasonable; she would understand if Roman explained it all to her nicely, sympathetically. For Ivriya it was simply too difficult to leave home, where everything, thanks to her mother's money and efforts, was set up for a wheelchair— wide passageways, ample turn spaces, ramps, even lowered counters to accommodate a seated housewife. It was always a major production for Ivriya to set out, and with all her entourage and paraphernalia she'd be far more trouble than help to Tikva at this hour, believe me. And Uman House, up two flights of steep, winding stone stairs in the Moslem Quarter of the Old City, would be, for Ivriya, a virtual prison. Even those who could get from here to there on their own two feet were prisoners at Uman House, surrounded as they were on all sides by Arabs with Kalashnikovs in their pajamas. But as for Ivriya, once she was carried in, she would be forced to rely on the kindness of strangers to be borne out again. It was just not enough for her to sit on the roof of Uman House and bask in the marksman's view of the Western Wall and the Temple Mount. She had worked hard and paid dearly for the pathetic morsel of independence she possessed; why would she voluntarily lock herself away at Uman House, even for a short time, even if Roman swore by all that was holy to spring her as soon as the baby was out? What's more, rumors had been circulating that Bruriah Lurie—the brilliant, imaginative matchmaker Bruriah Lurie—was planning to fix Ivriya up with that beggar—you know the one—who is parked each morning in front of the bank, propped in a wheelbarrow, the poor fellow who had been shot in the legs during the Yom Kippur War, whose thighs and hips had gradually been eaten up by gangrene until they had disappeared while what was left of him above the waist was consumed by faith. The subtle matchmaker Bruriah Lurie was just about the last person on earth that Ivriya wanted to deal with at this time, raw as she was from Shmuel's burial. No, it was simply not feasible. Tikva would certainly understand. From someone else it might be a small favor to ask, but from Ivriya, at this time and in her condition, it was just too much.

The beggar whose body ended at the waist was called Yisrael Gamzu, but soon after Ivriya was deposited in Tikva's room at Uman House she was calmed by the sense that Bruriah Lurie had no intention at all of proposing a match between her and that other invalid. Perhaps the image of such an obvious couple had flitted across Bruriah's mind at one time or another, and maybe she had even tested the notion on a friend or two—but just see how rumors start! The full thirty days had not even elapsed since Shmuel Himmelhoch's burial. It was absolutely improper to raise the possibility of remarriage at this time. And even if Bruriah managed to persuade her husband, Reb Lev, to rule that in Ivriya's case it would not be necessary to wait the full year—since who could say how long Shmuel Himmelhoch had already been dead?—still, the bottomless beggar

Yisrael Gamzu, however suffering and saintly, was the wrong bridegroom for Ivriya. What Ivriya required in a man, Bruriah reflected, was a complementary handicap, deafness maybe, or blindness perhaps, not the redundancy of immobility: someone damaged on top to complement Ivriya's lower-level disability— put together, they would form a whole person. Like those painted wooden babushka dolls from her husband's mother-land, the top and bottom halves clicking neatly together. How-ever hard she tried, Bruriah Lurie could never succeed in eradi-cating the secular imagery that had invaded and still occupied her mind.

The two beds in the Ungers' room at Uman House were pushed together, and Bruriah was sitting at the edge of Tikva's, nursing her youngest child and coaching the laboring woman as the contractions gathered and mounted. "Pant! Pant! Pant like a dog!" Bruriah urged. She had studied all the texts on the various natural childbirth methods, and each of her own seven deliveries had been a radiant triumph of technique. When the baby would emerge at last, the glistening and transfigured Bruriah seemed to rise like a grand actress bowing deeply at the end of a mighty performance: women who attended Bruriah have been known to applaud, to give her a standing ovation. Bruriah believed in the natural way of life almost as firmly as she believed in God and His chosen people. "Has it ever occurred to you, my dear wife," her husband, Reb Lev, used to tease, "that when the Messiah comes, quickly and in our time, the white robes he'll be wearing might be made of polyes-ter?" Bruriah breast-fed her children for as long as possible; that was her sole form of contraception. And she counseled women on their nursing problems: sore nipples, insufficient milk, triplets and only two breasts available—what's to be done? Bruriah was a crusader for breast-feeding. She was admirable, earnest, passionate, she always meant well, and she always tried her best. Tikva lay on her back, moistening her lips with the sugarless cherry lollypop Bruriah had given her, holding the hand of her best friend, Ivriya Himmelhoch, who had been set down beside her on Roman's bed. "She's having a contraction," Ivriya would inform Bruriah, for each time a pain rose like a wave and crashed, Tikva dug her fingernails into the palm of Ivriya's hand. Bruriah timed the duration of the contractions and the intervals between them, and she estimated that the cervix was about four to five centimeters dilated. "Ooh, it hurts so much," Tikva moaned. "You're not even in transition yet," Bruriah advised her. "You have five or six centimeters to go before you're fully dilated and can start pushing. The real fun hasn't even begun."

Shifra-Puah the midwife did not stir from her seat at the orange Formica table with the aluminum legs. When the time came to go into spectacular action, she would know it; the women trusted Shifra-Puah's knowledge. Bruriah Lurie heartily endorsed Shifra-Puah's minimal-intervention approach, but as for the ever-present stale cigarette between the old lady's lips, Bruriah disapproved fundamentally. Shifra-Puah the forteteller was gazing in deep absorption at the tea leaves that formed rich patterns at the bottom of the glass Ivriya had emptied. "There are volumes inscribed here for you, my couscous, believe me," said Shifra-Puah. On the only other stationary chair in the room sat Sora Katz, Ivriya's companion, sewing a brown corduroy vest that had belonged to her son, Shneour Zalman, altering it to fit Akiva Himmelhoch. She raised the garment for Ivriya's inspection. "What do you think?"

"Fine," Ivriya said. With a swift, by now automatic gesture,

Ivriya pushed forward the kerchief that had slid back down her narrow skull, exposing her fading hair. "What's the difference?" Ivriya added. "Akiva doesn't like a thing I put on him anyhow."

In his long, striped robe bedecked with a large pair of fringed and tasseled *tzitzit*, in his black velvet yarmulke perched between two extravagant sidelocks that had never been cut since birth, Akiva Himmelhoch was riding his mother's wheelchair back and forth, back and forth across the room, pretending it was a motorcycle, squealing "Vroom, vroom, vroom." Nonetheless, he was straining to catch every word of the women's talk. When he heard his name mentioned, he stopped short. "I don't want to wear this stupid robe any more," he declared. "I want to wear pants! All the boys at school laugh at me. They say I look like a girl."

"Enough, Akiva," Ivriya commanded. "You're not at home now. Not another word. This is how your father wanted you to dress."

"My abba's not here, so he doesn't have to know."

"Your abba is looking down at you from Gan Eden, Akiva. He's watching everything you do."

The boy cast his eyes up to the ceiling; a single bare light bulb drooped down a bit obscenely, and beside it hung a densely populated strip of flypaper. "My abba's getting a ride to Uman," Akiva stated firmly. "He doesn't care one bit what I'm wearing, and he can't see a thing I'm doing."

"Akiva!" hissed Tikva Unger. She was expressing Ivriya's outrage at the child's irreverence, just as Ivriya was giving voice to Tikva's labor pains. Shmuel Himmelhoch hitchhiking to Uman—what an idea! Where did the child pick up such stuff? It was time to put a foot down and compel Akiva to join the other children, who were playing so nicely in the courtyard. Where children were concerned, a little coercion was always in order. Enough with this nonsense, this coddling, this tacit encouragement of the boy's tendency to exploit his newly confirmed orphanhood for all it was worth. Someone ought to get Akiva out of this room at once. Pretty soon he would have to be expelled in any case, when the private female parts were undraped and the blood began to flow.

"Here, Akiva," said Sora Katz. She held out a handful of empty spools and an old shoelace. "Make a pretty necklace for your ima." Akiva sat down on the stone floor at Sora Katz's feet and began rummaging idly through her sewing basket. Sora looked down benevolently at the little button atop the velvet dome of the boy's skullcap. "He's such a little rascal, Akiva," she pronounced in her comical Hebrew. Then she switched to English, which Ivriya understood perfectly well, from the years she had spent in the streets of America. English was the language the two women fell into automatically whenever they didn't want Akiva to participate. Akiva was pointedly excluded, though not so Shifra-Puah, who, of course, had no English, either, but who did not, at this moment of imminent prophecy and revelation, experience the foreign tongue as a deliberate act of rudeness directed at her. As for Tikva Unger, her English, acquired in the sassy classrooms of the kibbutz, was harsh and stumbling, but she wasn't interested at this time in the women's trivial conversation, trapped as she was in her basic struggle. Sora Katz, like Bruriah Lurie, was an American, but, unlike Bruriah, Sora Katz was born a Southern Baptist in Macon, Georgia.

"You're just irritable these days, Ivriya," Sora Katz said in English. "You're going through a hard time, that's all. This, too, shall pass. How do I know? I know, believe me. I've been down, too. I've been down so low—you want to know how low I've been? Picture the lowest depths you can imagine, and then go fifty fathoms lower. That's where you would have found me." Tikva Unger groaned, but there was no other sound. Sora Katz interpreted this silence as license to proceed, even as bated-breath anticipation of what she would say next.

"I remember the morning after my wedding to Velvel Kravitz," Sora Katz reminisced. "I think they fixed me up with Velvel because I was a convert and already divorced, with a child to add to my attractions, he should live and be well, my sweet Shneour Zalman. Everyone knew that Velvel was missing something upstairs. Who else but me could they fish up so that Velvel could carry out the first commandment of the Torah—to be fruitful and multiply? And so there I was the morning after my wedding, alone in the house with Shneour Zalman—he was still only a baby then—and Velvel had gone to shul to pray. So I opened Velvel's closet to do a little cleaning. And what do you know? All those pornographic pictures came tumbling down, and the paraphernalia—it was, *mamish*, like a mini–sex shop for every taste and perversion. What to do? I picked up poor Shneour Zalman and headed straight to the rebbe's that very morning. I told him the whole story. So what does the rebbe say? 'It's your wifely duty to submit,' he says. Those were his very words—I'm quoting. So I thought to myself: For Velvel's dirty pictures I had to go to all this trouble of becoming a Jew? There wasn't enough *shmutz* back down home, right where I came from? But what could I do? I had no real options. So I obeyed the rebbe and went straight home to start submitting. It was, like, my karma—that's what I decided. But, then, all sorts of strange things started to happen. People would be walking along, minding their own business, and bricks would fall down, just missing their heads. One Friday night, no fewer than seven people nearly choked to death on chicken bones. Tires went flat. Store-front windows shattered. Stones were found in the Shabbos *cholent,* among the kidney beans and the barley. All over town people were putting sugar on their eggs and salt in their tea. Nobody could explain these events. Then, one Friday night, Blumie's braids caught fire from the rebbetzin's Shabbos candlesticks, and the whole street in front of the rebbe's place stank like a slaughterhouse bursting with singed chicken feathers. That's when the rebbe, her father, finally got off his throne and took some action. He concluded that the cause of all these disturbing events was nothing other than my Velvel's sex boutique. So they kicked Velvel out of town, they burned his junk, and they gave me my divorce. That, Ivriya, was the pits. But, you see, I came through. I survived. Look at me now."

Ivriya raised the back of her head slightly from the pillow, pressed her chin against her collar, and looked at Sora Katz. Indeed, Sora had survived. She was breathing, if Ivriya could believe the empirical evidence. Under the black pinafore apron Sora wore, under the black shawl wrapped tightly over her shaven skull with the long ends hanging over each breast, Sora's chest seemed to be rising and falling regularly. Ivriya looked and she saw. Sora had only lately taken on the extra burden of wearing these garments of the most devout. The face, framed by the black cloth, was more striking than ever in its paleness—the eyebrows and eyelashes almost white, the eyes a glassy light blue, the lips like a thin but emphatic underlining of the pinched, upturned Gentile nose. A nun, that's what she resembled more than anything else, a nun, Sister

Superior Sora Katz. Is this what it means to survive? Ivriya wondered. Is this how she would end her days, in a convent with Sora Katz?

"You're just a little short-tempered and irritable these days, Ivriya," Sora continued. "It's understandable. You need space to mourn, that's all. You should take some vitamin E. Everything will work out—I feel it in my bones. You know I have ESP. You just have to try to be a little more life-affirming. Good things are coming your way, Ivriya. God is on your team." Sora Katz was practically singing.

Sora Katz's nature was such that she couldn't bear the suffering of any of God's creatures. Her instinct was to comfort and relieve. Even the sight of a cat left for carrion on the road afflicted her sensibilities. Though, on the one hand, she might gaze at the dead cat and satisfy herself that the ecological process was running its course, she was, on the other hand, acutely dismayed by the indignities inflicted on the remains of a living being. She would find some newspaper, wrap it around the smashed cadaver, and throw the entire foul-smelling package into the big green trash bins that stood on the street corners. Then she would wash her hands vigorously. The cats of Jerusalem were singularly hungry and gaunt, their ribs angular beneath their meager fur. When the Orthodox men and boys held their demonstrations, protesting against autopsies or archaeological digs or Sabbath desecrations, or whatever was the abomination of the week, they would haul the great green dumpsters to the top of Mea Shearim Street, blocking the entrance just where the street narrows, and turn them over. The police would surge through the black-garbed throng, letting loose canisters of tear gas. Holding their hats, the demonstrators would scatter, like a great flock of startled black birds, leaving behind mounds of garbage and Sora's dead cats. "It's no accident that her name is Sora Katz," Bruriah Lurie used to say.

Her name might be Sora Katz now, but there had been a time when she was known to one and all as Pam Buck, and this was a historical fact that Bruriah Lurie could never totally assimilate. If the leap from Barbara Horowitz of Brooklyn, New York, to the Rebbetzin Bruriah Lurie of Uman House was of such breathless magnitude, how much more difficult, perhaps even impossible, was the leap from Pam Buck of Macon, Georgia, to Sora Katz of Mea Shearim, Jerusalem? Bruriah was instinctively in the camp of those who discouraged and distrusted converts. "It's just so unnatural," she said to her husband, Reb Lev. "Why would anyone in his right mind want to become a Jew? You'd have to be crazy, or a masochist, or something. For Sora Katz, Lev, this is just another trip. I know what I'm talking about. You don't understand Americans. It's deep down there, in her Southern heritage. She's being born again—born-again Christian, born-again Moslem, born-again Jew—what difference does it make to her? Only why did she have to pick on us?" For this attitude Reb Lev chastised his wife severely. Was Bruriah aware that Rav Nahman of Bratslav himself would be overcome with joy every time he was informed of a new proselyte? And the reason for this was that one of the classic signs of the imminent arrival of the Messiah—indeed, a prerequisite for His coming—was the conversion of the entire world to our faith, not necessarily as a result of any missionary activity on our part but, rather, of a clear and overwhelming insight into our unique truth. Bruriah listened with downcast eyes, and she took her husband's reprimand to heart. Thereafter, in all her dealings with Sora Katz, she made an effort to control her innate prejudice. In fact, she tended to overdo it with sweetness and favors, large and small.

The baby in the denim pouch on Bruriah's breast was asleep, its lips pursed and drooling a little moist stain onto the white cloth under its cheek. Bruriah placed her two hands on Tikva Unger's great belly and felt the massive heaves and surges of the laboring womb. The contractions were gaining in strength; they were lasting longer, sometimes even as long as ninety seconds, and they were coming closer together; Bruriah figured that Tikva was approaching transition, or perhaps had already entered that stage. "Six to eight centimeters dilated," Bruriah calculated. "Now it begins to get interesting. Now we can start to separate the men from the boys." Tikva was groaning in a deep bass, and Ivriya was moaning along with her in a shrill treble; it was as if the pain were being telegraphed through their joined hands and they were harmonizing it. "Breathe, Tikva, breathe," said Bruriah. "Don't clench your teeth. Relax. You're too tense. Loosen up, Tikva. Pant, pant—only don't hyperventilate. Tikva, let your tongue hang out." "Give me something for the pain—please, Bruriah!" Tikva cried pathetically. "Give me a joint or something. Get me some hash—I'm begging you, Bruriah." "Don't be silly, Tikva. Do you want to slow down the baby's reflexes? You're doing just fine." "Oh, shut up, Bruriah! Just shut up already!" "That's okay, Tikva, it's perfectly okay. Say whatever comes into your head. This is no time for inhibitions. You're doing great—I mean it."

Bruriah massaged Tikva's belly lightly, in wide circular strokes, with the palm of her hand. She performed this service competently and tirelessly, like a professional nurse, without even looking at Tikva. Her eyes were on Sora Katz, who continued to sew placidly at the orange Formica table opposite

Shifra-Puah, who, for her part, was still raptly engaged in the decoding of Ivriya's tea leaves. Akiva Himmelhoch was playing with the sewing basket at Sora Katz's feet, orchestrating a giant war between the buttons and the snaps: the needles and pins were the light weaponry, and the button side, which Akiva favored, had a missile called Abba—actually, a pair of scissors. "Do you really think he ought to be playing with those sharp things?" Bruriah casually asked Sora. "It's all right," Sora replied. "I'm keeping an eye on him. At least he's quiet." "Maybe too quiet," said Bruriah. "My mother always used to get worried when kids were too quiet for too long." Bruriah smiled at Sora, but Sora interpreted the smile as condescension. She resumed plying her needle assiduously. To Sora's ears, Bruriah's comments contained an unspoken allusion to their different heritages, a historical reality that Sora could never overcome, no matter how tenaciously she applied herself to the task of changing. But from Bruriah's point of view, she and Sora Katz were simply two female compatriots, chatting innocently in their native tongue about domestic matters and philosophies. Bruriah sighed. "Sora," she broached tentatively, "have you given any thought at all to what we spoke about the other day?"

"I thought about it a little," Sora admitted, and she was scalded by an uncontrollable blush. "Well, it's a pretty far-out idea, even for me."

"It all depends on how you look at it," Bruriah said. "You can look at it from the secular point of view, and then there's no question but that it would be considered polygamy, or maybe even worse—promiscuity, even. But if you have a holy mind-set and do it in the name of heaven, it's something else entirely. You know what I mean?" Sora Katz sort of nodded.

Bruriah went on: "Well, it's just that my husband and I had this idea of creating a sort of model community, like in the days of our forefathers, Abraham, Isaac, and Jacob. And when you think about it, it's really very natural for a man to have more than one wife. The medieval ban against polygamy of Rabbi Gershom Meor Hagolah is just that—a ban; it doesn't have the force of law. In my husband's opinion, it should be revoked, especially here in the Land of Israel, where the Arabs have such a high birthrate. Imagine how many more Jews we could produce if every Jewish man married two, or three, or however many wives he could handle. All our problems with territory and power and control would be solved. Anyway, Sora, let's face it: monogamy is a Western notion, and it must be shed along with all the secular and profane trappings of Western culture."

"Well, I was just wondering," said Sora Katz. "What do Rami and Golda think about the idea of welcoming into their happy home another wife, or concubine, or whatever you want to call the thing I'd be?" Again Sora blushed, and the embarrassment that evoked the blush was compounded by the added public mortification of the blush itself.

"Rami, for his part, is ready, willing, and able," Bruriah reported with satisfaction. "That's what he says, at least. And Golda says it doesn't make a difference to her one way or the other. Frankly, between you and me, I think Rami feels tickled to death. I think he feels honored to have been selected to be the first in this program—to be the vanguard. It's like being a trailblazer, you know, like a pioneer, or a spaceman."

Sora Katz looked at Bruriah Lurie. "In my opinion," Sora Katz said in a thickening Southern accent, "it would only be right that the honor and privilege of being the first in this noble experiment go to our leader, to Reb Lev." She pronounced it "Lay-iv"—melodiously, flirtatiously.

Bruriah flinched. "Of course, Sora. That will come, too, in its proper time." She patted her baby's rump, wondering if it might have awakened and be requiring her attention. "But don't forget, Sora," Bruriah forged ahead stoically, "there's also this other factor we need to consider. Reb Lev and I have been blessed with seven children so far, may they multiply and may the Evil Eye spare them and may they live and be well, while Rami and Golda are barren, you see. And you already have Shneour Zalman, so you've demonstrated your fertility."

"I'm thirty-seven years old, Bruriah," Sora Katz said despondently, "a little over the hill—don't you think?—to play the Hagar to Golda's Sarah?"

To Bruriah Lurie's overwhelming relief, at that moment Shifra-Puah jumped up from her seat with a sprightliness remarkable for her years, and hobbled over to the pushed-together beds where Tikva Unger and Ivriya Himmelhoch lay side by side. "Look here, Ivriya, my cucumber," Shifra-Puah cried, "see what I got for you." She tilted the empty glass she was holding so that Ivriya could examine the residue of tea leaves for herself. "See with your own eyes, my pudding. It's a man, Ivriya, a genuine man, *baruch Hashem*, thank God." She paused to allow her revelation to penetrate. "And," Shifra-Puah went on proudly, as if she were not only the interpreter of the leaves but also the bestower of their benefits, "as you can plainly see, Ivriya, my bageleh, it's far from an ordinary man. Both more than a man and less than a man. Linked to Shmuel, but not Shmuel."

"It's only Akiva," Ivriya said sullenly.

"No, no, not Akiva, my raisin. Obviously not Akiva. Can't you even read? It's an authentic man—full-grown, ripe, beyond ripeness. A man who is both dead and alive. But not Shmuel, definitely not Shmuel. You will be honored and blessed."

"But will I be happy?"

"You will be. Happiness is the voice of the bridegroom and the voice of the bride."

A scream. The mouths of the two women on the bed, round, dark: the single sound that had issued from their two throats hovering low, demanding action. "Her water broke!" Ivriya cried. "Oh my God—Akiva!" cried Tikva. The fluid gushed from between Tikva's legs, surging like a torrent; the women could actually hear it. And there on the floor, at Sora Katz's feet, Akiva Himmelhoch continued to sit quietly, the pair of scissors with which he had just hacked off one pristine sidelock still smoking in his chubby fist.

When Bruriah Lurie steered Akiva Himmelhoch by his newly exposed and painfully naked ear into the study hall where the men were gathered—and delivered the boy with a "Look what this child has done to himself!" and a "He's your responsibility now, the baby's coming any minute!"—she interrupted a discussion that was about to split Uman House in two. Such is the healing power of a child. All learning and prayer had ceased in that room, and the dozen or so men gathered there were rigid with the expectation of an impending declaration of total war—not wanting it for the havoc it would wreak but for the excitement it would generate. Reb Lev Lurie faced Abba Nissim across the big table, his flaming beard quivering, his light flashing a warning signal. "They call us the Dead Hassidim!"

Reb Lev roared. "And they're right!" Then Akiva Himmelhoch was delivered, pincered by the ear, looking lopsided, one sidelock a rich and flamboyant unplucked wild flower, the other raggedly shorn and disgraced. And the news, also delivered with Akiva, that the baby was moving down and out inexorably, threw Roman Unger into such a state that he groaned and doubled over, clutching his stomach. He required the immediate comforting ministrations of Shyke Pfeffer, who, luckily, was present at Uman House that afternoon with his son, Einstein, a boy of about twelve. "Relax, Roman, relax," said Shyke Pfeffer. "Breathe easy. Tikva will screech like a cat in the night, but she's as strong as an ox, take my word for it. Everything will come out okay, Roman, trust in God and believe me. For all her howling and yowling, Tikva will give you a splendid boy, just like she gave me." Shyke Pfeffer patted Einstein on his black-suited, recoiling shoulder.

How did all the trouble begin? Innocently, innocently. As Tikva Unger travailed among the women, Abba Nissim, in the study hall, was giving a brief discourse on a fine point in the *Tikkun Hakelali* of Rav Nahman of Bratslav. Then he happened to remark—appropriately, it seemed in retrospect to his supporters, including Shyke Pfeffer, Shimon Breslau, and some others—that although it was not yet the festival of Hannukah, it was nevertheless not too early to begin planning a trip for next Rosh Hashanah, with the help of God, to the holy grave of Rav Nahman of Bratslav in Uman. And this time perhaps they ought to consider taking along some of the children— Einstein Pfeffer, who would soon become a bar mitzvah, for instance (it was never too late to prevent wet dreams); Akiva Himmelhoch, certainly, fatherless and adrift as he was; Shneour Zalman Katz possibly, and maybe also one of Reb Lev

Lurie's sons, Eldad or Medad. "My sons will never go to Uman," Reb Lev said emphatically.

"Is that a prophecy or a prohibition?" Abba Nissim inquired archly. For this was not the first time that ideological disagreements had arisen between Reb Lev Lurie and Abba Nissim, although in the past they had been provoked by Reb Lev's liberal tendencies in matters of law ("Like Hillel the sage," it was affectionately pointed out by his disciples Roman Unger, Rami Marom, Einstein Pfeffer, and some others) in contrast to Abba Nissim's more fundamental and purist interpretations. But never before had Reb Lev Lurie deviated publicly on the issue of the importance of making the pilgrimage to Uman.

"The age of seers and visionaries is over," Reb Lev said. "You know the Gemara as well as I. After the destruction of the Temple, prophecy was removed from the prophets and given over to madmen and children. When the Holy Temple is restored, quickly and in our time, you may accuse me of prophesying, Abba Nissim, and I would be delighted to admit to the charge. But as things stand now, I'll put it to you plainly: I would not allow my sons to go to Uman."

"I assure you"—Abba Nissim, speaking with exaggerated courtesy and solicitude—"that your sons would not be exposed to any extraordinary dangers merely on account of the fact that their father is an émigré from that atheistic, anti-Semitic land, may its name and memory be blotted from the face of the earth."

"Really, Abba Nissim! If I were the type who shielded his children from danger, would I permit my family to live here at Uman House, right in the heart of the Moslem Quarter, surrounded by our enemies on every side? There are risks and there are risks, and we must carefully pick and choose, weigh and balance, the ones that are worth exposing ourselves to."

"Have I heard you correctly? Do you mean to tell me that you do not consider the prevention of nocturnal pollution worth the risk of taking the cure—not worth the risk of traveling to Uman to recite the *Tikkun Hakelali* by the sacred grave of Rav Nahman of Bratslav, may his merits protect us?"

"Excuse me, Abba Nissim, but there's no one in this room who takes the danger of nocturnal emissions and all they imply more seriously than I do. Why should I be obliged to prove my sincerity? Who else in this room can state that he has sat by the holy grave in Uman, tending it lovingly and faithfully for two years, as I have? When I was still in Russia, after I had completed my studies in mathematics at the university, I remember how I woke up night after night, sweating and bereft, and I would ask myself, Is this it? Is this all there is? There must be something more, I cried out in my anguish, something beyond what I can prove so elegantly with all my numbers and all my theories. That was how I began my quest, Abba Nissim. Then the Creator of the Universe, in His loving-kindness and mercy, granted me the privilege of discovering the few remnants of Rav Nahman's followers around Kiev—men of such other-worldly intensity that they seemed to have clawed their way up from the bottommost layers of the slaughter mounds of Babi Yar. For two years I prayed and wept and studied and fasted and broke my heart and poured out my soul and screamed silently and out loud by the grave of the sainted Rav Nahman in Uman. It was there in Uman that I acquired the light that has not left me yet. My credentials are immaculate."

"I've never doubted you, Reb Lev. In the past you've always been exemplary in encouraging our young men to risk everything to take the treatment at Uman. Think of Shmuel

Himmelhoch and all he endured to be brought to Uman, thanks in large measure to your good influence. But this new shift in your position is nothing less than alarming. If you ask me, it's a betrayal of Shmuel Himmelhoch and the whole struggle of his last years."

"You know, Abba Nissim, in the *Likutei Moharan*, when Rav Nahman first speaks of the *Tikkun Hakelali* as the general remedy for nocturnal emissions, he doesn't specify that the ten psalms must be recited by his grave. He says many interesting things there—that the numerical value of 'Psalms,' *Tehilim*, four hundred and eighty-five, is the same as that of *Lilit*, four hundred and eighty, plus five, for the five letters of the accursed name of that demonic seductress. Rav Nahman makes many subtle and enigmatic points in that passage of the *Likutim*, but the clear implication is that the *Tikkun Hakelali* would be effective wherever it's administered."

"What nonsense you talk, Reb Lev, you should excuse me. Why would Rav Nahman have referred to his grave at that time? He wasn't dying yet. Only later on he says that the *Tikkun* will operate best at his graveside. And it wasn't that he was trying to arrange for visitors because he was afraid he might get lonely. Now, Reb Lev, I'll give you an example. Suppose your son had a terrible disease—cancer, let us say, God forbid, it shouldn't happen to us. And suppose, also, that there was a known cure for his cancer, and its chances of success were pretty good if taken at home, but they were excellent if you traveled with him a great distance. What would you do? Is that a question, even? The answer, of course, is obvious! Nocturnal emissions are nothing less than the symptom, the external manifestation of a severe general spiritual cancer. Those rancid drops are a warning, a symptom that only a fool would ignore."

"You do me a great injustice, Abba Nissim, if you assume that I've yielded even one centimeter in my war against wet dreams, and you're definitely mistaken if you assume that I'm denying the beneficial effect of a journey to Uman. But there are times when other concerns must take precedence, and this, I believe, is one of those times."

"What can be more important than utter dedication to the goal of spiritual purity?"

"Come here, I want to show you something." Deferentially, Reb Lev Lurie took his older colleague by the elbow and directed him to a door in back of the study hall that opened onto a small, rubble-strewn terrace with a collapsing parapet. They did not venture out, but through the narrow doorway they could see down to the Western retaining Wall of the Second Temple, sprouting tufts of grass, birds fluttering and alighting, Jews pressing burdened foreheads to its pulsing, humming stones, and, above and beyond this, the glittering domes and minarets of the two great mosques, the well-tended gardens and walkways, the sparkling mosaics and fretwork of the Temple Mount. Rev Lev stretched out his arm, like a lord showing his domain. "Just look at that," Reb Lev said passionately.

Abba Nissim squeezed his eyes shut. "With the help of God, the Messiah will arrive, quickly and in our time," he pronounced fervently. "We lost it for our sins. And so we must strive every day to elevate ourselves. To hasten the coming of the Messiah ben David, and the rebuilding of the Holy Temple, amen. In the meantime, we must always try to be joyful, but the truth is, as the Talmud tells us, that heaven is not so blue and love is not so sweet as when our sanctuary stood on Zion. Still, had Rav Nahman himself been shown the sight you just showed me, he, too, would have said we must wait."

"No, I don't believe that. The exalted Rav Nahman, may his merits protect us forever and ever, would have gazed lovingly at what I showed you, with a heart cleft in two, and then he would have turned to his followers and declared that the time of mourning and grieving was now officially over. The time for bold and decisive action had arrived!"

"I beg your pardon, my dear Reb Lev Lurie of Uman, but you know as well as I that when the revered Rav Nahman, may the light of his merits intercede in our behalf, disembarked, after great peril and travail, at the port of Haifa in the year 5559 from the Creation—or 1799, in the usage of strange nations—he walked just four cubits on the soil of the Holy Land and then he was ready to return home. Why? The reason, I believe, was that Rav Nahman was burning to effect the coming of the Messiah as quickly as possible, and the way to accomplish that goal was not by glamorously wrenching the holy sites out of heathen hands, not by usurping the role of the Messiah, but, rather, by returning home—home to preparing for His coming through the daily, tedious, repetitious tasks of self-improvement and self-perfection."

"I'm afraid that's only part of the story, Abba Nissim—the part you're inclined to favor. Rav Nahman was not such a passive leader. On the contrary. We of the innermost circle know very well that, despite the criticism and uproar he knew it would provoke, Rav Nahman revealed himself as the Messiah ben Joseph, the harbinger of the Messiah ben David. This occurred around the year 1806 by the profane calendar, or, counting from the Creation, 5566, which, incidentally, is numerically equivalent to 'Messiah ben Jospeh.' "

"Such nonsense! If I didn't know you better, Reb Lev, I

would call your words by a stronger name—blasphemy, heresy! Where in the world did you get such ideas?"

"It's all recorded. In *The Burned Book.* In the manuscript of *The Hidden Book,* to which only the most trusted and proven of Rav Nahman's disciples are privy. I don't mean to suggest that I'm among them. What I just said about Rav Nahman is common knowledge." The two men stood and probed silently, as if to determine whether the other were among the privileged, whether his eyes had rested on those mysterious and holy pages. For the initiate was forbidden to reveal that he was among the chosen, nor was he granted the knowledge of who the others were. And because of this remorseless secrecy, it also happened at times that an impostor claimed special knowledge, for none of the true initiates could step forward to shame and gainsay him.

Reb Lev Lurie of Uman House continued: "In the year 5724 from the Creation, or 1967 of the Common Era, the Almighty performed a *ness* of awesome proportions, in fulfillment of His promise to our forefathers Abraham, Isaac, and Jacob that their seed would inherit the land. What else could it be called but a miracle when a small, frail nation such as ours humiliates the multitudes and hordes of its Arab foes, and wrests back, after nearly two thousand years of tears and hand-wringing, our beloved city of Jerusalem? So what do we Jews do? No sooner do we reach the Western Wall, the pathetic remains of our glory, our Holy Temple, than we put down our guns and start immediately weeping and wailing. Do you know what Rav Nahman would have said? '*Yidden, Yidden,*' Rav Nahman would have said, 'postpone your crying for a little while. Climb Mount Moriah. Reclaim our Holiest of Holies. Destroy the mosques.' Why not? We have seen in the past how the world tolerates and absorbs atrocities of every sort. If our Temple could be defiled and burned and razed to the ground, why not their mosques? How much could they really care about those Temple Mount mosques anyway? They prostrate themselves five times a day, bowing their heads toward Mecca while pointing their unclean behinds toward Jerusalem. It's only their third-holiest site; for us it's the first, the *first!* 'Finish the job, *Yidden,*' Rav Nahman would have said. 'Then, after you've finished, since you like to cry so much, and over the millennia have gotten into the habit of filling your cup of tears to overflowing, you may slip back down the mountain and cry to your hearts' content. But first take the Mount. Then, and only then, shed your tears, beat your breasts, and bang your heads against the Wall!' "

"You're a very confused man, Reb Lev. Truly, I'm sorry for you. I'm worried, really I am. I'm worried about what you've done to your soul. As deeply as it hurts me to say this, I think that Shmuel Himmelhoch can thank God that his own fragile soul is safe from your present influence and indoctrinations. I wish I could feel as secure about the delicate souls of all these other young and impressionable men gathered here in this room."

Reb Lev drew in his breath as if he were struggling to stop himself from leaping off a ledge. "You know, Abba Nissim, it's very painful for me to hear you say that I'm deliberately harming the souls of the students who have entrusted themselves to me." He shook his head, like one deeply hurt, and continued. "I'm certain that if Shmuel Himmelhoch were alive today he would agree with me completely. There's no doubt in my mind. Shmuel's ideas would have developed in the exact same fashion as mine."

"In that you're wrong, I'm happy to say. Shmuel would not have deviated one millimeter from the program for self-improvement as set down by Rav Nahman. He would still be struggling to be brought to Uman—if not to the physical Uman, then to the spiritual Uman. His goal would still be to receive the general remedy for his weaknesses and failings. Read his journal closely, Reb Lev. What further proof do you need of Shmuel's total devotion to the efficacy of Uman? No, no, Reb Lev Lurie of Uman. Shmuel Himmelhoch would never have collaborated with your band of hotheads in preempting the Messiah. Never! Shmuel would have waited. And he would have waited in fine style—in accordance with the teachings of Rav Nahman of Bratslav. We Jews are past masters in the art of waiting. That's how we have survived: we can outwait anyone. The Messiah can be prodded only through our acts of repentance and our righteous deeds. Therein lies our activism. Work on yourself, Reb Lev, work on yourself, for each one of us must work on himself. That's the only way to hasten the coming of the Messiah. Other than that, we must wait. We must wait patiently for the redemption, as the holy Rav Nahman has demonstrated. Even as the Messiah procrastinates, we must wait!"

Reb Lev Lurie smashed his broad palms down on the table, propping himself up as he leaned more than halfway across the stained white cloth, across the open volumes, the cold glasses of tea and nibbled lumps of sugar. His red beard bobbing, his green eyes glowering at Abba Nissim of Safad, Reb Lev Lurie bellowed, "They call us the Dead Hassidim! And they're right!"

Fortunately, at this moment Bruriah Lurie bustled into the room, remaining only long enough to deposit the absurdly barbered Akiva Himmelhoch, and to launch Roman Unger into a state of near frenzy with her bulletin from the women's quarters, and to hand her own baby over in this emergency to the interim care of its father, Reb Lev.

Abba Nissim walked over to Akiva Himmelhoch and plaintively fingered the ragged remains of the boy's silken earlock. "Such a pity, Akiva," Abba Nissim said somberly. "If only you could remember the joy that flooded your dear father's heart when you had your first haircut, on Lag BaOmer day in Meron, by the tomb of Rabbi Simeon bar Yohai. That was the holy event that inspired him to start the journal we cherish so highly." Abba Nissim went and got the lucite case containing Samuel Himmelhoch's journal, and set it down in front of Akiva. "For you, Akiva, he wrote this journal. Not for me, not for anyone else in this room, but for you. And now look what you've done to your hair, to your precious *payah,* which the great cabbalist Rabbi Isaac Luria of Safad, the holy Ari, taught us is numerically equal to eighty-six, the exact same value as *Elohim,* God. You'll excuse me, Reb Lev, but, as you can see, you don't have a monopoly on Gematria calculations. Do you know what our Torah teaches us, Akiva? 'Ye shall not round the corners of your head.' That's what our Torah teaches us. Oh, you're a very, very bad boy, Akiva! Your father is weeping in heaven over what you've done." Samuel Himmelhoch's son tilted his head upward, shielding his dark eyes as if from the storm of his father's tears. "You had an excellent father," Abba Nissim went on, "and you have disappointed him, Akiva. You're an ungrateful child. Your father asked me to give you this." Abba Nissim raised his aged hand and delivered a smart slap to the boy's cheek. There was a piercing scream. "Now, stop your blubbering, Akiva, and sit down beside me to learn a little Torah. Your father left me specific instructions regarding you. He asked me to take care of you. I have a mandate. He put me in charge."

The scream came out of Ivriya Himmelhoch. When Bruriah Lurie rushed back to the women's room, she instantly recognized that the high time had arrived. The ancient Bokharan midwife Shifra-Puah had already taken her place at the foot of Tikva Unger's bed. Shifra-Puah always knew exactly when to act. Now, as she concentrated intently on palpating the massive rising and sinking belly, outlining the baby's position and shape, the years began to fall off Shifra-Puah. Already Shifra-Puah looked plumper, smoother, a quarter-century younger at least. The skin at her throat no longer sagged; teeth flashed in her gums; her hair shone rich and dark. "You little silly, Tikva," Shifra-Puah said. "You've done it all backward, as usual. The baby is upside down. I have to turn it." And before Tikva could utter a question or a protest, Shifra-Puah inserted her arm up to the elbow, high into the birth canal, through the trap door of the cervix, and rummaged and rooted in the dark, rocking womb. Ivriya screamed. Shifra-Puah's arm, when she drew it out again, was cleansed of its brown blotches. The skin fitted snugly, no longer wrinkling like a loose glove. "It was a pretty little baby tush-tush I felt in there, darling," Shifra-Puah reported, "but, as much as I'm looking forward to seeing it, I'd prefer to be introduced to the head first." Forty years had glided like oil off Shifra-Puah's voice.

Tikva began to cry. "What kind of kid can this be who plans to come out ass first? He can't be worth all this trouble. Oh, let's quit now, Ivriya. Let's go home and forget the whole thing." Then Tikva Unger remembered she was home. She squeezed her legs together and held her breath, pummeled into silence as a deep and long contraction overwhelmed her.

"God have mercy, Tikva," Bruriah Lurie cried, "you're doing everything wrong! Breathe, for goodness' sake. Pant. Please, Tikva. Don't tighten up. Relax. And—my God!—open up your legs! How will the baby ever get out if you seal yourself up like that?" Bruriah turned to consult with Shifra-Puah. "We ought to get her squatting down on the floor. That's the natural way. That's how I did it." Tikva groaned and buried her face in her pillow.

"It's not modest," Sora Katz intervened. "Who knows what else would come out with the baby?"

"Stop being ridiculous, Sora," said Bruriah. "It's only natural. Besides, we're all women here."

"Don't worry, Tikva," Ivriya Himmelhoch reassured her friend, "you won't have to squat. She can't make you do it. I won't let her." And Ivriya smoothed Tikva's damp hair back from her clammy forehead, kissing her and crooning, "It's all right, Tikva'le. It's okay. Everything will be all right. I'm here, Tikva'le. It's all going to be okay."

"Oh, Ivriya, I feel like I'm having a bad trip. I feel so spacy, Ivriya, I'm all spaced out."

"*Baruch Hashem*," said Bruriah Lurie, and she raised her hands in gratitude to heaven. "Thank God, it's the natural high."

Now the midwife Shifra-Puah began to sing without moving her lips, to dance motionlessly in her place. She was like a woman in the full power and strength of her thirty years. Bruriah Lurie she stationed at her right, Sora Katz at her left, and assigned to them the task of grasping Tikva's knees and holding the legs apart, like velvet-curtain openers making way for royalty. "Push, Tikva my darling," Shifra-Puah sang. "Push, my life! With all your might, darling. Listen to the push song inside you, my love, and sing out loud with it. Push, my soul!"

"Oh, I'm dying, I'm dying. Ten thousand kilos are on top of me. Squashing me to death! I'll never make it! I can't do it! I have to get out of here! You're tearing me apart! You're killing me! I'm being tortured! I'm dying!"

"Push, my sweet. Push, push, my love." Drumbeats and dance steps accompanied Shifra-Puah's song.

"You're killing me, Shifra-Puah. Oh, Mamma, Mamma, Mamma. Where's my mother? I want my mother."

"Here it comes, you silly. Look—the head. Ah—the shoulders. Here. Out—that's it, out. A fish, a delicious little, slippery little fish." Shifra-Puah received it in her hands—this tethered-at-the-navel, blood-and-paste-smeared, wrinkled, ancient baby. The midwife Shifra-Puah, white and rose, radiant and triumphant, like a young girl.

In the study hall, the men heard the cry. "There's your son," Reb Lev Lurie announced to Roman Unger.

The cord still uncut, the baby was passed up to Tikva Unger to suckle as Shifra-Puah kept watch for the afterbirth. Shifra-Puah, the midwife, was now aging stunningly, and when the placenta emerged at last, she collected it in her trembling, withered, spotted hands.

Bruriah Lurie hastened to the study hall to consult her husband on a pressing matter of law: Was placenta kosher? Why not? People regularly chewed parts of their own bodies—fingernails, loose skin, hair, and so on. And if placenta *was* permissible, was it necessary to salt and soak and rinse it like meat? She had an excellent recipe for placenta, with all sorts of natural herbs; placenta was extremely healthy and nourishing, not to mention delicious, for a woman who had just delivered. Animals ate their placenta as a matter of course. Therefore, it was natural, perhaps no worse than when human beings swallowed parts of themselves, such as their saliva. Bruriah and Reb Lev conferred with such solitary intensity over this matter that Roman Unger became alarmed. He approached diffidently. "Is everything all right?" he asked.

"Oh, Roman," said Bruriah, as if she had not recognized him for a moment and needed to clarify his identity. "Yes, of course, of course everything's all right, *baruch Hashem!*"

"Amen," Roman intoned, "thank God."

"Excuse me, Roman, I'm so sorry. I've been in such a hurry, I forgot to congratulate you. *Mazal tov.* You have a beautiful little girl. Forgive me, Roman."

"A girl? But your husband just told me it was a son!"

On two occasions later, in the heat of argument with his wife, in the depths of irrationality, Roman will put the blame directly on Tikva. "If you had listened to me and gone to the hospital," he will say the first time, "God would have given us a boy." The second time he'll say, "To Shyke you give a son, but to me—look what you give!" Now, however, he only grinned and accepted the congratulations, like an added administrative responsibility. "I'd better start saving for the wedding," he said.

Roman and Tikva Unger's daughter was born in her mother's bed at Uman House in the Moslem Quarter of the Old City of Jerusalem, achingly close to Mount Moriah, upon whose pinnacle Abraham raised the gleaming slaughter knife over the tender throat of his son Isaac. Upon the black rock that Jews call *even hashettiya,* stone of the foundation, and

Christians *omphalos mundi*, the bellybutton of the world, Abraham bound the half-brother of his eldest son, Ishmael. From this black rock the prophet Mohammed was launched into heaven, leaving behind his most delicate footprint, and over it, to honor his passage, his followers erected the sparkling golden dome. This black rock, perhaps the site of the priestly offering in the Holiest of Holies, is certainly the absolute center of the earth; dislodge it, and all of creation would be sucked into the hole, like a whirlpool down the drain, back into chaos and void and nothingness. In the shadow of this black rock, Roman and Tikva Unger's baby girl was born on a Thursday, between afternoon and evening prayers, during the first week of the month of Kislev. Winter was closing over the city. Women in woolen kerchiefs and long dresses, with rosy cheeks and chafed hands, trudged up the twisting stone stairway to Uman House, their breath pluming in the cold air, to visit the mother and her new baby. In their arms they carried fresh loaves of bread, pots of hot soup, and bundles of sticks to feed the black cast-iron stove that stood like an altar in the center of the room. Tikva Unger, the new mother, invited her friend Ivriya Himmelhoch to remain with her at Uman House through the Sabbath, when the baby would be given a name. Naturally, the selection of the name was ultimately the father's prerogative. But if Tikva could prevail, the child would be called Shmuela, to carry on the life and to honor the memory of Ivriya's husband, Shmuel Himmelhoch, peace be unto him. However, the beacon of Uman House, Reb Lev Lurie himself, was pressing a strong case for the name Moriah: "To symbolize our highest aspiration, our claim to the center of the earth; to stand for our strongest imperative, the rebuilding of our Holy Temple upon its original site." And Abba Nissim was agitating just as passionately for the name Geula, "Redemption," may it arrive speedily and in our time.

After the departure of the Sabbath Queen, Ivriya Himmelhoch was sitting in her chair in the Ungers' room at Uman House. Her coat was folded across her lap, her carpetbag was stuffed and ready beside her on the floor, and she herself, like another item of luggage, was packed into her wheelchair. She was waiting for Sora Katz to finish her prenuptial interview with Rami Marom in a distant room, where Bruriah Lurie, match-maker and catalyst, unobtrusively sorted laundry in the corner. Bruriah's presence was necessary by law, for under no circum-stances could an unmarried couple be permitted to occupy a closed chamber alone; in addition, the presence of a second woman would provide valuable training for this particular mar-riage, which stipulated two wives for starters. As soon as the meeting between Sora and Rami was concluded, Roman would load Ivriya and her entire entourage into the Uman Boys Band van, and drive them home. Over the Sabbath, Ivriya had con-tinued to share the Ungers' room with Tikva; Roman was banished to the single men's dormitory, where he would re-main for several weeks, until Tikva's period of uncleanliness came to an end. Besides, if he stayed in the room with the mother and her night-howling infant, how would he ever get any sleep? And he needed to be well rested to do God's work in the morning.

Now Tikva was sitting up in bed, her baby in the crook of her arm beside her. Akiva Himmelhoch was sprawled on the other side of the baby, and Tikva's full attention was devoted to guarding the infant from the sudden thrusts and jabs of

Akiva's frisky limbs. "Watch it, Akiva!" warned Tikva Unger. "You might poke Moriah Shmuela Geula!" What a name! Roman was such a softie, such a mush-brain, such a spineless, good-natured fellow, that he didn't have the heart to hurt anyone's feelings on this matter of the name. And now, look at the monstrous name to which he had yoked his own tiny daughter. Diplomatically, he had striven to satisfy everyone, and, in the end no one was genuinely pleased. To show her loyalty to her husband, Tikva valiantly addressed the baby by all three names, but pretty soon, she resolved, she would give up and call her just plain Moriah, and that would be the end of that.

Tikva had just finished telling Ivriya the latest about Golda Marom, a story for which she had whetted Ivriya's appetite in Meron, on the day of the funeral of Samuel Himmelhoch. She might have told her friend the story on the Sabbath, but just in case the tale was tainted by slander, just in case it was an unintentional manifestation of the evil tongue, it would be doubly reprehensible to indulge in it on the sacred day—no? Now, as Ivriya sat in her wheelchair waiting for Sora Katz to conclude her prenuptial meeting with Golda's husband, Rami, she reflected on the story as she had it from Tikva. Golda Marom's absence from Samuel Himmelhoch's funeral, as well as her total reclusiveness during this weekend of the baby's birth, had not passed unnoticed. Ivriya had always cared for Golda, and Golda for her—or so she thought—and that made it all the more odd that Golda hadn't emerged from her room at Uman House when she knew Ivriya was visiting. Ivriya couldn't climb up the stairs to Queen Golda; that was a sad fact.

What was it about Golda that had always appealed to Ivriya?

Golda was obviously no beauty—pudgy, round-shouldered, thick-spectacled, her chin colonized by a small band of pimples once a month, her dull hair thinning under her kerchief. A strange wife for the artist Rami Marom, for whom visual pleasure had always been paramount—but perhaps Golda's physical appearance was another aspect of Rami's penance. Maybe it was Golda's intelligence that had always drawn Ivriya: Golda had the reputation of a mathematics prodigy, but after she graduated from M.I.T. in America, Golda had relinquished her scholarships and fellowships, her array of grants and awards, and had come to Israel to live with Bedouins in the Sinai. Ivriya could not help admiring Golda's boldness; for two years Golda had lived with her lover, a Bedouin fisherman named Munis. Come to think of it, Golda would have been a perfect match for Reb Lev Lurie—together they could have exalted the Lord with numbers—but Golda had always been attracted to Eastern men. What was she searching for? Dark passion to counteract an overdose of cold Western calculation, to shoot full of color the black-and-white, orderly, lifeless world of the rational intellect. But Munis the Bedouin fisherman had beaten Golda mercilessly—she still bore the scars—and in his lovemaking he was swifter than an eye blink.

Golda came limping out of the desert. Then, not long after she became a penitent, the marriage was arranged between her and Rami Marom, the Oriental, the Moroccan—for even in arranged marriages, consideration was given to personal tastes and inclinations, and, besides, very few people, including penitents, would do business with a Moroccan. A sweet man, Rami Marom, and good, but simple, a little dull, disarmingly uncomplicated, an artist in the primitive style, whose former passions had been soccer and disco dancing. How could Golda complain? Yet she wasn't content. And when she petitioned to attend the university to take a degree in sociology, Reb Lev Lurie granted her leave, despite Rav Nahman's strenuous warnings against the dangers of secular learning, for he, Reb Lev, reasoned that if he forbade her she would abandon the fold entirely, whereas if he made an exception in her case she would go, get what she needed, and carry her learning back to Uman House to brighten and advance their cause. And now—or so Tikva had just reported to Ivriya—Golda had fallen in love with her sociology professor, a convert from Germany—from Munich, as a matter of fact. Everyone knew about it, Rami included. Oh yes, Rami's feelings, naturally, were hurt—but you know Rami, he was never particularly hot-blooded. A simple man, an easily contented man, Rami; Shmuel used to say that Rami praised God with each brushstroke. And here was Bruriah Lurie, busily pushing her scheme for the model patriarchial, polygamous family. "Now all the pieces are beginning to fit together," Ivriya remarked to Tikva. "As soon as the first wife, Golda, slips off the stage, the second, Sora, will be waiting in the wings. Bruriah's not such a revolutionary after all. She's more of a pragmatist, it seems to me."

A knock on the door, and simultaneously it was pushed open. Shyke Pfeffer's head popped into the room. "Everyone decent?" he sang out. And he entered without waiting for a reply, trailed by Abba Nissim. Abba Nissim stood in the background, his head turned away from the women. He always took pains to avoid looking at women directly, for he strove to attain a level of holiness equal to that of the saint in the Talmud who never noticed, until her funeral, that his own wife had a wooden leg. As soon as Akiva Himmelhoch spotted Abba Nissim, he leaped frantically off the bed into the safe haven of his mother's lap, causing the wheelchair to lurch wildly, for Ivriya had neglected to push down the brake. Shyke Pfeffer, nimble as a wood sprite, halted the chair as it was about to crash into the cast-iron wood-burning stove that was the centerpiece of the room. "You could have started a fire, Akiva," Ivriya said forlornly.

"We came to say good-bye," Shyke Pfeffer announced. "We're leaving for Safad in a few minutes."

"How are you going?" Tikva asked, slipping automatically into the wifely mode in relation to Shyke Pfeffer.

"Hitching. How else?" And Shyke Pfeffer displayed his well-worn thumb.

"Well, then. Go in peace and arrive in peace." Tikva stroked her downy baby. "What about Einstein?" she asked tentatively.

"That's what I came here to talk to you about, Tikva. Our difficult son refuses to return to his boarding school in Bnei Brak, and he won't go north with me, either. He's always been a problem, you know. I guess, coming from such a combination as you and me, what would you expect—eh, Tikva?" Shyke grinned rather proudly. "Anyhow, nothing I said to him did any good. I tried to convince him to come with me, Tikva, so don't you start accusing me of giving in to him in order to sabotage you."

"Why? What does the boy want to do?"

"He wants to stay here at Uman House and become one of Reb Lev's warriors. I tried to talk him out of it, Tikva, but you know how stiff-necked he can be. He gets that from you, by the way. Look, I told him as forcefully as I could that Reb Lev is no true disciple of Rav Nahman. You'll excuse me, I even went so far as to suggest that Reb Lev is a charlatan and a fraud and a misleader of youth. I tried to show him how Reb Lev cynically twists the teachings of the holy Rav Nahman in order to justify his personal ambitions—his designs on the Temple Mount, his desire to be acclaimed as a hero and a savior. Even Abba Nissim here tried to talk to Einstein, tried to influence him, but everything we said fell on deaf ears. The boy will not leave Uman House, and that's it. I tried my best. My hands are clean. Reb Lev agreed to take him in. Your son says he wants to prepare for his bar mitzvah here at Uman House. He promises not to bother you."

"It's mean of you, Shyke, really, it's mean of you," Tikva cried. "Here I am trying to get myself back together again and start a new life, and you manipulate Einstein into staying at Uman House to haunt me with the past. You're just sabotaging me. You should never have brought him here in the first place."

"I brought him to celebrate the birth of his sister." Shyke pointed to the baby. "She is his sister, after all."

"Einstein can stay with me at my place, Tikva," Ivriya offered.

"Oh, Ivriya, you just don't understand. This is typical Shyke Pfeffer manipulation and sabotage. First he informs me that Einstein insists on staying, and then, in the same breath, he tells me that the boy promises not to bother me. Now, how do you suppose that makes me feel? Like an unnatural mother— that's how it makes me feel, if you want to know the truth. And Shyke knows it very well. I just don't get along with Einstein— it's a bitter fact that I've had to face. There's nothing I can do about it. Einstein just reminds me too much of Shyke." And Tikva turned her face away, to sob softly into the powdery blanket of her comforting baby, this baby who loved her without qualification or reservation, this baby who cared—cared—when her mother was unhappy.

"I'm a witness that Shyke tried his best to dissuade your son from remaining here at Uman House," Abba Nissim spoke. "I, too, tried, but it was hopeless. I recognized that at once. Nevertheless, I tried. For a young boy, Lev's style is practically irresistible—romantic, adventurous—a boy has to be very special indeed not to be seduced by all that glamour and superficiality. What could we offer him in exchange? Daily prayer and self-scrutiny are not for every taste. Holy war is much more alluring when you're twelve years old and your blood is boiling. I tried to point out the inconsistencies in Lev's interpretations, the out-and-out errors—but what good is reason in the face of passion? What Lev fails to understand is that the redemption must come by supernatural means, like the liberation from Egypt, for if salvation is brought about naturally, by the logical intercession of man, then doubters will persist. Can you imagine—Lev claiming that we're called the Dead Hassidim because of our seeming inaction and passivity? What an absurdity, what a dangerous bit of ignorance! Even a child of three knows that the disparaging term 'Dead Hassidim' does not refer to us, the disciples of Rav Nahman, but to the followers of Reb Arele, who sit for hours in a rigid stupor, in a trancelike, deathlike state. But those who mistakenly call *us* the Dead Hassidim do so because we have no master other than the holy Rav Nahman, and Rav Nahman is dead and buried, yet he has not retired, for even from his grave in Uman he corrects and repairs our souls. No, we are not like the other Hassidim, with their royal courts, their dynasties, their rebbe-worship that borders on idolatry. We have never taken the easy road. And if for that reason they call us dead, then being dead is our glory and our honor. *That's* what I should have said to Lev."

"Well, maybe you'll have an opportunity to say that to Reb Lev some other time," Ivriya put in crisply.

"Ah, the widow of Shmuel Himmelhoch," said Abba Nissim, revolving majestically, but still not looking directly at Ivriya. "A good week to you." It was as if he had just noted her presence there in the wheelchair, among all the other furniture. Akiva curled himself up even smaller in his mother's lap, warming his hands between his thighs. "I have a message for you," Abba Nissim informed Ivriya.

"Really? For me? You're joking. A message? Who could be sending me a message?"

"It's from your husband, Shmuel Himmelhoch, may his memory be a blessing." And Abba Nissim drew a folded piece of paper out of the pocket of his velvet coat, and, his eyes averted, dropped it on Ivriya's knees. "Please, do me this kindness—don't read it until we've left."

Ivriya looked down at the frayed paper without touching it. "Where did this letter come from?"

"If the widow finds it easier to believe that her late husband, Shmuel Himmelhoch, peace be unto him, prepared this letter before his passing and placed it where he was sure it would be found, then she is free to believe so. But a person of true faith would understand that for the Creator of the Universe, who has performed such startling miracles as the splitting of the Red Sea, sending a mere letter from the next world is not such an incredible wonder."

"The postage must have been exorbitant," Ivriya murmured into Akiva's hair.

She continued to stare down at the letter after the two old men had taken their leave; and even Akiva, for some reason, refrained from touching it. It was as if the paper were composed of some celestial substance that would either crumble to dust between their fingers and then never impart its secret, or sear them indelibly. "Well, read it already," cried Tikva. "Read it, Ivriya; I can't stand it another minute!" Ivriya lifted the smudged piece of paper, unfolded it, and read:

To my Widow, Ivriya bat Frieda, Long May She Live:
For the sake of our son, Akiva ben Shmuel, greetings! Do not doubt for a moment that the writer of this letter is your husband and master, Shmuel ben Hayim Himmelhoch. I am no longer of this world. I parted from you in haste, without bidding you a proper farewell, without asking your forgiveness, without putting forward the final request due the dying. So, good-bye, my widow. Forgive me for any wrong I may have done you, knowingly or unknowingly. Forgiveness is the essential ingredient of a marriage. Belatedly I ask you, as your last kindness to me, for the sake of my soul's peace in my new life, to secure for our son a suitable father, a father who will guide him in the path I have carved out, and who, as your husband, will reflect glory on you and serve as further testimony to the world of your consistent high standards in the selection of a mate. The man I have chosen to be a father to Akiva, and, in certain respects, to you as well, is my friend Abba Nissim of Safad. Learn from him, honor him, and love him in moderation—you have my permission.

THE DEAD
WILL RISE

Sora Katz's marriage to Rami Marom was sealed at Uman House on Purim day, and despite the maxim cautioning against mixing two different types of rejoicings, the Purim feast and the wedding feast were combined. There's wisdom in this maxim, surely, for each occasion for happiness ought to be granted its own special hour, but since there existed absolutely no standard rituals for the taking of a second wife by a man still married to his first, the idea was to slip in this irregular wedding as discreetly and as innocuously as possible, camouflaged by the grand annual celebration commemorating the day that Queen Esther of Persia and Mede rescued her people from annihilation at the hands of Haman the Jew-hater. For the festival of Purim, Reb Lev Lurie's followers traditionally went all out. It was the only time in the year when they were given license to draw upon the skills and knowledge they had perfected in the secular world before their penance. But now the dancing, the music, the imaginative soarings, yes, the levity, the wildness, the intoxication, were indulged not to achieve a state of loose, profane abandon, but to reach the heights of sublime rapture. It's a great good deed to be constantly happy, Rav Nahman said, but especially on a holiday such as Purim, and if there's a wedding thrown in, then how much more reason—indeed, duty—have we to rejoice. As long as it's in the name of heaven.

The decision of what to wear to her wedding preoccupied and agitated Sora Katz far more profoundly than the decision of whether or not to marry Rami Marom at all. The latter she dispatched one morning between her ablutions and her devotions, and she announced it as she rotated Ivriya's toes, one by one, an aspect of the daily foot-massage routine Sora had instituted for her friend's sake. "The way I see it," Sora explained to Ivriya, "it's the best I can do. I'm no spring chicken—okay? And even if I have a lot of common sense and I'm not a bit stubborn, which are the two main qualities that matchmakers look for in a girl, everything else is against me. It's a market situation—you know what I mean, Ivriya?—brutal and cutthroat. And as for me, not only am I used merchandise, but— let's face it—I've also been manufactured in the wrong factory." Sora took a cake of tiger balm out of her apron pocket and began to rub it into the soles of Ivriya's feet.

"Using such reasoning, then I suppose I ought to jump at the chance of marrying Abba Nissim," Ivriya observed. "Thank God I can't jump," she added dolefully.

"Rami's a decent guy—right? He's definitely not a sex maniac, like my second husband, Velvel Kravitz. And he doesn't seem to have the proverbial hots for Gentile women that some Jewish guys have—take Beryl Katz, for instance, Shneour Zalman's father. He's pious, he's not physically repulsive, and he's not too old, either. In fact, I think he's about five years younger than me."

"Abba Nissim is more than twice my age. Bruriah says I should marry him."

"Really? How about that! I was sure she'd be dead set against it, on account of losing you and Akiva to the rival camp."

"That's what I figured, too. But I think she fancies it as a novel idea, a stimulating abstraction, a relief from boredom—never mind that there are some living souls involved. Guess what she said to me? She said—and I'm quoting—'It's a real trip to be married to a holy man.' Those are the immortal words of the distinguished Rebbetzin Bruriah Lurie of Uman House."

Sora Katz was slapping Ivriya's feet to coax the blood down into them. "I'm going up to Uman House this morning, Ivriya, to tell Bruriah okay. Bombs away—the blushing bride is willing. Should I give her the go-ahead on you and Abba Nissim, too, while I'm at it? So what if I have to share Rami with another wife? If Goldie doesn't mind, why should I? The fact of the matter is, I'm convinced that a married Moroccan is just about the best I can do."

The selection of the perfect outfit to wear to her wedding, however, evolved into a far more serious and complicated concern, because, to Sora Katz's mind, her bridal costume would make the definitive statement to those people who truly mattered about where she had come from, where she stood at the present moment, and where she intended to go. Having been married before, she could naturally not wear white; nor could she wear off-white, or any shade of white at all, or any light color, for that matter, since she had been previously married not once, but twice—twice, that is, since her conversion. Although some rabbis rule that a widow or a divorced woman, to render herself more appealing to a prospective mate, may remove the head covering that signifies her married status, Sora Katz continued to bear the burden of this wifely badge even between marriages, and under her tightly wound scarf, in the manner of the ultra-Orthodox, her head was shaven. She was extremely rigid in upholding the externals; the externals would seep inward, she believed, be absorbed, so to speak, and raise the level of inner holiness. The issue of feminine modesty was particularly important to Sora Katz. Having had some training as a graphic artist in her Pam Buck life, she used to print signs carefully on bedsheets, and she would string up these signs from porch to porch across Mea Shearim Street, first taking care to slit them to counteract the distorting wind: "Rules of Modesty for Daughters of Israel: Absolutely no makeup, nail polish, or perfume, God forbid. For the unmarried, hair neatly combed and pinned away from the face. For the married, hair completely, one hundred percent covered, no exceptions. High necklines. Sleeves down to wrists. Long, loose dresses. No pants, God forbid. No tight belts to accentuate the form. No loud, vulgar colors. Opaque stockings. Low-heeled shoes that do not make offensive, clacking noises." Sora Katz would fold back the curtain on her balcony door to observe the young women below as they paused in the middle of Mea Shearim Street to read her admonition and take correction.

The sense she had of having done her share to straighten these women out through the power of her message never failed to satisfy and inspire Sora Katz.

One possibility that Sora Katz considered and then rejected was simply to wear her Sabbath clothes to the wedding; that is, instead of a black kerchief a white one, instead of a black apron the nice white one with the ruffles, and under that a freshly starched dress, the blue cotton print, maybe. Such a costume would have the desirable effect of toning down what was already a highly unusual, even flamboyant, occasion. On the other hand, if she appeared in that attire, what she would resemble more than anything else in the world would be a proper housewife who had bathed and rearranged herself after having spent the whole Friday standing over the hot stove, stirring chicken soup, sculpting gefilte fish, sampling tzimmes; and what in the world would a proper housewife be doing getting married, even if the groom is already a husband, albeit not hers? No, Sora Katz was at a turning point in her career, and the bridal costume she chose must reflect the radical change that was about to take place. Two factors seemed paramount: that she was marrying an Oriental Jew, and that, by becoming his second wife, she was entering the patriarchal stream, which was at once revolutionary and ancient. To accommodate these two distinguishing factors, Sora Katz selected for her bridal costume a brilliantly embroidered robe sewn together from patches of antique cloth that had originally been designated for the trousseaus of Bedouin girls. In fact, it was Golda Marom, destined to become Sora's senior wife, who helped Sora put together the robe, for Golda had what they called an "excellent hand"—she was an accomplished seamstress and embroideress, a skill she had picked up during her years in the Sinai with Munis, her Bedouin fisherman. She had been instructed in this art by Munis's other wives. Under the robe, Sora Katz wore pants, drawn in at the ankles by colorfully embroidered bands, in the Yemenite way; pants were acceptable, as long as they were underneath, an Eastern style that was, when you thought about it, far more modest and sensible (when climbing, for instance, or bending, or shopping on a blustery day), and as long as they in no way resembled the equivalent male garment, with a row of buttons or a zipper in the front, say. To cover her head, Sora first tightly wrapped her smooth skull in a pale-green scarf, with a border of coins dangling in a straight line across her forehead, and over that she artfully draped a mesh veil the color of sand, ornamented with sequins, which some believed was meant to be worn exclusively by Moslem women who had made the pilgrimage to Mecca, but this veil was so delicate, so nomadic, so emblematic of the wilderness, so like what the matriarchs might have worn to shield their heads from the desert's scorching sun, that Sora Katz could not resist. She was happy in this bridal costume of her own invention, she was exhilarated, for she had never thought she would ever be so lucky as to be given a legitimate excuse to dress up so exotically. Ivriya commented that if some tale-bearer went and informed the police that a polygamous marriage was about to take place and the cops raided Uman House, they could always claim that Sora was not really a bride at all, but Queen Esther of Shushan, dressed up in costume in honor of Purim. And Golda Marom found that notion so right that, for the sake of consistency, she decided to attire herself as Vashti, the Purim queen in the scroll who was liquidated after she refused to heed King Ahashverosh's drunken summons to appear before his courtiers—naked, some say. As for

Shneour Zalman Katz, Sora's son, he insisted on dressing up as a cowboy—it was Purim, after all, and all the children wore costumes—and so, in addition to the regular fringes on his *tzitzit,* Sora Katz sewed fringes along the seams of his black trousers and across his black vest, and in the market of the Old City she found a battered old Stetson hat that came down so low over Shneour Zalman's shaven head, it almost entirely concealed his sidelocks.

Akiva Himmelhoch was playing by himself in the entry courtyard of Uman House, constructing tepees out of bits of old lumber pocked with rusty nails, when Shneour Zalman Katz came up the steps wearing that Stetson. It seemed to Akiva at that moment that nowhere on this earth was there a hat more glamorous, more desirable, than the one that adorned the undeserving head of Shneour Zalman Katz. What did Akiva care for the velvet-and-gilt crown of King Ahashverosh that his mother had constructed for him so long ago, and that he was compelled to wear every Purim in order not to hurt her feelings? What did a robe and a royal cape trimmed with fur mean to him, for whom an ordinary pair of jeans and a T-shirt with a football insignia would have been a far more novel costume? So, as Shneour Zalman swaggered by bowlegged, his thumbs thrust into his waistband, Akiva pounced out of a tepee, snatched the Stetson, and pulled it down on his own head, right over his crown. "Hand over your gun, too!" Akiva demanded, stretching out his arm to collect the weapon. Shneour Zalman took a swipe at Akiva's open palm, and was about to make a lunge to reclaim his prize hat, when he was distracted by a small dog with matted beige fur that had run up the steps, followed by an extraordinary array of photographic equipment, to which a man with impressively large white teeth was appended. As the man paused to screw on a lens to photograph the interesting urchins, Akiva grabbed Shneour Zalman's hand and pulled him under cover. "Shoot the dog instead!" Akiva yelled to the photographer from inside one of the tepees.

Then Akiva gave Shneour Zalman's costume a ruthless once-over. *"Nu,* so where's the gun already?" "Don't have any," Shneour Zalman replied; "my mother don't believe in guns." "Some cowboy!" Akiva said disdainfully. Shneour Zalman stuck his head out of the tepee. "Here, doggie, doggie," he called. Promptly, the dog sauntered in and took a look around. "Smart dog," Shneour Zalman said, "I tell him to come in, and he comes in." "So now tell him to get out," said Akiva. But the mutt just sat there. "It's really a dumb dog," said Akiva. "It's probably a goy." The truth of the matter was, Akiva was not particularly fond of dogs, and though he would not have cared to acknowledge it, he might also have been a little afraid. But the dog just sat on unperturbed, as if it were an invited guest. Akiva considered kicking it, he considered poking it with a stick or maybe throwing stones at it, but then he simply rose, hitched up his robe, pulled down his pants, and urinated on its tail. The dog fled. "This is my gun!" Akiva declared. "Trrrrrr!" And, clutching his penis with two hands, he aimed it to the four winds, mowing down the enemy hordes.

From Uman House the music came strong and delirious, and the sound of dancing feet pounding the stone floor was magnetic, drawing Akiva and Shneour Zalman out of their tepee and toward the building, to check out the action inside. The Uman Boys—Roman Unger on guitar; Shimon Breslau, drums; Uzi Tepel, trumpet—were blasting away ecstatically, their faces flushed, their eyeballs rolling, great stains of perspiration spreading over their white shirts. In the study hall, the men were swigging little tumblers of whiskey, wiping their mouths on the backs of their hands, dancing and stomping heavily, and in the smaller room next door the ladies were holding hands and revolving daintily in a circle. Akiva and Shneour Zalman joined the children in their vivid costumes and masks, as they hovered around the band, leaping and frolicking, and even the little girls were not prevented from drawing close to the musicians in the men's study hall on this Purim day. The children twirled their noisemakers and slammed one another over the head with squawking plastic hammers, adding to the gaiety. The beggar Yisrael Gamzu— the one who ended at the waist—was dancing, too, waving his arms and clapping his hands as he was borne aloft on the shoulders of one of the men. And in the women's room, wearing her trademark green rags, Frum-Frumie, the beggar from the Wall, was swaying entranced in the center of a ring of women, blowing her famous shofar, which she customarily blasted to reward any kind soul who dropped a few coins into her cupped palm; but those who turned coldly away from her entreaties and did not take the trouble to plunge their hands into their pockets and rummage for some charity, these she cursed. The photographer who had tried and failed to steal the images of Akiva and Shneour Zalman had been politely relieved of his idolatrous equipment by Reb Lev Lurie, and now he was attempting to dance with a group of men, lifting one leg after the other tentatively, stamping clumsily, like a white man among the natives, earnestly trying to do what is customary and correct. This, as it happened, was Avraham Ger, Golda Marom's sociology professor from the university, the German convert. He had prevailed upon Golda to persuade Reb Lev to allow him to observe the unique fundamentalist rites of this cultic sect as part of an ongoing, multivariable study. "Tell your rabbi that I'm thinking of becoming a penitent and of enrolling in his group," Dr. Ger said to his protégée, and Golda, thrilled that there was something she could give him that would not violate her religious precepts, obeyed. Each band member had a bottle of arak beside him, and at any break in the music would reach down to bring it up to his lips, throwing his head back, showing egg whites in his eye sockets, sighing contentedly, exclaiming "Ah!" By the time they went into a fervent rendition of "Bring Us to Uman," all the musicians were wonderfully drunk, and then Shimon Breslau was so suddenly and so agonizingly gripped by the memory of how the opportunity to be brought to Uman had been snatched away from him, of how he had attempted to foil Rami, Roman, and Samuel Himmelhoch by denouncing their false documents, of how he had been led out of the airport like a madman in utter humiliation—this memory clutched Shimon Breslau and caused him such excruciating pain that he flung down his sticks and began beating the taut sheepskin of the drum with his own head, screaming all the while, "Flunked! Flunked! I flunked! Flunk! Flunk! Flunk!"

It was an alarming sight, truly, Shimon Breslau banging the drum with his head instead of sticks, yelling "flunkflunkflunk," but the children were thrilled by the spectacle, charged, and they stamped in rhythm with their feet—"flunk! flunk! flunk!"—and with their plastic hammers pounded on one another's heads; in a way, it was like amplified heartbeats in moments of terror—flunk! flunk! flunk!—like breast-beating on the Day of Atonement—flunk! flunk! flunk!—but there was no denying that this was the festival of Purim, and there was a wedding to boot, and there was music and merriment and plenty of food and drink.

In the midst of all this confusion, no one could pinpoint the exact moment of entry of the monumental Arab woman covered from head to toe in a black chador. She proceeded gravely into the ladies' section. The alert Bruriah Lurie immediately rose to shoo her into the men's quarters, for she assumed that the visitor was actually one of the more recent male penitents, still a little borderline and mischievous, costumed for Purim as a devout Moslem lady and attempting, in this fashion, to infiltrate the women's sanctuary and elicit a few shrieks to add to the fun. Ivriya Himmelhoch was maneuvering in her wheelchair alongside the tables, setting out napkins, cutlery, and glasses, for although it was Purim and all mourning gives way to a holiday, it was also a wedding, with lively and joyous music, and the only way she could properly participate while she was still in her year of mourning over her husband, Samuel Himmelhoch, was by rendering some necessary service. As the Moslem lady intruder passed by, Ivriya commented to Tikva Unger, "I heard somewhere that those women are widows who, forever after their husbands die, voluntarily elect to view the whole world through a black veil." "Haven't you ever wondered what they wear under those tents?" Tikva asked idly. "I know," said Golda Marom; "harem pants and a bra, even the fat ones like her."

The black-robed woman sailed forward to the study hall, where the men were celebrating, and where Shimon Breslau, looking like a casualty with a dish towel wrapped around his throbbing headache, was rubbing valerian and skullcap into his forehead, and drinking glass after glass of camomile tea to relax the ringing nerves. At first the black-clad matron was ignored, because it was again assumed that she was merely one of the men in disguise, having a little Purim joke, another benign prankster; already among the yeshiva-student revelers there were several ersatz Arabs—keffiyas draped over yarmulkes, scimitars thrust into *gartel* s. But then Akiva Himmelhoch drew all eyes to the stranger by running up to the dolorous figure, throwing his arms around its knees, and crying, "Abba! Abba! Look everybody! My abba's returned!" And Reb Lev Lurie of Uman House and Abba Nissim of Safad approached, displaying a united front on this public occasion that involved an outsider, and welcomed the guest, who spoke up in a husky cigarette voice, which, upon reflection, might or might not have been feminine. Rami Marom translated: "She says she was sent here by our Moslem neighbors. She says we're making too much noise with our religious observances. She says we're disturbing the peace of the whole neighborhood. She says that if we don't quiet down, they're going to call the police." "Ask her about their muezzin!" yelled Shyke Pfeffer. "Five times a day and an optional sixth, he blasts away over the loudspeaker, calling the faithful to prayer. Talk about disturbing the peace with religious observances!" "A woman! A woman!" cried the more fanatical penitents. "What's a woman doing in here? Get her out! Quick! Quick!" And, brandishing whatever they could lay their hands on—a chair, a broomstick, an empty soda bottle, so as to avoid direct contact with the female—they sought to prod the trespasser out of the room. "Don't touch her," Reb Lev Lurie commanded; "you'll get us into trouble." He ran to fetch his wife, Bruriah, who quickly arrived with another woman, and together, like professional, no-nonsense bouncers, they briskly escorted the veiled stranger out.

A few minutes later, Bruriah Lurie reappeared in the men's

study hall. This time she was escorting a veiled woman in—the bride, Sora Katz. A way was rapidly cleared for the procession by the vanguard of Ivriya Himmelhoch's wheelchair, pushed at daredevil speed by Akiva, still wearing Shneour Zalman's Stetson. The men pressed against one another in their eagerness to let the women have a wide berth as they proceeded to the door that opened onto the rubble-strewn terrace overlooking the Temple Mount. Here, in the hour approaching sundown, under the frank Jerusalem sky, the wedding canopy was set up.

With his guitar hanging around his neck from an embroidered strap, Roman Unger strummed the open strings with his right hand, while he linked his left arm into Rami Marom's, the bridegroom's, and they propped each other up in their stumbling march to their places under the velvet canopy. Rami had just finished explaining to Roman his perspective on the situation. "The way I see it, it's no big deal. Each wife will have her own little apartment at Uman House, so everything will be completely separate. Now, the way I'll work it will be like this. Every night I'll drop in first on one, and then on the other, and very politely I'll inquire, 'Yoohoo, what's for dinner?' And whoever is fixing what I like more, I'll stay with her that night." But such a strategy could encourage an unhealthy, even dangerous, rivalry, Roman pointed out sagaciously. "Yes, but it'll all be in my best interests," said Rami, and with the flat palm of his hand he traced delicious orbits over his tummy. But now, as he headed toward his wedding, robed in the plain white *kittel* that Rav Nahman of Bratslav likened to the garment of the dead, Rami Marom tried to focus his mind on lofty thoughts. He lowered his head and closed his eyes, allowing himself to be steered like a blind man by Roman Unger, his friend and fellow traveler.

So much rubble and debris had accumulated on that terrace over the years that only a small section could be cleared in time for the wedding—an apron, a saucy tongue sticking out from the study-hall door. The students who had hauled and carted the heavy stones had been gratified to learn from Reb Lev Lurie that their labor would not only earn them the *mitzvah* of enabling a marriage, but would also serve as the first stage in the renovation of Uman House, for there were serious plans to enlarge the study hall by constructing an annex on this terrace. In addition to the stones that had cracked and broken and gone unrepaired during the nearly three decades that Arabs had occupied this Jewish-owned building ("They're so lazy and slothful, God have mercy, the sons of Ishmael—for their neglect alone they've forfeited any claims on this property!"), there were also archaeological strata of rubbish and trash ("And how filthy they are—I don't have to tell you!"). Even while the students worked, piling stones on stones, fashioning a low wall so that the area they were clearing for the wedding resembled a small fortress, garbage and slop were dumped on their heads from Moslem windows. There were ominous fist-shakings and shouting and cursing on both sides, and only just in the nick of time did Reb Lev Lurie prevent one of the more hotheaded students from hurling a small boulder and precipitating an international incident. Garbage continued to rain down, even during the wedding itself. The small group huddled under the canopy, as under a shelter in a storm. The canopy sagged from the weight of all that had been cast down upon it. When the canopy was taken down after the ceremony, it was found to contain enough rotten vegetables for a good-sized salad of desperation.

Because of this unremitting barrage, and because, also, the

wedding might be regarded by some as illegal and it was in everyone's best interests that it be gotten over with as quickly as possible, Reb Lev Lurie speeded up the ceremony so deftly, remarkably skipping not a single requirement or word, that it was like a film run in fast motion—stiff, choppy, disjointed. The bride raced around the groom seven times, followed by her panting female attendants, Bruriah Lurie and Ivriya Himmel-hoch. A sharp jab—the ring was stuck on her finger. His words—"Behold thou art consecrated to me"—squeaky, car-toonish, incomprehensible. Veil lifted, wine cup in face, veil dropped—slice, clip, cut. His shoe landing on the glass—bang, pop—and then a flash of light, a scream. They thought for a heart-stopping moment that the Arabs had tossed an explosive into their arena until the voice of Professor Avraham Ger cried out, *"Ach, mein Gott! Mein Leica!"* No one had even known until then that Avraham Ger had joined the wedding party—at Golda Marom's suggestion, he had squeezed himself in—and now it was evident that he had managed to hold on to a small Leica camera when the rest of his equipment had been confi-scated. Regrettably, he had yielded to temptation and taken it out to record and give reality to this unique wedding. Just as the lovely Leica flashed, Einstein Pfeffer sprang into action. In his youthful fanaticism and zeal, Einstein Pfeffer knocked the camera out of Dr. Ger's hand. There it lay on the stones, what had once been the most subtle of mechanisms, the proud expression of Teutonic technology, smashed to smithereens, like the glass under the bridegroom's sole, the latest contribu-tions to the historical chronicle on the terrace, written in garbage. Professor Ger crouched forlornly over his loss, making the mistake, as he did so, of moving out from under the protec-tion of the wedding canopy just when a Moslem housewife stepped onto her balcony and overturned the pail of ammonia-laced water with which she had just mopped her kitchen and bathroom floors.

The humiliation of the German convert and sociology professor Dr. Avraham Ger was thoroughly unfortunate and unjustified, Ivriya Himmelhoch believed, because had it not been for the flash of his contraband camera, she would never have looked up from reading the letter that Abba Nissim had dropped in her lap after she had finished spinning the bride around the groom and her official duties were over. In this letter, Abba Nissim informed her that her husband, the late Shmuel Himmelhoch, may his memory be a blessing, had appeared to him in a dream the previous night and had urged him to go to the widow and demand a swift and favorable decision on the future of the boy Akiva Himmelhoch, as had been recommended in the missive that he, Shmuel Himmelhoch, had sent from such a great distance at such great expense. Thank God for the flash of Avraham Ger's idolatrous camera, Ivriya maintained, for it caused her to raise her eyes from this disturbing letter just in time to notice Akiva teetering on the edge of the terrace parapet, watching the slow and lamentable descent into the street two stories below of the beautiful Stetson hat. Ivriya let out a scream. Abba Nissim, who happened at that moment to be directly behind the boy, grabbed him around the waist and, clambering nimbly over the stones, delivered him, legs flailing at one end and howls erupting from the other, into the empty lap of his petrified mother. Abba Nissim said: "I am confident the widow recalls the words of our sages, that he who saves a person's life, it's as if he has given birth to him. Whether I desire it or not, I now have an even greater paternal responsibility for the well-being of this child."

Akiva cried so long and so hard after this incident that it was not until the bride and groom had emerged from seclusion, and the blessing was recited over the bread, that he quieted down sufficiently and the sobs subsided enough for him to tell his mother what had happened. Ivriya hugged and kissed Akiva with passionate relief, yet simultaneously, with the same intense relief, she scolded him vigorously: What where you doing climbing the stones? How many times have I warned you? What do you mean, you were running away from Abba Nissim? What nonsense, Akiva! Why in the world would Abba Nissim want your hat? For goodness' sake, Akiva! What do you mean, he didn't think the hat was proper and seemly for a son of Torah? What are you talking about, Akiva? Stop your babbling, you bad child—I'm telling you. Why would an old man be chasing a little boy for the sake of a stupid hat? Who cares about that ridiculous old hat anyway? But when Shneour Zalman Katz heard the disastrous news, that his gorgeous Stetson cowboy hat was lost for good, he took over the bawling for his now calm friend Akiva Himmelhoch, and for a long time Shneour Zalman wailed and shrieked and would grant no repose at all to his mother the bride.

The food was now being brought up on great wooden trays from the communal kitchen downstairs. The men served the men first, as is proper, and from what remained the women gladly served the women. Most of the members of Uman House were vegetarians, even from the period before their repentance, but to honor the Sabbath, or on festivals, or for such special joyous occasions as weddings and circumcisions, fish was also offered. Golda Marom was the one who had supervised the women down in the kitchen during the long week of preparations in anticipation of Purim and her husband's marriage; she volunteered in order to demonstrate her utter good will and her complete lack of hostility toward the impending union. Under the direction of Golda Marom, the women braided the long challah loaves, studded with raisins and sweetened with honey. They folded cookie dough or pastry dough over dollops of prune or poppyseed or apricot filling, shoving into the sooty black oven tray after tray of triangular little hamantaschen cakes. There was a nice baked fish, sprinkled with butter, lemon, paprika, and parsley, and there were all sorts of dumplings—spinach, mushroom, cheese, potato. There were plates of zucchini and bean-curd pancakes, and great bowls of steaming brown rice, kasha, barley, noodles. There was a nourishing lentil soup and a lighter cucumber soup made with yogurt and dill. There was a tempting selection of cold salads—beet, carrot, eggplant, cabbage, tomato, hummus and tahini, pickles and olives. There were woven baskets of oranges and grapes. And, for drinks, there were dark bottles of sweet malt beer, and white beer, too; there was soda water and apple juice, arak and wine, herbal and regular tea. No one went hungry. Plenty of challah was left over for the women and girls, so they could acquit themselves of the *mitzvah* of partaking in the feast by pronouncing the blessing over the bread. And there were lots of extra hamantaschen, too, though mostly poppyseed in cookie dough, which were apparently the least popular on the men's side. There were also dates and figs and pistachio nuts and sunflower seeds and dried green peas and chick peas, and some untouched salads as well. Everyone was satisfied and no one complained. The food raised everyone's spirits. There was even a small portion of fish saved for the bride, graciously served to her by Golda Marom. "May you multiply like the fish in the sea," Golda said as she set the plate down in front of her co-wife. "I hope you haven't put any poison in this," said Sora Katz Marom good-naturedly. Everyone was in a delightful mood.

Ivriya Himmelhoch took a little mother-of-pearl-encrusted pipe out of her pocket. From a pretty brown velvet drawstring pouch she drew out a silver folding knife and a nice chunk of hashish. "On Purim it's allowed," she said. "Even my crazy fanatic Shmuel, may his memory be a blessing, used to say so." She sliced off a bit of the hashish, stuffed it into the pipe, and set the match to it. Then she closed her eyes and sucked at the stem long and deeply. "I'm just trying to get it started," she explained. "Of course, it's only right that the bride be honored first." She passed the pipe to Sora, who took a good long pull and then handed it to Golda Marom. "I defer to you, head wife," Sora said jauntily. From Golda it went to Tikva Unger, who wondered if the hashish would get into her breast milk. "Well, why shouldn't my baby Moriah be a little extra happy on Purim, too?" Tikva declared, and she indulged. Then she gave it to Bruriah Lurie, and so it went from hand to hand around the table. When it came home to Ivriya, she filled it again.

"You know what I feel like doing right this minute?" said the bride, Sora Katz Marom. "More than anything else in the world, at this very moment in time, I really feel like giving someone a foot massage!" She turned to Golda Marom. "Let me do it for you, Goldie, please. It's so relaxing, I can't tell you. And, besides, it'll be proof positive that I know my place." Golda Marom, usually so shy and reserved about exposing or letting anyone handle any part of what she considered her ugly body, now, with no hesitation whatsoever, stripped off her shoes and stockings and dumped her big feet—corns, bunions, calluses, blisters, and all—into the bride's lap. Sora worked on these feet assiduously, pausing only to draw on the pipe of hashish whenever it reached her. "Oh, it's so good," said Sora Marom. "It's like—*gewaldig!* It's absolutely heavenly. I feel like I'm soaring. Through submitting—by surrendering—we rise. Who can deny it? From the lowest to the highest, from the feet to the head. You first have to smash into the ground hard before you can take off as light as a bird. God, nobody understands that! It's, *mamish,* exactly what I understood when I knew I had to become a Jew. Nothing dramatic, no revelation or vision or anything. I just knew. It had the purity and simplicity of truth, exactly like Rav Nahman said, *'Prustig! Prustig!'*—'Simplicity! Simplicity!' It came to me like that— pure and simple recognition. I wanted to be absorbed. I wanted to be swallowed up. I just wanted to prostrate myself, I wanted to have no choice but to be brought to my knees before the true God. How can you explain it?"

"Isn't it something, though?" said Bruriah Lurie. "No outsider can understand the absolute beauty of the Jewish woman's position. To the outsider, it looks like we're downtrodden and oppressed, like we're low, lower than low. We eat the leftovers. We're barred from the study halls. We're regarded as inferior and unclean. We're excused or simply forbidden from performing many of the rituals and *mitzvot,* from studying the more complicated and interesting texts. We get no help at all in the house." Bruriah shook her head mournfully as she expanded the catalogue and allowed its details to seep in. She sighed. "That's how it looks from the outside," said Bruriah. "But we know the truth, don't we?"

"We know the truth, all right," Tikva Unger agreed, "no matter how it looks from the outside. The women on the outside think they're the liberated ones, but their so-called liberation is actually a subtle form of enslavement. You know, on the kibbutz where I grew up, when you reached puberty you were expected to lose your virginity. It was as simple as that. Totally—and I mean totally!—secular and corrupt. They put a lot of pressure on you. If you didn't do it you were considered abnormal, repressed, unnatural—see? That's liberation? I ask you!"

"Good-bye to liberation," sang Ivriya Himmelhoch, who was by now respectably stoned. "Good-bye to *Kama Sutra*. Hello, *Baba Kama.*" She smiled, marveling at the profundity of the last turn of phrase, at how she had managed to link by the sounds they shared the ancient Indian text on erotica with a group of tractates in the Talmud. She wondered if she'd remember her clever word play after the sweet hash wore off.

"Who dares to come forth and deny the glory of the Jewish woman?" Bruriah Lurie was now declaiming. "She, the domestic beacon, the unmatched administrator, who bears and raises the children, who manages the household, who goes out and earns a living to provide for her husband and family while he sits all day in the *kollel* and learns Torah! Is there any greater privilege in the world than what is accorded to the Jewish woman? And as her husband grows in wisdom and in holiness, she, too, is elevated and exalted. He endows her with sanctity. From him she receives her spirituality. It is his gift to her, which is made possible only through her gift to him. Between a Jewish man and his wife who live together in accordance with the precepts of the Torah, there is a partnership of equals in the truest sense of the word. Only a fool would call us low, when, in fact, we are so high!"

"Boy, are we high!" said Ivriya Himmelhoch, and the women exploded into gales of hilarious laughter, which continued for a full five minutes at least, rising and cresting in wave after wave. Each time one of them attempted to get serious, the convulsions began again, rattling the silverware on the table and setting the cups dancing.

"Stop already!" yelled Tikva Unger, wiping away the fat tears that were streaming down her face, and pressing her fingertips to her cheekbones, which throbbed and ached from the stretching of laughter. "Compose yourselves—please! I want to tell you something—about a dream I had around the time I was breaking up with Shyke. God, what a heavy time that was! All sorts of changes were going on in me that I couldn't account for. But one thing I knew for sure was that I couldn't go on leading my old futile, wasteful, self-indulgent, meaningless life in a cave in a wadi with a hoodlum like Shyke Pfeffer. So I started studying, but it was all very complicated. There was Einstein, of course, who was already showing his mean streak and giving me a hard time, and then the rabbis added to my woes by decreeing that I had to get a divorce from Shyke even though we had never married—common law, a child, and so on, it's all extremely complex. And of course Shyke refused at first, and tried to squeeze all sorts of concessions out of me. Oh, it was awful! What did I want to say? Oh yes. In the middle of all this, I had a dream that really blew me away entirely. I can't even remember the whole thing, but certain parts I'll never, ever forget. In this dream I was trying to climb something—a ramplike thing, very steep and slippery—and I was constantly falling back, making hardly any progress at all. But then a giant hand rescued me and lifted me up—I was like a speck of dust in its palm—and it placed me in a hole in a steel wall. I stuck out at both ends. Then a great hand started to beat me, it beat me and beat me, all over my body. And I cried out, 'When will I get there, Father?' and a voice answered—so sweetly, so tenderly—'Have patience, my daughter, you will arrive.' And all the while I was still stuck in the wall and the beating continued and I was shrinking, becoming smaller and smaller, growing younger and younger, purer, cleaner, and 'When will I get there, Father?' I would keep on asking, and 'Have patience, my daughter,' the gentle reply would come." Great milk stains appeared on Tikva's blouse. "That's all I remember," she said.

Golda Marom turned to Ivriya Himmelhoch. "Do you remember the condition I was in, Ivriya, when I came out of the desert? What a wreck I was! I was black and blue all over from being beaten by Munis. My teeth were rotten and broken. I was filthy, disgusting. I stank. I was sick, covered with a rash and boils and bruises. I was sure I was dying. It turned out that, to add to everything else, I had hepatitis, and I came to your door, my darling. You were pregnant with Akiva at that time, but still you took me in." Golda Marom laid her head in Ivriya's lap, and she remained in this position silently, her head with Ivriya, her feet with Sora.

Ivriya stroked Golda's kerchief. "Well, we were just lucky that Shmuel, may his memory be a blessing, wasn't home; he was gone, thank God, on one of his trips to Uman. God was watching over you, Goldie, when He gave Shmuel the idea to set out. I believe that that was the trip when Shmuel tried to encourage the ladies to be a little more modest, as a matter of fact. Because if Shmuel had been at home, I'm afraid I could never have earned the *mitzvah* of performing that *hesed* for you, Goldie, of taking you in and nursing you back to health with loving-kindness. As it was, he burned your mattress when he returned, and everything else you'd touched, as a precaution against the impurities. Oh, not because of the germs, mind you. Shmuel never believed in the existence of germs. You know, he wouldn't even allow me to get Akiva vaccinated; I had to go and have my mother do it on the sly. But Shmuel, may he rest in peace, was concerned about your spiritual effect on the baby in my womb, and he was very angry at me for letting you in. It was nothing personal against you, Goldie— really! It was mainly a matter of concept and ideas."

"What did you do for the hepatitis?" Sora inquired. As a herbalist and acupuncturist of some reputation, she was always interested in home remedies.

"I used the only method I knew," Ivriya said. "You were the one who taught it to me, Bruriah—do you remember? See, I got hold of about two dozen pigeons. I took the first one and I placed it with its anus directly on Goldie's bellybutton. I held it there until it kind of wilted and died. Then I did the same thing with the next pigeon, and the next one, and so on, for seventeen pigeons, and they all filled up with the poisons that exited from Goldie via her bellybutton and entered the birds through their anuses, and they all crumpled up and died, one after another. But the eighteenth pigeon lived, so I knew that all the poisons had been sucked out of Goldie and she was cured. And she really was! To tell you the truth, Bruriah, I always thought this method was mildly insane, if harmless, except, of course, to the pigeons. I guess my disbelief was one of the consequences of having been brought up in a medical household. As a matter of fact, when my mother heard about it, she was very upset with me for bringing such filthy, disease-carrying birds into the house. But my mother was wrong this time, just like she's been wrong many times before and since, she should live and be well. In another life I might have agreed with her, but I saw it with my own eyes. I did the pigeon procedure on Goldie and it actually worked. It was incredible!"

"And isn't it interesting," Bruriah said complacently, "that the cure was accomplished on pigeon number eighteen, or *chai*, which means 'life'? It's not the first time, by the way, that it has worked on the eighteenth."

"I want to tell you, Ivriya," said Golda Marom, "that it was thanks in large measure to your mercy to me when I was in such deep distress that I rejected my old way of life and returned in penance. Because after I became thoroughly disillusioned with the so-called romantic Bedouins and got up enough courage to escape from Munis the monster, I remember how I trudged through the desert, broken, dirty, sick, and despised, and I prayed out loud, 'God in heaven,' I prayed, 'show me some kindness, bring me some comfort, prove to me that the life of a single individual matters, give me a reason to live, give me a reason to believe in You.' And He heard my prayer, and He acted through you, Ivriya. I really believe that. I owe everything to you."

"I just don't know what to say, Goldie," Ivriya spoke. "I hope I haven't done you a disservice in the end, substituting a spiritual ailment for a physical one."

"What a dreadful thing to say, Ivriya!" Bruriah declared. "You ought to be ashamed of yourself."

"I am, I am, I am really and truly ashamed of myself. It's

161

a terrible sin, my old cynicism and disdain. It's because of the hash—I shouldn't ever indulge, not even on Purim. It makes me run and slaver at the mouth, uttering nonsense, dribbling foolishness, saying obnoxious things I don't mean at all, Bruriah, not at all. I can't help it. Because you know, Bruriah, perhaps better than anyone, what it has meant to me to return, and if I had to do it again, I would return again, and yet again. Even without my accident. Even without Shmuel's encouragement and pressure. There's no comparison between my life now and the way it used to be when I lived in my mother's house and after I left, when I practically threw myself away like trash. Please forgive me, Bruriah, I didn't mean it. It was idle talk. Because the truth is, I believe a person can change. I believe in penance. I believe in *teshuva.* I believe in the return."

How long had it been silent on the men's side? The women seated around the bride's table now experienced as one the weight of the hush, felt it almost as a physical presence. They noticed that many of the other women had left their seats and were clustering against one another at the door opening into the study hall, trying to get a glimpse inside. Reb Lev Lurie was delivering his talk. Yet even though they could not see him, his words—and, more powerfully, the force behind his words—penetrated as brightly as his rod of light.

"Blessed are we to share in two joyous occasions—this Purim and this wedding. For in the Megillah we read how Hadassah the Jewess intermarried, she submitted to a stupid Gentile king and, for the sake of her people, became Queen Esther. And we have here with us today Professor Dr. Avraham Ger, formerly of Germany, may its name and memory be erased, a convert from the seed of Amalek, from the descendants of Haman, from the most vile anti-Semites in history. No words can express. And now he has become one of us, he has been detoxified and defanged, he has been turned into a hamantasch, and can no longer do us any harm. To the stranger and the convert we must show no malice, our Torah teaches us. And the bride herself is in the long and honorable tradition of women who have been brought into the faith—of Tzipporah the Midianite, the black wife of Moses our teacher, of Ruth the Moabite, the great-grandmother of King David, who lives everlastingly. The revelation to Moses our teacher on Mount Sinai was a wedding, for it is written, 'His mother crowned him on the day of his wedding.' The numerical value of 'Sinai' is one hundred and thirty, exactly the same as *sulam*, 'ladder.' This is the wisdom of our master, Rav Nahman of Bratslav. The dancers at a wedding do *pristakes*—they go up and down, they raise their bodies and they lower their bodies, they dance along the ladder of Sinai. But the Talmud in Ketubot teaches us that 'A woman may rise with her husband, but she does not descend with him.' And it is written in the Torah that 'Moses went up' and that 'God descended onto Mount Sinai.' The wedding at Sinai was a combination of ascent and descent, of up and down, a union of the superior and the inferior, of the low and the high. For this reason it is customary for the dancers to do somersaults at a wedding. And also it is customary at a wedding, just as on Purim, for people to get up and say humorous things, to gladden the hearts of the bride and groom, to heighten the holiday's joy. But every time you get up to entertain and amuse, you must begin by saying, 'I shall rise!' Let us all ascend to the wedding, let us all ascend Mount Sinai. I shall rise! I shall rise! We shall rise!"

In that instant, according to several eyewitness accounts,

Abba Nissim of Safad levitated. From our level it is impossible to confirm or to deny these reports. For the peace of mind of the skeptics, however, suffice it to say that at that moment Nissim rose in the estimation of many. And to the women who could not see him, his words, when he spoke, seemed to be landing on them from above. "Your talk has moved me, Reb Lev, my friend. I am so deeply inspired, I cannot tell you. And I wish to propose something in honor of your excellent discourse and for the sake of *shalom bayit,* domestic peace, here at Uman House. Let us have *shalom,* let us have peace. Let us forget our squabbles and our differences and our disputes. Let us forget for a while about going to Uman. Let us also forget for a while about reclaiming the Temple Mount. Let us, instead, go together into the desert, as it is written, 'I shall follow you into the wilderness, to an uncultivated land.' Let us climb Mount Sinai. Let us re-enact the moment of revelation. Perhaps when we reach the summit of the holy mountain, it will be revealed to us where we should journey next—whether to Uman or to Moriah. Let us elevate ourselves. Let us cast off our old shells and expose our inner core of purity. Let us grow and expand in spirit. Let us rise to the pinnacle of Mount Sinai and await the answer!"

There were cries and moans from both the men's section and the women's: "I shall rise! Let us climb Mount Sinai! Let us rise! I shall rise! We shall rise!" Bodies swarmed in deep prayer; eyes closed in passionate supplication; fingernails raked faces ecstatically. And at her table, with a pencil stub she had sharpened with her teeth, Ivriya Himmelhoch was scribbling desperately on the back of Abba Nissim's letter: "If you can get me up to the top of Mount Sinai, and shed your grace upon me, then I shall submit and do as Shmuel wishes." This note was delivered to Abba Nissim on the men's side. The messenger was Shneour Zalman Katz, because Akiva Himmelhoch had refused absolutely.

Then the comedy sketches and the farces began, for the amusement of the bride and the groom, and in the Purim tradition of mocking gaiety and irreverence.

"I shall rise": Two revelers, costumed as Reb Lev Lurie of Uman House and Abba Nissim of Safad, got up. (The women strove in vain for a glimpse of the show, straining their necks over the added obstruction of the seat that had been placed in the doorway for the bride.) The mask of the Reb Lev jester had a red light bulb for a nose that flickered wanly on and off. The Abba Nissim impersonator had birds perched all over him, upon his head, on his shoulders, trailing down his arms. The two frolickers belted out their jingles simultaneously, trying to drown each other out. The Reb Lev clown's song consisted almost entirely of numbers, which, according to the refrain, added up to "Messiah," "Moriah," and "IBM computer." The Abba Nissim's song was a war chant: in the dark of night he would give the order to his avian legions, who would fly over the sleeping Reb Lev and launch their foul droppings onto his eyes, bringing cataracts—physical blindness to match the spiritual blindness, punishment from above, as had been inflicted upon Tovie in the Book of Tobias.

"I shall rise": A prankster disguised as a pregnant woman with one baby in a sling on her chest, one in a sack on her back, one on each hip, and a few more tugging at her skirt—the actor's buddies, actually, great bearded fellows in frilly baby bonnets, white towels for diapers, thumbs stuck into drooling mouths. Who was this supposed to be? Bruriah Lurie, of course. Over the babies' piercing shrieking and screeching, the

Bruriah impersonator sang in an unmistakable gonadal baritone. "It's Only Natural" was the title of the song: The IDF frisks us when we go down to the Wall. Don't worry. It's only natural. The cops hassle us when we come out of the hall. Forget it. It's only natural. The street kids throw rocks at us when we step out of the stall. No problem. It's only natural. The Moslems curse and spit at us so we get into a brawl. Big deal. It's only natural. And so it continued for several verses, a good-humored litany of the ordinary trials and tribulations of life at Uman House.

"I shall rise": A masked celebrator strumming a guitar, pretending to be Roman Unger—who else?—crooning a long, melancholy ballad, the words consisting entirely of a minute-by-minute breakdown of his daily schedule, from his awakening at six in the morning to the drawing up of his feet into his bed after the rising for the midnight service, each entry anxiously listed and followed by the lament "oy-yoy-yoy-yoy-yoy": 6:00 A.M., wake up ("oy-yoy-yoy-yoy-yoy"); 6:01, put on yarmulke and wash *nagel vasser* ("oy-yoy-yoy-yoy-yoy"); 6:03, recite *Modeh Ani* ("oy-yoy-yoy-yoy-yoy"); 6:05, put on and bless *tzitzit* ("oy-yoy-yoy-yoy-yoy"); 6:08, go to toilet ("oy-yoy-yoy-yoy-yoy"); 6:55, return from toilet ("oy-yoy-yoy-yoy-yoy"); 6:56, greet wife, not overfamiliarly ("oy-yoy-yoy-yoy-yoy"); 6:57, finish dressing and rush out for Shaharit before she hands you the baby to change ("oy-yoy-yoy-yoy-yoy"). More than once the singers were interrupted by the real Roman Unger himself, rushing up to call their attention to details in his day they had omitted.

"I shall rise": A Rami Marom impostor, identifiable by the artist's beret on his head that he still affected, and by the two women tugging at each arm, tearing him apart, screaming:

He's mine; Oh no, he's mine—it would require the wisdom of a Solomon to negotiate. Alas, Solomon, honored far and wide for arbitrating between the two mothers with the only child, but the mighty king himself, husband to one thousand mighty wives, could do nothing at all to save himself from being chewed up into a thousand little pieces.

"I shall rise": A player now came forward, completely masked and disguised, releasing "Who-is-it?" buzzings throughout the study hall and beyond, into the women's section. As he advanced to the platform, his head lowered, he sang in total inward concentration of the pangs of the Messiah— here they come, here they come, today. He was costumed, it soon became shockingly evident, to represent the High Priest in the Temple: a towering miter on his head with a golden crown, the words "Holy to the Lord" carved into it; a splendidly embroidered apronlike ephod to which a breastplate was attached, embedded with twelve precious stones—carnelian, topaz, emerald, turquoise, sapphire, amethyst, jacinth, agate, crystal, beryl, lapis lazuli, jasper—engraved with the names of the twelve tribes of Israel; upon the breastplate the oracular Urim and Thummim were placed; at the hem of the long blue robe, under the ephod, pomegranates of dyed wool and linen hung, and golden bells that tinkled as he moved. When he raised his face to the audience, they saw that it was completely swathed in white gauze, like a victim of a terrible disfiguring burn. He sang, and there was no spreading stain of moisture where his mouth should have been: "Shmuel Himmelhoch is my name / Of mystical posthumous fame / The Temple altar awaits my flame / I've come to stake my claim."

Over and over the stranger in the priestly garb chanted this verse. From his gauze-shrouded face, across the distance of the silenced rooms, his voice was cast like an echo from elsewhere.

Then the spell was broken. Abba Nissim was on his feet. He was shouting. "This is absolutely outrageous! It's a desecration of the Name! If this is your idea of a joke, Lev, then I don't know what to say. You have sunk low, very low indeed!"

Reb Lev Lurie rose manfully to face the charges. "I beg your pardon, Abba Nissim. What can you possibly be thinking of?"

"You planned this, to lead the innocent astray, to make them think that Shmuel would have wanted them to join your benighted ranks in an assault on the Temple Mount!"

Reb Lev Lurie looked truly hurt, and his lips trembled as if he were close to tears while he sought to compose an answer, but no one was destined to hear his reply (except, later on, his wife, Bruriah, as she placed a comfry-root tea pack on his back; to her alone he was reduced to confiding what he would have said, but the opportunity was now lost to him, lost forever). For just as Reb Lev Lurie was about to demolish once and for all the unjust accusation of Abba Nissim, a stone struck him on the back. And then more stones were hurled into the study hall, and there was screaming and confusion, pandemonium, as men ducked under the tables and scurried here and there, covering their heads in panic. But the stranger in the priestly garments moved calmly toward the door that led to the terrace, which had been flung wide open. Three young Arab men in sunglasses stood amid the rubble, stones in their fists, their pockets bulging. The sight of the ghostly bandaged face froze them. The priestly stranger stretched his arms out before him at shoulder height, palms forward, the first two fingers leaning against the thumb, separated from the last two in a fan-like configuration, and he advanced inexorably toward the attackers, droning, droning: "A holy nation, a kingdom of priests, a holy nation, a kingdom of priests." As he advanced, lights began to flash—from the engraved gold crown around his miter, from the onyx stones on his shoulders, from the breastplate studded with the twelve precious jewels, from the Urim and the Thummin. So dazzling was this display of lights that afterward no one could be found who could pinpoint with any degree of reliability the exact moment that the Arab attackers turned their backs and leaped over the parapet. And when order was restored in the study hall of Uman House and in the women's section, it was discovered that the priestly visitor had also vanished.

In the report that was filed with the Israeli police by the Moslem community, it was alleged that an unidentified member of the zealot sect had reacted to the peaceful disturbance-of-the-peace complaints of three Arab neighbors by suddenly lifting his robes, dropping his trousers, and indecently exposing his private parts. It was further noted that whereas on most occasions they, the Moslem neighbors, could not tell the zealots apart because they all looked and dressed exactly alike, in long black coats and black hats, with fringed garments and fringed faces, this time the one who had indecently exposed himself was clearly distinguishable by so weird and fantastic a costume that he seemed to have come from another world.

MOUNT
SINAI

A short while after the Uman Boys Band van passed the luminous oasis of Dahab, it turned west off the coastal highway and began penetrating deep into the southern portion of the Sinai Peninsula along a rough desert road, steep and strewn with rocks. Roman Unger, the driver, at first paid scant attention to the ominous change in terrain under the wheels of his vehicle; he had taken due notice of the sign directing the wayfarer to the Monastery of Saint Catherine and to Mount Sinai, a distance of about one hundred and sixty kilometers, and he had turned right accordingly. His thoughts at the moment were stuck at the memory of Shyke Pfeffer's eulogy for Samuel Himmelhoch, Shyke's nostalgic account of the paradisiacal time spent dancing naked on the sands and in the clear waters of this very spot flying by, this golden spot, Dahab—Shyke, Shmuel, and the two women, Ivriya and Tikva, in their fallen days. Now Tikva was Roman's wife, and where was she? She was home at Uman House, attending to their baby, Moriah, distant from him in space now as she had always been distant in spirit. Roman was not Tikva's first love; he was not the bridegroom of her youth; he would never be true blood and kin to her; never would she allow him to know her. Roman wondered if Ivriya, too, was remembering, as Dahab passed them by, remembering those nights when she danced.

But then the van began to bounce, to spring, to fly, and Roman slipped one palm off the steering wheel and smacked it hard against his forehead. "My God! My shock absorbers!" he cried out loud. Oh, he should never have consented to this mad escapade; he should never have allowed Reb Lev Lurie to talk him into it. For perhaps the first time, Roman Unger permitted himself the luxury of a resentful thought against his teacher. But Reb Lev had presented the case so rationally, how could Roman have done otherwise but acquiesce? To Abba Nissim Reb Lev had said, "The Midrash teaches us that the world is securely established by virtue of the two great mountains: Moriah, where Abraham brought Isaac for sacrifice and where the Holy Temples stood in splendor, and Sinai, where Moses received the Torah in thunder and flames. You, Abba Nissim, can have Sinai. I'll take Moriah." They were like two mighty conquerors dividing up the empire. Furthermore, Reb Lev pointed out, except for the prophet Elijah's ascent in quest of sanctuary from the wrath of King Ahab and Queen Jezebel, and but for the revelation Elijah experienced up there, there is no real Jewish tradition of making pilgrimages to Mount

Sinai; as for the rabbis, their deepest interest had always been riveted in *what* was given upon the Mountain of God, not in *where* it was given. "Besides," Reb Lev Lurie concluded, "all Jewish souls, past, present, and future, were at Sinai for the giving of the Torah. So if you don't mind, my dear Abba Nissim, I won't go this time, since I've already been there!" Privately, Reb Lev had confided to Roman Unger, "This is Nissim's project, Roman. It wouldn't be fitting for me in my position to endorse it by participating. On the other hand, I don't want to be petty and spiteful. I can't withhold my support entirely, especially since Nissim proposed it on Purim to patch up our differences. So we'll have to let them use your van, and you'll have to drive it as my representative." What choice did Roman have? And now, in addition to everything else, such woeful punishment was being inflicted by this miserable Egyptian road on his loyal van—his pal, his buddy—that never, never would it be the same again.

For Akiva Himmelhoch and Shneour Zalman Katz, however, sprawled on the floor of the van, across rolled-up sleeping bags and knapsacks, wedged between the cartons of biscuits and apples and the jerrycans of water that formed a barrier separating the male from the female passengers—for the two merry little boys, every bump and roll translated into a thrill, a squeal, a hurtling into the air, a sly look at the clenched disapproval on Abba Nissim's face before descending for an exhilarating plunge into the cushioning. And what treasures there were to be found in Roman's van—harmonicas, tambourines, drums, flutes! Abba Nissim was obliged to shush the raucous children far too many times, until he had no choice but to confiscate the instruments, one by one, for the legends about Mount Sinai with which Abba Nissim was preparing Rami

Marom were necessary and good for the children to hear as well. Of how Sinai, unique among the mountains because idolatry had never been practiced there, was chosen. Of how Sinai had never expected the honor, for it considered itself far too low and unprepossessing, and by virtue of its modesty it was exalted. Of how God caused Sinai to hover menacingly over the heads of the children of Israel, and He roared, "If you accept the Torah it will be well with you; if not, here will be your burial." Of how the carnality with which men had been pierced by the serpent in Eden departed from them at Sinai when they declared, "We shall do and we shall listen." Of how, at Sinai, there were no unclean persons; there were no lepers, no imbeciles, no lame, no deaf, dumb, or blind; and at Sinai, there was no dissension among the Israelites. "For perhaps the first and last time," Abba Nissim added dolefully.

"We cannot hope to achieve a level of purity like that of the generation of the wilderness," Abba Nissim said, "but if we ascend to a fraction of their height, it will be a blessing, far more than we deserve." His audience consisted solely of Rami Marom, for the two boys were irretrievably lost in blissful crashing and springing, while Roman Unger, the driver, was cursing the road, moaning each time the dear van was struck, and the fourth adult male passenger, Professor Avraham Ger, could not hear a word Abba Nissim was saying because his head was poked well out of the window; he was clicking his camera incessantly, recording the magnificent changing landscape, as the steep mountains of black rock gave way to sandstone formations cut through by narrow canyons and surrounded by brilliantly colored walls, and then the flat valleys that were rendered emphatic by sandstone blocks in queer shapes opened into the gorges and the massive granite peaks of which Jebel Musa, the Mountain of Moses, was only one. Dr. Ger had been granted permission to bring along his photographic equipment, provided he didn't aim it at any of his companions, but even this stricture represented such a deprivation for him that he would become uncommonly excited by any sign of life in the inanimate scenery—a Bedouin squatting under an acacia tree, a camel grazing by the side of the road. The children got into the habit of clicking their tongues each time they spotted a camel, to alert Dr. Ger. It was as if they were pressing a magic button: the professor would instantly, automatically, jut half his body out the window and shoot. No two camels are alike, Dr. Ger instructed the boys pedantically, and the boys certainly did not contradict him, enthralled as they were by their power to jolt him into action.

The matter of whether or not to allow Avraham Ger to join the expedition in the first place had been carefully deliberated by Reb Lev Lurie, especially in the light of Golda Marom's well-known and lamentable infatuation with the man—nobody could understand what she saw in him, but, then, Golda, so intelligent in other spheres, had repeatedly demonstrated her stupidity when it came to choosing men, and she was only lucky enough to be one of the wives of such a nice, decent fellow as Rami Maron, everyone agreed, because the marriage had been arranged. But the deciding factor in Ger's favor, as far as Reb Lev was concerned, had been his repeated and vehement insistence that he was seriously considering becoming a penitent. As it was, Reb Lev had a problem accepting Avraham Ger as an authentic convert, for although Ger had shown the sincerity of his desire to become a Jew by undergoing circumcision at such a mature age—an experience he had rather enjoyed, according to his own account—his training and preparation for joining the faith had been transacted through the mails, in a correspondence course. Still, the prospect of another penitent convert was not to be taken lightly; it was an additional stone in the pathway being paved for the coming of the Messiah, a necessity that the master, Rav Nahman of Bratslav himself, had acknowledged and promoted, for Rav Nahman had declared that the Temple altar would be made whole once again through the casting off by each person of his old faith for the redemptive faith of Israel. And how could such conversions be encouraged? By acts of charity, which had the power of smoothing away and dispelling the disturbances in the air that interfere with communication between people. It would be a charitable act, indeed, to allow Avraham Ger to join the pilgrimage to Sinai since he expressed the desire so ardently. It would be cynical to question his motivation, Reb Lev Lurie decided, and when you considered the hardships that the convert was prepared to put himself through, his avowed interest in atonement could only be regarded as genuine.

Abba Nissim, for his part, was not at all pleased with the idea of including this Herr Professor Dr. Adolf Germani, as he called the convert. It was the gravest folly on Reb Lev's part to take to his bosom this snake, this phony with his cheap conversion, who was still, in his every tic and nuance, startlingly Prussian. Why, after all, should Abba Nissim care—he whose family had lived for generations in Safad, and had been unmolested by those savages, those Huns? But Reb Lev Lurie of Kiev, of the charnel pits of Babi Yar—he should know better! This was just another example of Lev's softheaded liberalism, which had been typically displayed in matters of law and practice, now manifesting itself in the political and social arena as well, where it was nothing less than self-destructive.

176

Still, if the shining Reb Lev Lurie of Kiev insisted, Abba Nissim was willing to take Ger—he was hardly more than a buffoon in any case, with that bladelike star of David under his shirt; yes, Nissim would make room for this clown and charlatan, Dr. Adolf Germani, provided that Lev gave up, in exchange, that absurd project of his, that Einstein Pfeffer come along, too, for the purpose of having his bar mitzvah solemnized at the top of Mount Sinai. Oh, Abba Nissim was well aware that it was fashionable nowadays to enact the bar-mitzvah ceremony at all sorts of novel and outrageous sites—Masada, Meron, the Herodion, Caesaria, and so on—but Mount Sinai? First of all, they wouldn't even find a *minyan* of ten men up there for prayers. And second, since that fateful moment when Einstein Pfeffer had smashed Professor Ger's precious camera under the wedding canopy at Uman House, the boy and the man were mortal enemies. As Abba Nissim put it to Reb Lev Lurie, "I'll do you the favor and take one or the other, but not both. God forbid that I be the conveyor of dissension to the top of Mount Sinai!"

Abba Nissim certainly had his hands full—the children, the convert, Rami, and Roman, not to mention the women—and he felt himself responsible for both the spiritual and physical well-being of all his charges. But, blessedly, as the van continued to climb heroically into the mountainous region of the southern Sinai, the silence of the women in the back seat deepened until it was almost possible for Nissim to forget they were there at all. The last time the women had had a conversation of any length was over a hundred and fifty kilometers back, somewhere between Taba and Nuweiba. Their voices and their trivial murmuring had constituted a distraction to Abba Nissim as he struggled to expound on the lofty topic of the significance of Sinai, and, accordingly, he had instructed Akiva Himmelhoch to order the women to be quiet. After that, Ivriya and Sora would occasionally bestir themselves when the children became too boisterous, but each time they ventured to speak, Akiva or Shneour Zalman would inevitably retort with Abba Nissim's words: "The women should close their mouths!" And soon enough the mothers recognized the advantages of their situation. They surrendered the irritating burden of supervising and disciplining the children to the men, who might speak, and gave themselves over to thinking without interruption.

Golda Marom sat with her forehead pressed against the window. This was the first time she had returned to the Sinai since she had left Munis. The configuration of the landscape was familiar to her, an already indelible aspect of her internal landscape; she knew it intimately from the days when she had followed her fisherman, carrying his nets beside his other wives as they walked along the shores of the Red Sea, up and down the Gulf of Akaba and the Gulf of Suez. Who could be sure that the black-clad Bedouin woman moving in the distance over there was not a classmate of hers from M.I.T., burning to taste life? And look at poor Professor Ger here—so ridiculous, so plaintive and touching, really, with his assortment of lenses—another type entirely.

Why was she always drawn to types? Ger had exploited her to gain entry into Uman House—she understood that very well—he claimed her research and her insights as his own; all his dazzling statistical formulations were hers. Perhaps it was her weakness to be attracted to selfish and cruel men, to Arabs, to Germans, to the persecutors of her people. Ger scorned her, she knew, because she wasn't outwardly pretty, and yet he took advantage of the devotion she couldn't hide, well aware that he was perfectly safe from the traditional forms of female aggression, that she would never demand any commitment from him, because, to compound her woes, she was a married woman and a religious woman. And she really was religious. Adultery was a grave transgression, explicitly singled out to be included among the commandments handed down on the tablets here at Sinai; but even her adulterous thoughts were radically sinful, and they tormented her. Arrogance and adultery are bound together, Rav Nahman of Bratslav said. Truly, she was guilty of excessive pride. But perhaps she needed temptation, tension, conflict, to challenge her and keep her steadfast to the faith, just as, it has been speculated, Jews need anti-Semitism to go on preferring the sorry comfort of having been chosen. For the survival of the Jews—not as individuals, naturally, but as a race—we have the anti-Semites to thank. So, thank you very much, Munis; thanks a lot, Dr. Ger. And her husband, Rami, listening so patiently and mildly over there to Abba Nissim—how much, after all, did Rami absorb of the words of the old mystic of Safad? He, her sweet, harmless Rami, was like that Hassidic saint who never once learned a complete lesson from his master, for each time the master began with the words "And the Lord spoke," the saint would soar in rapture, would cast himself about, crying, "The Lord spoke, oh, the Lord spoke!" That was enough for him. That was sufficient profundity for this saint, joy enough to boost his soul to the celestial spheres. It was here at Sinai that the Lord spoke most generously. But she, cursed woman that she was, she demanded to know what He said, and the meaning of His spoken words, while Rami, in the simplicity of his faith, took true delight in merely attending to the resonant melody of Abba Nissim's words. Truly, it was in her, in Golda, that Abba

179

Nissim of Safad ought to be investing his mysteries, for she possessed the intelligence, she had the passion, she had the fire; she—not any of the males in this van, not even Ivriya, and certainly not her co-wife, Sora—was endowed with a spirit that had within it the potential to be utterly transformed and illuminated by the ascent to the top of the mountain.

At the other end of the back seat of the van, Sora was dipping into a little volume called *The Praises of Rav Nahman*, and letting her thoughts drift pleasurably. Rav Nahman, she read, would sometimes be so stricken with embarrassment when standing before God and addressing Him in prayer that he would blush—that is, Rav Nahman would blush, not the Almighty, God forbid—he would actually blush! As for her— not that Sora was in any way comparing herself to the master, *l'havdil*—she tended to blush so easily, all her life it had been a chronic source of mortification. Perhaps it was physiological, related to the fact that she was so fair, but these perfidious blushes had always been like flash bulletins of what she was feeling; they sabotaged any attempt at self-possession. Her mother had declared that she was born blushing, probably because she was naked at the time.

There was no point in thinking about her mother on the road to Mount Sinai. Her mother had always maintained that she, Sora, was a prude, an authentic puritan, that her obscenely rebellious days before her conversion to Judaism represented an artificial effort to thwart the basic frigidity and prudishness of her nature, and that in the end she had opted for the destiny of what amounted to a Jewish cloister because to become a Christian nun would have been too ordinary and conventional. This was how her mother thought and explained things. Her mother had been in analysis all her adult life; it was her career.

And because the mother did not wish to deprive the daughter of any of life's advantages, she had started Sora in analysis at around the age of four, right on the cusp of the Oedipal phase. Sora often thought that she had converted simply to get out of analysis, that she had only enough strength within her to give up the psychiatrists for their cousins the rabbis. It was the mother's fault entirely that the daughter had developed such a dependency on Jewish types.

And the rabbis really were adorable little darlings—weren't they?—much cuter than the psychiatrists. Just look at Abba Nissim over there, laboring so hopefully over her husband, over her Rami. Which half of Rami was Abba Nissim working on anyhow, hers or Goldie's? Well, it was probably the spiritual half, above the *gartel;* the physical half, below the belt, was what she shared with Goldie, and not very enthusiastically, either. Poor Rami! Two wives, and he hardly enjoyed the benefits of one. But it didn't seem to bother him much, thank God; they must have run out of hormones when it was his turn on line. Goldie didn't seem to be particularly interested in the conjugal aspect of their marriage, and as for Sora, because she was already in her late thirties, she was subject to all sorts of gynecological irregularities—spots, stains, leaks—and she considered each of these, no matter how minor, to be exactly the same as a period; she would separate and count the days, a minimum of twelve. Rami was lucky if he got one clean night a month out of her. You know what Rami really needed? What he needed was a third wife. Maybe Ivriya—why not? Goldie and Sora got along perfectly well, and both of them loved Ivriya. They would be the three inseparable wives of Rami Marom, the three Maromeers, the three witches. Sora turned to Ivriya, sitting there in the back seat of the van, between her and Golda. Ivriya's eyes were closed, but Sora could tell she wasn't sleeping. "I just had a great idea, Ivriya," Sora began. "The women should close their mouths!" piped up her son, Shneour Zalman.

Well, impudence or not, the child's interference was just as well, Ivriya thought, because she was not particularly in the mood, at the moment, to consider another one of Sora's great ideas. The trip through Eilat, south past Coral Island, had evoked keen memories in her of the six months she had spent living there alone, among the ruins of the Crusader's Castle. That was before her accident. Shmuel had visited her there, too, paddling out to the seclusion of her island in a yellow submarine, bearing fragrant offerings to smoke and burn and taste. Like a pagan priestess, she had been. She used to tie a beautiful old Spanish shawl around her hips, like a sarong, but always she went bare-breasted. As she had up at Rosh Pinna, too, when she galloped on her horses. Shmuel later maintained that it was for her bare-breasted wantonness that she had been punished. Then why didn't she get breast cancer? Why did she break her back? Not that she was expressing any particular preference. God works in mysterious ways, Shmuel had advised her, but there was no doubt that it was for her deficiency of modesty that she was punished. For flaunting her physical gifts, she was chastised physically; for her pride in her beauty, for her vanity, she was struck down. Yet there, on Coral Island, he, too, had taken idolatrous pride in her beauty, delicately cupping a breast in each hand with such exquisite veneration, she felt she could break. And she did break. But why not Shmuel? Why wasn't he punished in such a way for such sins? Why, when she could no longer take a single step, was he able to walk—to walk, and walk, and walk away? "Look, Ivriya sweetheart," her mother used to say after the accident, "it's just something that happened. For my sake, darling, if not for your own, stop torturing yourself by always asking why, why, why. Whoever said there was any justice in this world? It's not as if you did anything to deserve this. What do you think? It's not because you ran away from home, and danced all night, and bummed your way all over the world, and in general nearly worried your poor mother to death, that now you can hardly budge an inch without my help. I never want you to think that, honey. Above all, don't blame yourself."

They were all accomplices in comforting her in those days after her accident, but she would not be comforted. Her mother, her friends—all of them collaborated in the pretense that nothing essential had changed: Hey, it's all right if paralysis is your thing, as horses were once, as travel, as poetry, as dancing, as relationships; hey, so now you're into wheelchairs—it's okay, it's cool. But she recognized that in their hearts they dismissed her, crossed her out as a potential rival, discounted her as a threat; she no longer mattered; there was nothing she could ever again accomplish that would incite their envy. They would forever indulge themselves in feeling noble and virtuous by wishing her well without a single qualification. They pitied her! They pitied her! What was most infuriating of all was their pity! God, how she despised their pity! There was nowhere she could run to escape this curse—not to Amsterdam, not to New York, not to Marrakesh, not to Rosh Pinna, not to the Crusader's Castle on Coral Island. Her affliction was the trap, the blighted universe she carried with her wherever she went.

What a revelation it had been, then, after the bitterness and the pain had yielded up their raw edge, to discover that, though her body was doomed to remaining heavy and inert, her soul could still leap, could lightly dance. And in those early days of her penance, how she had been swept away by the possibilities opening up to her: of mystery, of transcendence, of ecstasy, of union with the divine. Abba Nissim had said to her then that such exalted states were indeed possible, even for a woman, and well worth striving for, though in fact the female did not commonly achieve high levels of holiness because she was fettered by nature and by circumstances to practical, mundane affairs; indeed, she, Ivriya Mendelssohn, physically earthbound as she was, was the paradigm of all womankind. Nevertheless, there was hope for her, Abba Nissim had said. How could she have forgotten? It had been Abba Nissim—hadn't it?—in the bitter days when, no longer able to take physical steps, she had taken her first tentative steps toward returning, it had been Abba Nissim, after all, who had reminded her that often it's the case that the righteous suffer while the wicked thrive. Look how Rav Nahman of Bratslav himself had suffered: the death of his son and of his wife, sickness and his own untimely passing, not to mention the calumny and hatred and contempt of his contemporaries, their total lack of understanding of his teachings, their complete failure to perceive his uniqueness. So her suffering was in the grand tradition—not that she intended in any form to flatter herself through such a comparison. And perhaps her suffering in this life marked her as one among the righteous, refined her soul, prepared her for the rewards of the next world. Why had she allowed herself to forget the great comfort she had derived in the past from the mystical words of Abba Nissim? Of course, Abba Nissim was often harsh with her now, but so had Shmuel been. It was the natural way of men who had dedicated their lives to attaining higher and higher degrees of holiness. With the great work before them, there was no time to waste on frivolous amenities. Besides, the harshness was good for her; it gave her standards to aspire to, forced her to be constantly alert to ways in which she might improve and elevate herself. And, yes, Akiva was terrified of Abba Nissim's severity, but wasn't it just this sort of consistency and rigor that she failed to provide that the boy needed in order to develop properly, like a sapling that must be ruthlessly lashed to stakes in the ground if it is to grow straight?

Oh, which one of those glowing peaks rising up ahead was Mount Sinai? It was a spectacle that made her heart beat in chords! Abba Nissim had promised to get her up there; he had said he could do it. Into his blessed hands she would deliver her crippled body, her gravity-diseased body, and he, Abba Nissim, would bear it, would bear it up to the top of the mountain and launch her soul.

It was almost dark when they began to unload at a campsite in the wadi outside the gates of the Monastery of Saint Catherine, at the foot of Mount Sinai. The night was cool and crisp, a sweet relief after the hot day caged in the van. Twice on the way the van had overheated, and Roman had tenderly slaked its thirst, emptying one jerrycan after another. Here in the wadi, as spring capitulated to summer, there were still a few pools of water from the rain-filled days of winter, but already it was mostly dry. It had happened at this season of the year, too, more than three millennia ago, that the desert Jews, the liberated slaves of Egypt, had camped in this wadi to receive the yoke of their spiritual bondage. Here at the foot of Mount Sinai they had stood in the late spring, trembling bridelike, in anticipation of consummating their mystical union with God through the medium of His law. "Well, maybe it wasn't in this wadi at all that the old Hebrews camped," said Professor Ger, reading from a German guidebook. "Maybe it wasn't even on that mountain over there that they received the Tablets. There's a lot of scholarly debate on the subject of the exact location. Some even claim it was Jebel Halal, in the northern Sinai."

Ger was buzzing around the women, who were scarcely paying any attention to him, busy as they were with setting out the provisions, preparing the dinner, and arranging the bedding for the night. Even Ivriya—although she was lying down, because the long day seated in the van had been a great strain on her—was occupied, washing and changing Akiva, and arguing with the child because he insisted on going barefoot. "I *have* to take off my shoes," Akiva declared, "because this is the spot of the Burning Bush!" And he proceeded to quote from the Book of Exodus: "Remove your shoes from your feet, because the place on which you are standing is holy ground." No question about it: Akiva was a smart aleck, like his father before him.

"The boy is correct, you know," said Ger. "Inside that compound over there"—and he pointed in the darkness to the fortresslike stone walls of the Greek Orthodox monastery—"there's a living descendant of the Burning Bush, right near the spot where Moses is said to have seen it, where he had his first vision. And I've also heard that there's a spring in there, with the sweetest and coldest water in all the Sinai. Wouldn't you like to go and get some of that fresh water to drink?" Ger addressed his tantalizing invitation directly to the two children, Akiva and Shneour Zalman.

"You know it's forbidden to enter a church." Softly, Golda Marom said this to Ger, as if by gently enlightening him she would save him from the public embarrassment brought on by ignorance. After all, how could he, a newcomer to the faith, be expected to know every single one of the thousands upon thousands of customs and laws?

"And do you know what else they have in there?" Ger went on in a storybook rhythm, exclusively for the children's sake. "They have a special room in there called an ossuary, filled with piles and piles of skulls and bones—thigh bones and arm bones and back bones, any kind of bone you'd ever want to see. And these skulls and bones are all that's left of the monks who lived and died in the monastery over the generations. Whenever a new monk dies, they dig up the remains of the monk who had been buried longest and put them in the ossuary. Then they bury the new monk in the old monk's spot, because they only have a small cemetery and they don't have enough space. And presiding over all the heaps and heaps of skulls and bones in the ossuary is a shrunken little skeleton dressed in a purple robe and a cowl. This skeleton was once a monk named Saint Stephanos, who lived long ago. He used to listen to the confessions of the pilgrims who made their way to Sinai, and he would examine them for piety."

"Well, it's lucky for you he's dead," Ivriya spoke up smartly, "because you'd flunk the piety test for sure. Why are you bothering the children with your ghoulish Black Forest fairy tales?"

"Kids love spooky stories," said Ger. "The crueler the better. Anyhow, I don't see any reason why I shouldn't be allowed to take them into the ossuary at least, and maybe get a few shots of it myself. It's not the church, after all, with the crucifixes and the icons."

"Sorry," said Ivriya. "Akiva's staying right here with me, where he'll be safe and sound."

"You see that mountain over there?" Ger continued, pointing for the children's sake to the shadowy outline of Jebel Katherina. "That's the tallest one in the region—two thousand, six hundred and thirty-seven meters high. Do you know what they found up there? Up there they found the bones of the martyr Saint Catherine, whose head had been chopped off after she was first strapped to a spiked wheel that turned and turned, but, miracle of miracles, it didn't tear her to bits and pieces."

Sora Marom had stopped peeling carrots and was listening attentively. "What did she do to deserve such a gruesome punishment?" Sora asked quietly.

"Proselytizing. She was a little too zealous at it." The two converts, Sora Marom and Avraham Ger, exchanged a long look. "Anyhow, the monks carried her body to the top of the mountain, and when her bones were found many years later, they exuded a scented oil that, supposedly, could cure any disease. In the Middle Ages, drops of this oil were sold as a panacea all over Europe for very high prices. And that, they say, is how this monastery acquired all its valuable treasures."

"Is that so?" said Sora. "There must have been something in that oil. I wonder what it was."

But if Avraham Ger possessed this information as well, he was prevented from transferring it, for just then Roman Unger approached, after having been prodded by Abba Nissim, who was disgusted by Ger's unseemly socializing with the women.

Roman, for his part, had been all the while resenting the way Ger was avoiding the heavy work, but, tolerant soul that he was, Roman refrained from exercising his authority. With difficulty he yielded to Nissim. Rather coldly, Roman inquired if Ger wouldn't mind helping the men out a bit by setting up the propane burner to heat the water. Then Roman couldn't stop himself from going on and explaining apologetically: "We want to eat and pray and finish up and get to bed as early as we can, because the plan, as it now stands, is to wake up around three A.M., God willing, and to climb Mount Sinai before daybreak, before it gets hot. That way, with God's help, we'll reach the top at sunrise, just in time for morning prayers."

Ivriya managed to coax Akiva into eating three carrots, a cucumber, and a tomato, which he bit into and finished off exactly as if it had been an apple. The only point in her childrearing program on which her husband, Shmuel, had ever complimented her was the way she had trained Akiva to prefer vegetables over junk. But Shmuel had never been privileged to hear Akiva's regular litany whenever they passed the kiosks in the streets—"Buy me a falafel!" "Buy me an ice-cream!" "Buy me a cola!" "Buy me a pizza!"—for this was a litany that Akiva would never have dared to recite while walking with his father. And once, when Ivriya's mother had offered to buy Akiva a bicycle, he declared that he'd rather have a chocolate bar instead. "You see the consequences of sweets deprivation?" her mother had cried triumphantly. "They become just another taboo, like sex. Ivriya honey, I just hope I'm still alive and kicking when this terrific kid grows up, because it'll be a real treat to watch the fireworks when he rebels against you fanatics like nobody's business." How her mother pursued her and invaded her thoughts, even to the foot of Mount Sinai!

189

It took all of Ivriya's strength to get Akiva to quit jumping around, to sit down properly while eating, and to recite the correct blessing over the fruits of the earth. But on no account would he wash his hands and say the blessing over a slice of bread, for that would oblige him to repeat the long, the interminable grace after a meal, and there, over there on the men's side, the gas burner that Avraham Gar was igniting was flickering, glowing, beckoning irresistibly. Like the Burning Bush, the spectacular lighting effect that the Lord, the greatest lighting engineer of them all, had set up in this desert to lure the shepherd Moses as he walked beside his father-in-law's flock, a bush burning in fire but not consumed. "The difference between the Creator of day, night, and all the heavenly bodies, and mortal lighting specialists," Shmuel used to say, speaking as an ex-professional in the early days of his return, "is that whereas we use light to attract for the purpose of obscuring, He, may His name be blessed, uses it to attract for the purpose of illuminating." But then the light went out; there was darkness. Akiva let out a bitterly disappointed, reproachful yelp, and it was impossible for Ivriya to contain him a moment longer. He ran off to the spot where the light had been, and then that scream of his, his mortal scream, was thrown up into the air like a burst of black smoke; it rebounded to her like a blow in the stomach. She couldn't move. She wasn't even in her wheelchair: she was lying on a sleeping bag on the ground. She began to push herself forward, crawling on her belly, groveling like a snake, sand and ash filling her mouth, and all the time his screams were coming, punching her, pounding, pummeling, tearing her to pieces, ripping the cords that held her together; she would never survive this; she could see him thrashing desperately; she could see Roman lift him up under

190

the armpits and dip him again and again into a pool of water, a forced baptism.

Then Roman placed him in her arms and turned the bright headlights of the van on the child's burned foot. The skin of the toes and side had curled up like the flimsiest of things, peeled away, roasted; the pulpy red-and-blue flesh underneath was scooped up and turned inside out. "You should have made a stone boundary to mark the spot where you were setting up the heater!" Roman Unger said to Avraham Ger. "You should never have let him go barefoot!" Avraham Ger said to Ivriya Himmelhoch.

Akiva cried and cried in his mother's arms, his compact little dancer's body alternately twitching and going limp, his eyes shutting and opening to reveal whites tinged with the blue of one still new to this earth. He was in pain! Just a few minutes earlier he had been fine, full of high spirits, brimming with curiosity, and now look at him! Just a few minutes ago, she, Ivriya, his mother, had felt herself to be in command of her little corner, in control. Now she was helpless. Her child was in pain, yet the earth did not shudder nor the mountains collapse.

The pilgrims of Uman House gathered around the mother and child, offering remedies and advice. "Munis used to put egg whites on burns," said Golda Marom. "It forms like a skin, kind of sealing it off and protecting it." "Oh, I could just kick myself for leaving my herb basket at home," wailed Sora Marom. "Aloe vera is the only thing to put on a burn, and maybe a comfry tea taken internally. How could I be so stupid? I'll just never forgive myself!" "Let him drink a little rose water," Rami Marom said. "Did anyone bring along some rose water? I'll sit down right now and make him an amulet, a *cameo* of some sort." "He is not burned," said Abba Nissim. "I shall pray to the One Above to make the child realize he isn't burned." "The main thing is to keep it clean," said Roman Unger. "There's a first-aid kit in the van. I think there's some gauze and some dressing in it." And Avraham Ger, as he brought over the kit, pointed out that they ought to put some medication on it, too, to prevent infection. "Look at this!" Ger exclaimed, as he flipped up the lid. "Aren't we lucky tonight? Here's some iodine! Just what the doctor ordered!" And since Ger was the closest in their group to an official doctor, the others deferred to him.

The first daub of iodine that Dr. Ger smeared on the burn caused Akiva's leg to shoot straight out convulsively, as if he had been shocked with an electric current. His screams grew even more piercing now, louder, more agonized than ever. Stoically, Ger continued to apply the iodine to the burn. Akiva was thrashing about, screaming, and Ivriya was compelled to be an accomplice in holding him down. Now she had direct confirmation of what professional torturers have always known: break the parent by forcing him to witness the torture of the child. But what could she do? Here they were in the middle of the desert, in the middle of nowhere, and the wound had to be kept clean, it had to be kept safe from infection. Tears ran down Ivriya's face, soaking her glasses, blinding her, she was sobbing, but she went on pressing all her weight on Akiva to hold him still so that Dr. Ger could carry on with his work. As he painted the wound with iodine, Dr. Ger chanted soothingly: "Ah, *schmerzen,* Akiva, *schmerzen!* Ah, Akiva, *schmerzen, schmerzen!*" And Akiva screamed into the dark desert night, "You're killing me! You're killing me! Murderer! Murderer! You're killing me! Murderer!"

Afterward, neither Ivriya's despair nor her baby's suffering hindered the others from dining heartily at the end of an exhausting day of traveling, from attending to their varied duties and needs, from slipping with pleasure into their sleeping bags, and, within seconds of mumbling their prayers, from falling soundly asleep. Akiva drowsed fitfully, jerking his leg spasmodically, moaning and crying in a troubled half-sleep. Ivriya held him in her arms, drawing him as close as she possibly could to the warmth of her rooted body, crooning: Oh, Akiva, oh, Akiva, oh, oh, Akiva, you'll never know how much oh! As the others slept, Ivriya listened to the faint groans and rumbles that came down to her from Mount Sinai, an encore of the theophony given for her and her child alone. The eerie sounds soothed rather than frightened her, celestial music for a privileged audience. It was as if she and Akiva were the sole survivors of a global calamity, as if these were their last hours, but the theme of the mountain's music was clear—all would be well with them, there were personal guardians who loved them. Then there came a dissonant clashing of metal against metal, not from the mountaintop but from close at hand. Ivriya's heart swooped: the local Bedouins, the Jebeliya, were on the prowl, desert Cossacks in the mood for a little pogrom. But everyone except Avraham Ger went on sleeping deeply. Ivriya observed the convert as he rose, clumsily gathered together his cameras and equipment, and set off in the direction of the monastery. A bright light was beamed into her face. It was Roman Unger, pointing a flashlight. She must have dozed off after all. "Do you think he can climb yet?" Roman asked, jutting his beard in Akiva's direction. Ivriya shook her head. "Then we'll put off the ascent till the afternoon," said Roman. "Abba Nissim is very firm about Akiva's going."

Akiva's face was breaded with sand when he woke up late that morning. The first thing he wanted to know was if they had made the climb without him and had already descended. When his mother told him that they had decided to wait until he was strong enough to ascend with them, the sand that encrusted the boy's face cracked as his cheeks stretched in a dazzling smile. Oh, she had never loved him so much! "But, of course, you don't have to go up at all, my darling. In fact, I think it's better that we shouldn't. Roman will drive us over to the airport and we'll take the plane to Eilat. We'll go straight to the emergency room at the hospital and have the burn treated properly. Maybe they'll even give you a pair of crutches, or a wheelchair just like mine. Mother-and-son wheelchairs—wouldn't that be nice?" But Akiva wouldn't hear of this. He was feeling just splendid. Before she could get out another word, he strapped his sandal on his left foot and stood up; on the burned right foot, over the bulky bandaging, he was wearing two white socks that belonged to Abba Nissim. He began hobbling about, rapidly improving his maneuverability, demonstrating his agility, to his mother's amazement and joy. His agony of the night before now acquired the substance of a dream. "You see, Ima? I'm perfectly fine. I want to climb the mountain. I have to see what's on top. And you want to go, too, Ima, I know you do. You have your heart set on it. You'd be very sad if we lost our chance. Don't deny it, Ima. I know you really want to go." Tears were forming in his bright eyes, threatening to spill over and turn the sand on his face to mud.

At last, a male who really cared about what she wanted, and, moreover, knew what it was without requiring her to go through the humiliating process of telling him herself. Ivriya gave Akiva some bread and cheese to eat and some juice to drink, and so tender and indulgent did she feel toward him at that moment that she overlooked the rituals of the blessings and washings and simply sat there reveling in the pleasure of watching her child eat with such appetite. Her own mouth opened, quite instinctively, each time Akiva brought another piece of food up to his mouth. She was engrossed in this lovely vision of Akiva's restored well-being and did not notice the approach of Abba Nissim. "Eating without a *kippah*, Akiva?" Abba Nissim said severely. Ivriya started, and quickly set down the forgotten skullcap on Akiva's shaven head, between the descending columns of the two sidelock ringlets. "And it looks as if you haven't even washed," Nissim went on. "Sand is raining into your food. I'm afraid to ask if you've said the blessings. That you should be so neglectful here, of all places, at the foot of Mount Sinai!"

Ivriya looked down at her hands, as if they had just been slapped. "He's feeling much better, thank God," she said to Abba Nissim, who towered over her.

"*Baruch Hashem.* I expected no less. We are in a place of miracles."

"I want to climb the mountain!" Akiva spoke up boldly.

"Of course you'll climb the mountain, God willing, and I happen to know He is." For the first time, Abba Nissim granted the boy a smile. "I've brought you something to help you along." Nissim showed Akiva an excellent stick, knobbed and peeled, and just the right height for a boy his age. "This will be your walking stick, Akiva. It may not be as wondrous as the staff of Moses our teacher; it may not have within it the power to be transformed into a snake or to inflict plagues or to part seas, but it can be leaned upon for the purpose of reaching the top of Mount Sinai, and, like Moses's rod, which

he used to hit the hard and unyielding rock, it can also strike."
And Abba Nissim gave Akiva's backside a stinging little smack
with the stick before handing it over to the boy.

"Moshe wasn't supposed to hit the rock," Akiva said gravely.
"He was supposed to talk to it. And you know what happened
to him because he hit instead of talked!"

"What?"

"He never made it to Uman!" Akiva declared with unre-
strained glee.

"What a child! What a cunning little child!" exclaimed
Abba Nissim, tugging Akiva's ear affectionately. "Now, if only
we can take your cleverness and channel it in the service of
heaven!"

Abba Nissim squatted down on his haunches in order to talk
to the boy at his level. "Akiva, do you remember the story
about how Moshe our teacher became a stutterer? He was a
child then, even younger than you are today, Akiva, and, as you
know, he was being raised in Pharaoh's court. But Pharaoh's
wizards and conjurers warned the king that little Moshe was
destined to grow up and overthrow the sovereign. So, in order
to determine whether or not the boy really had any sinister
designs on the throne, they subjected him to an ordeal. They
placed before him two dishes. In one dish was the royal crown,
and, in the other was a pile of burning coals. If Moshe reached
for the crown, that would be proof of his dangerous ambition.
Of course, Moshe was only a little baby then, and, naturally,
like any little baby, he was attracted to the glittering jewels and
the sparkling gold of the royal crown, so he put out his hand
to grab it. But see what happened next! An angel of God
quickly sprang down, seized that chubby, dimpled little hand,
and placed it in the dish of hot coals, for little Moshe's own

good. Poor little Moshe our teacher! Immediately, just like any ordinary baby, he stuck his scorched hand into his mouth, and—what?—he injured his tender mouth as well. That's how he became slow of speech and of a slow tongue." Akiva, with his hand in his mouth, listened intently to this story, though he had already heard it many times before. "Do you know what I think, Akiva?" Abba Nissim went on. "I think that last night an angel of God caused you to step barefoot on the burning spot where the gas heater had just rested, because you, Akiva, were without a doubt on your way to stepping somewhere else, somewhere you had no business stepping at all, and the angel of God who is personally in charge of you immediately jumped in to save you from sin. You are a very special boy, Akiva. You must thank God for sending His angel just in the nick of time. It's not every child who is considered worthy of such clear and immediate correction."

"*Baruch Hashem,*" Ivriya said. "God has been very kind to my little Akiva. Look at him now, *baruch Hashem.* And Akiva has been so considerate of my wishes and feelings this morning, Abba Nissim, I must tell you. I truly think it is as you say—he's a special child. Shmuel used to believe that, too."

"But you're not the only good child," Abba Nissim went on, addressing himself exclusively and pointedly to Akiva. "Do you see what I have here?" Now Abba Nissim drew a sandal out of the other breast pocket of his long striped satin robe. "This is Shneour Zalman's right shoe. It's much larger than yours, naturally, since he's a few years older than you, so it will fit very comfortably over your bandages. Shneour Zalman has agreed to let you wear it to climb the mountain, while he will wear on his right foot your small shoe. Now, tell me Akiva—isn't that devotion of the soul? Isn't that an act of extreme loving-kindness on the part of Shneour Zalman Katz? What do you think? I hope, Akiva, that you will prove yourself worthy of this shoe."

At about three o'clock on that hot afternoon, the wayfarers of Uman House set out for the summit of Mount Sinai, 2,285 meters high. Roman Unger's van pulled up behind the Monastery of Saint Catherine and disgorged. To reach the route they had chosen for the ascent, they first had to walk a short distance across a dry, stony wadi. Abba Nissim and Akiva Himmelhoch, each one wielding a staff, led the group at a brisk pace, the boy straining to keep ahead of the old man, as if it were a point of honor, a race with important consequences. Akiva scrambled over the stones so nimbly, his burned right foot seemed never to touch the ground. Next came Rami Marom and Avraham Ger, with Shneour Zalman in between, limping exaggeratedly in the squeeze of his right shoe. Rami and Ger were debating the merits of photography versus painting. "A painting," Rami said, "bestows something extra upon its subject, while a photograph steals from it." "A photograph," said Ger, "is proof that you exist and experience. If none of these pictures comes out, it will be as if I'd never been to Sinai. I'd be compelled to return to get new pictures." The finest attribute of Rami's soul, Reb Lev Lurie had once remarked, was its natural simplicity; that he was capable of discoursing on such mundane and secular topics even at the most sacred of sites was confirmation of the unassailability of his essential purity. Behind Rami and Ger came Roman Unger, the ox, as he called himself, lugging Ivriya's wheelchair. And last of all were the women, the two wives of Rami Marom, bearing their friend Ivriya Himmelhoch—Golda clutching her under the armpits, and Sora under the knees, after first making sure that Ivriya's skirts were properly arranged to prevent any hint of lewdness. Despite all these burdens—an injured child, a child in an ill-fitting shoe, a cripple, women—Abba Nissim hoped, with the help of God, to arrive at the peak of Mount Sinai in time for sunset and evening prayers. Abba Nissim said: "We shall ascend in light and descend in darkness, instead of the other way around, as we had originally intended. This is the correct way, the holy way. You understand, now, how Akiva's accident and suffering of last night were meant for our instruction and benefit."

The paved road that zigzagged up the mountain, at some spots more steeply than at others, was wide enough to accommodate the passage of a small cart. Here it was possible to set Ivriya down in her wheelchair and push her up. Golda and Sora grasped the handlebars of the wheelchair and pushed together. At the steepest inclines they bowed their heads low, and their bodies stretched out rigidly behind them in a straight diagonal, their feet a good distance away from their hands, always obliged to catch up. It was a difficult climb. Ivriya was apologizing throughout for the material burden she was, every single one of her molecules adding to the burden, while Golda and Sora were constantly reassuring her. "Carry me back to Old Virginny," Sora couldn't stop herself from singing: God help us, her mind was clogged with the flotsam and jetsam of her profane Gentile career, and required merciless fumigating. The women had to rest often. On several occasions, they considered giving up the venture entirely and waiting in one of the stone shelters that had been erected along the path for the descent of the men. "Yes, let's just give it up," Ivriya said. "It's much too hard." But then, without consulting each other, Sora and Golda would once again apply the force of their muscles to the back of the wheelchair and persevere in the arduous ascent. The path ended at the cleft between the greater and lesser peaks of Jebel Musa. Here, beneath the radiant pinnacle, the men had been waiting for close to an hour.

While they waited for the women, Abba Nissim, who considered it his duty to divert the pilgrims' thoughts away from secular matters toward the awesome spirituality of their present undertaking, asked each one, as in Rav Nahman of Bratslav's "Tale of the Seven Beggars," to describe his earliest memory. Roman Unger remembered being lost in a field of wheat stalks many times taller than himself. "It was near a DP camp, I think," Roman said, "outside of Berlin." Avraham Ger's first memory was of creeping on a patch of grass, observing the inexorable approach of the revolving blades of his father's lawnmower. "It's a very Freudian memory, if you know what I mean, Abba Nissim," said Professor Ger. Rami Marom remembered biting into a bunch of bright-red cherries he had plucked off a lady's straw hat, and discovering they were artificial. Abba Nissim said that his first memory was of the color blue. Shneour Zalman remembered a great throng. "An eye," Akiva Himmelhoch said: "the first thing I remember is an eye."

Roman's memory, Abba Nissim interpreted, is both old and new, both a racial memory and a personal one; it is of the holy Moses our teacher hidden among the bulrushes, and of the Jews in the Diaspora, wandering and lost, yet temporarily secure, concealed among the powerful and indifferent giants. Avraham Ger's memory is linked to Roman's, a companion memory, for Ger's is the memory of Amalek, the classic foe,

of the eternally damned tribe who pounced upon the un-
protected Israelites as they wandered in the desert; Ger's lawnmower is advancing to cut down the sheltering wheat stalks for
the purpose of exposing Roman, of laying him open for an
assault. The bright-red cherries on the straw hat in Rami's
memory stand for the State of Israel; though tempting and
alluring, they are stolen, and when tasted are discovered to be
false, stone-hard, tooth-cracking. So, too, the limited goal of
the Zionists, to ensure the physical survival of the Jewish people, is false and misguided, and it is accomplished at the expense of spiritual survival. "The Jews may endure, but when
we become a nation like all other nations on this earth, what,
may I ask, will be the fate of Judaism? This is a very deep
question. Why do we need nationhood? That will come to us
in its own hour, I assure you, with the arrival of the Messiah,
may it be soon and in our lifetime. No amount of bombers and
missiles, paratroopers and tanks, will hasten the event. For
generations my ancestors have dwelt in the Holy Land, and we
have done so perfectly well without the benefit of a state. The
blue of my earliest memory is the blue of the mystical city of
Safad, which flooded my vision when I opened my eyes and
looked out the window as I emerged from my mother's womb.
As for Shneour Zalman, he is recalling the other time he was
here, when he stood at the foot of Mount Sinai to receive the
Torah among all Jewish souls, past, present, and future. The
great throng is very vivid in his memory, for he could see it all
stretched out before him, since his place was at its edge, among
the strangers and the converts. The eye in Akiva's memory is
truly mysterious and holy. It stands for the letter *ayin,* which
also means 'eye.' Yes, *ayin* means 'eye,' but it also means
nothing, and the letters that form the word 'nothing' also

compose the word *ani*, 'I,' for the 'I is nothing. *Ayin* is also the first letter of Akiva's name. What Akiva is remembering is so sacred and ancient, it surpasses understanding. It is the memory of the chute through which he descended to this earth when he was born. This chute is in the shape of the letter *ayin*, and is endowed with all the holy attributes of that letter. Through this very same chute Akiva must strive each day to make his spiritual ascent, by singing hymns and praises to God, by confessing, by penitence and prayers, by struggling to remain always in a constant state of joy. Akiva's eye, his *ayin*, has gazed upon the *ayin*, the nothingness, the chaos and the void, before the creation of his soul, before he became an I, an *ani*, and descended in the chute shaped like the *ayin* of the first letter of his name, and appeared to us on this earth in the form of Akiva ben Shmuel Himmelhoch. Just as it happened in the tale of the exalted Rav Nahman, may we be protected by the light of his merits, the oldest memory belongs to the youngest."

Then Abba Nissim told this story: "During the period of the British Mandate, there was an active underground group of misguided Zionist terrorists making trouble in and around the holy city of Safad, where I and my ancestors before me have always lived. I was a much younger man at that time, of course, and, to my shame, despite the injunction of our sages against exploiting the Torah as a practical tool, I earned my living as a teacher of the cabalistic mysteries. I survived, also, by dispensing amulets and cameos and blessings to sufferers who came to me with their little notes, their heartbreaking *kvitlach*, pleading in their mothers' names for my intercession in their behalf with the Creator of the Universe. I had a small following then, and we lived simply and joyously. I was known in those days as Abba Nissim the Kidnapper. The reason for this was that often I would go out among men with the purpose of swaying them away from their sinful lives, and I made a special effort with respect to the hotheaded Zionist terrorists, for these were men of great passion; what wonders they could accomplish if only their passion were deflected in the name of heaven! My activities, as you can see, were similar to those of the Master of Prayer in the story by Rav Nahman of Bratslav, may his great virtues protect us eternally. And, as it happened, like Rav Nahman's Master of Prayer, I, too, succeeded, and soon sons and fathers and brothers and husbands were disappearing from their homes and following me. This is why they called me Abba Nissim the Kidnapper. It was an honorable title, a royal title. But because I was frequently observed consorting with known members of the Zionist underground, the British, whom God in His wisdom had never endowed with any vision beyond the third dimension, the British assumed that I, too, was a terrorist. So they arrested Abba Nissim the Kidnapper and threw him into prison, where I remained for more than a year.

"I recognized at once the hand of God in my imprisonment, for He was rebuking me for having earned my bread from His Torah. But it was a mild form of chastisement, after all, for in His boundless wisdom and kindness, He provided me with the opportunity to correct my ways. It was during this period of my confinement by the British that I learned my English, so that upon my release I was able to take up my present occupation as a tour guide in the old cemetery of Safad, where I am also the caretaker. Of course, my chief work is still that of a teacher and a 'kidnapper,' but no longer am I a teacher for the purpose of gaining a prize. And lest you bestow a garland of undeserved glory upon me because of my imprisonment, I must hasten to

203

tell you that I hardly suffered at all during that period. On the contrary, in addition to perfecting my English, I was able to continue my 'kidnapping' labors, for my jailers were extremely generous in providing me with a constant stream of Zionist terrorist cellmates, who possessed silken souls, well worth the snatching. And the British, though a spiritually limited race, are fair and decent; if they tend to be a bit punishing in their personal habits, they have, as a general rule, lost the viciousness and brutality that distinguish the character of their distant Germanic ancestors. So my simple, joyous life continued virtually uninterrupted in that British jail. I was not barred from roaming freely within the prison compound, and I was also permitted to enter the courtyard after the midnight hour, to smear ashes on my forehead and lament the destruction of our Holy Temple, to break my heart and pour out my soul before the Lord.

"After the midnight hour, the prison courtyard was inhabited by strange and mysterious creatures. In the corner sat a British officer named Godd, only he did not spell his name in the same fashion as the English word for the Creator of the Universe: this Godd wrote his name with an 'o' instead of a dash. Godd sat there in the corner of the prison courtyard night after night, with a companion who tickled him continuously, and as the companion tickled and tickled, Godd sat there in the corner weeping and weeping. 'All my senses are dulled,' Godd wept to me one night. 'I have not been happy for a single moment in my life. Show me how to rejoice, Kidnapper!' For even through my mourning over Zion, even through my heartbreak and outcries, this Godd could discern the joy that burst out of me like a ray of light, and others could see it as well. In the prison courtyard after the midnight hour there were many who came to me to seek the source of my joy, and to strive to acquire it for themselves. 'You must serve God in happiness, and come before Him in joy,' I taught them. 'You must sing praises and hymns to Him and plead with Him to grant us happiness in proportion to the days He had tormented us, the years we have witnessed evil.'

"After the midnight hour in the courtyard of the British prison, I had great success as a kidnapper. I remember one young terrorist I kidnapped, not much older in years than fifteen, dark and comely, and his name, as it happened, was also Akiva. He came into the courtyard one night with a can of gasoline in his hand, and so absorbed was he in his intention that he did not notice me as he systematically poured the gasoline over his clothing and prepared to ignite himself. I dissuaded him, thank God, from so terrible a sin of sadness and desperation, and after that he joined me in the courtyard night after night, and we hunted for his joy; for there exists a personal lode of joy marked for each man, only he must make an effort to find it. One night I told this Akiva that I would carry him up to the very heights, that I would help him fly. So we dug a pit in the dirt of the prison courtyard and descended into it, this Akiva the terrorist and I. We held each other in an embrace, like a father and son, and I let out a piercing whistle, rising spiritually in preparation for our material ascent. 'It is our duty to praise the Master of All,' I prayed out loud without moving my lips, in a high-pitched screech well beyond the range of normal hearing. 'It is our duty to praise the Master of All, to exalt the Creator of the Universe, who has not made us like the nations of the world, and has not placed us like the families of the earth; who has not designed our destiny to be like theirs, nor our lot to be like that of their multitude. So we bend the knee and bow. . . . ' "

In the cleft between the lesser and the greater peaks of the Mountain of Moses, overlooking the Moslem shrine to the prophet Elijah, Abba Nissim, the joyous Kidnapper of Safad, bent his knees and sank down to the ground in a deep bow, just as the three women approached. "I see that my story is destined to remain unfinished, like so many of the tales of Rav Nahman," Abba Nissim commented. "Suffice it for those who are wise to understand my meaning." Yet he did not rise from his place, but continued to remain there on his knees. From this position he addressed the two wives of Rami Marom without gazing at them directly. He instructed them to lift Ivriya Himmelhoch out of her wheelchair and place her on his back. "I have promised the widow that I would bring her to the top of Mount Sinai," he said. "I am ready now to fulfill my promise."

To reach the summit of Mount Sinai from this point between the greater and the lesser peaks, the pilgrim must climb three hundred curving steps that long ago had been reverently chiseled out of the granite by the hands of the monks. Each step is irregular and unique, and the distance between one and the next varies in such a way that at times it is necessary to stretch the leg to the painful limit while climbing, and at other times one must ascend mincingly. The surface of some of the steps is rough and treacherous, and of others slippery and treacherous, worn so smooth that they slide, melt into one another. Penitents have ascended these steps upon their knees, and convicts in shackles. The air is thin, the climb is tortuous;

therefore, the eye must be unwaveringly fastened upon the shimmering goal.

But Akiva—Akiva practically flew up those steps. Among the pilgrims of Uman House, Akiva Himmelhoch, with his burned right foot, was the first to step on the top of Mount Sinai. Behind him came Rami and Roman, deafened by the shrill wind, singing, chanting as one of being brought to Uman; words tumbled out on the heels of words, to allow no gaps in between for the intrusion of earthly thoughts. Then came the women, Sora and Golda, their eyes closed, their arms linked like two blind sisters guiding each other upward, their lips moving in prayer: O Merciful One, send us Elijah the prophet of goodly memory, and let him bring us news, good news, salvations, salvations and consolations. Some distance below the women, Shneour Zalman Katz limped in his pinched shoe beside Avraham Ger. "You have to be healthy to make this climb," Ger panted. "That's what one of the monks in the monastery down there said to me. Even he's climbed it only twice!" And many steps below these stragglers, Abba Nissim continued the laborious ascent with Ivriya Himmelhoch on his back. Abba Nissim was a strong and supple man for his age, accustomed to walking at a brisk pace in valleys and hills, and Ivriya was a light woman, a wisp, but it was a hard climb. Nissim never said a word, though many times he had to set his hands on a higher step to pull himself up, pitching his body forward and advancing on all fours, and even through the padding that had been laid across his back to prevent her body from making an impression, Ivriya could feel his strained breathing. She was a horsewoman, delicately attuned to the condition of her mount; she had been thrown once before and her body crushed; her soul would be trampled if she were dropped once again. On the back of Abba Nissim, Ivriya Himmelhoch ascended toward the shining summit of Mount Sinai. Between her and Abba Nissim not a word or a look was passed. She struggled to elevate her thoughts as he raised her body, but not always did she succeed. The best way to avoid looking at a woman is to set her as a load on your back; this was one of Ivriya Himmelhoch's baser thoughts, to her shame, in the course of her ascent to the top. She was so close to Abba Nissim—did her thoughts seep into him? Did he know her for what she was?

Abba Nissim, with Ivriya Himmelhoch on his back, was fewer than fifty steps from the summit of Mount Sinai when Akiva came running down toward them, waving his stick and calling out jubilantly: "Oh, Ima, it's so beautiful up there, Ima, you must hurry up before he goes away." "We're coming, darling, as fast as we can." "In the cave there, Ima, where Moshe our teacher slept—I saw him there." "You saw Moshe our teacher?" "No, Ima, it was Abba I saw there." "Abba is right here, Akiva; you can see that plainly. I'm riding on his back to the top of the mountain." "No, Ima, it was *my* abba I saw up there—it was Shmuel, my father."

Abba Nissim squatted down on one of the steps and gently wriggled Ivriya off his back. "The widow will forgive me," said Abba Nissim. "I am obliged to break my promise." Swiftly Abba Nissim vanished up the curving stone steps toward the pinnacle of the mountain.

Ivriya lay there forsaken on the steps. Akiva stroked her kerchief as she cried softly. "It's my fate," she lamented, "my fate. Always I give up just before the end. I give up, or I'm given up." "Come on, Ima," Akiva implored, "don't be sad,

please, Ima. I want you to come up with me to see my abba.
He's waiting up there for us. We're almost there. Just a few
more steps. I'll help you do it." Ivriya looked up at this child;
since the burn he seemed to have been touched in a new way.
It was as if he had been refined in a heavenly flame, and all his
physical grossness had departed from him; he was almost an-
gelic, like the Yanuka, the holy wonder child of the Zohar who
clarified the mysteries for the wise. Guided by his voice, which
seemed to her now to possess a divine inspiration, Ivriya turned
over and sprawled on her belly along the steps. Using her arms
and shoulders, which had developed a singular compensatory
strength since her accident, she began to pull herself up the
steps, dragging her inert lower limbs behind her. "Come on,
Ima," Akiva sang; "come on, Ima." He walked along at her
side, assisting her arms, boosting her at the waist, bringing her
heavy legs up after her like baggage. "Come on, Ima, come
on!" Her arms and legs were bloody and scraped, her face was
battered, her clothing shredded. "A few more steps, Ima. It's
only around the bend. It's coming now, Ima. We're almost
there." The sun descended. They arrived. The flat granite peak
of the border between heaven and earth stretched out to receive them.

The Moslem caretaker of the small white mosque at the
summit approached. "Ah, Moshe Dayan is back, I see," he
greeted Akiva amiably. As far as Ivriya could tell, this was the
only stranger present who had not ascended with their group.
On one of the smooth ledges, Rami and Roman were transported in prayer. On another ledge, Golda and Sora stood
swaying side by side, their eyes shut, each woman with her arms
wrapped ecstatically around herself. In a nook, Abba Nissim sat
with a flock of white birds on his shoulders and head. He was

singing a melody that no one had ever heard before; he seemed, at that moment, to be creating it. Those who listened to the melody were overcome by a great wanting for something achingly beyond their reach.

Avraham Ger came up to Ivriya. He was hauling Shneour Zalman by a sidelock. "You want to know what this little bastard did?" cried Ger. "He threw all my used rolls of film off the mountain! I'm going to murder him! I'm going to shove him off right after them!" "It's because he's an *apikoros!*" Shneour Zalman said. "He's a big heretic! He went into the monastery! He told me so himself!" Avraham Ger looked down at Ivriya's bloody limbs. "You shouldn't have bothered," he pronounced coldly. "It probably never happened on this mountain anyway. It's the wrong mountain, you know. You've killed yourself getting up here, and it's the wrong mountain. Ha ha. Most likely, it was Jebel Sirbal over there." From the shallow cave beside the stone chapel, Akiva called out in desolation: "He's gone! We came too late! He's gone!" Akiva plunged into a crying fit, just like any ordinary child, whimpering and whining, turning up his face and howling that his burned foot was hurting him more than he could bear, that he refused to take another step.

Until the moon came out, they descended in darkness. Abba Nissim carried Akiva. Rami and Roman took turns carrying Shneour Zalman. Avraham Ger held the only flashlight. Golda and Sora carried Ivriya as far as the cleft between the greater and the lesser peaks, where the wheelchair had been abandoned. They descended in silence; they dropped, staggered, collapsed, fell. When they reached the van, they waited there for the arrival of Abba Nissim and Akiva Himmelhoch. They waited until the morning. Over the next few days, the area was thoroughly combed by the Jebeliya, the Bedouins of the mountains, and by the Israeli and Egyptian authorities, in helicopters, on the backs of camels and donkeys, in jeeps, and on foot. The Bedouins declared that the two lost Jews, the old man and the child, could not possibly have been killed; the presence of corpses in the area was always known. Seven days later, without Abba Nissim, without Akiva Himmelhoch, the pilgrims of Uman House returned to Jerusalem.

MOUNT
MORIAH

She called it the summer of her sorrow. Her mother said, Come
live with me, but Ivriya refused. Late one morning the scarlet
Mercedes came to a dramatic halt in front of the building in
the Bokharan Quarter, kicking up a bevy of dark urchins. The
formidable Dr. Frieda Mendelssohn slid out of the car, strode
resolutely to the rear, inserted the key in the trunk lock, and
unloaded a seemingly endless stream of elegant suitcases. She
snapped her fingers. Without requiring an articulated command, the swarthy street boys stepped forward one by one;
each grasped the handle of a suitcase, carefully lifted the arti-
fact off the pavement, and marched smartly with it into the
house. Throughout that summer of her sorrow, the scarlet

Mercedes remained a fixture on David Street. The children of the neighborhood hovered around it reverently, paying daily homage, but never, never daring to draw close enough to touch it with any part of their unworthy selves except their yearning black eyes.

"There's just no point at all in sitting around here doing nothing but crying!" Frieda Mendelssohn declared as she made her entrance into Ivriya's darkened room. "I'm not crying." "Well, in that case, that's even worse!" Ivriya was lost in the vastness of her wheelchair; on her gaunt face she wore the classic mask of grief. "Where are your glasses?" The daughter pointed apathetically down to the twisted metal and shattered glass under the wheels of her chair. "When did you do that?" "When I heard you pulling up. I told you I didn't want to see you." "I seem to remember reading something in the Bible about honoring your father and mother, to lengthen your days." "Never mind. I want to die." "Look here, Ivriya, didn't that insane Rabbi Nahman of yours say something about depression?" "What can I do? I'm a weak person. I'm worthless." "Well, what exactly have you been doing? Have you been doing anything at all?" "I've been praying." "Praying? We'll see just how far that gets you. Even God, I'll wager, doesn't want your little prayers at this time. What have you been praying?" "I've been praying, God help me! God help me, I've been praying. God help me! God help me! God help me!"

Within a day, Dr. Frieda Mendelssohn managed to convert her daughter's apartment into the central headquarters for the search. She exploited all her extensive connections with the police, the military, high government officials, and men of power, influence, and wealth. She placed advertisements in all the Israeli newspapers and in several newspapers abroad, and she deluged the cities of Jerusalem and Safad and their surrounding areas with posters containing the only existing picture of the child, one she had slyly snapped at his birthday party a year earlier when Ivriya's back was turned. The moment Ivriya had heard the click and had felt the aura of the flash, she had tried to snatch the camera away from her mother, but it's easy to elude a person in a wheelchair, and even a mother will take advantage when necessary.

In this photograph, the blazing-eyed Akiva is holding a brilliantly glittering sparkler in front of his face; it had been Ivriya's idea, to Akiva's boundless delight, to stick sparklers into the cake instead of ordinary candles. This picture of Akiva became famous throughout the land. He became known as the Stolen Sparkling Child. Photos of Abba Nissim, the alleged kidnapper, were not at all difficult to locate. They appeared in the scrapbooks of numerous tourists, from Tokyo to the Bronx. Frieda Mendelssohn arranged for the distribution of thousands of posters, offering a generous reward for the apprehension of Nissim, who was shown against the background of the old cemetery of Safad, a flock of white birds on his shoulders pecking at the bread crumbs in his venerable beard.

No possible avenue was allowed to remain unexplored by the energetic Frieda Mendelssohn; she spared no expense whatsoever. A private detective agency was hired and set to work on the case, and similar resources were tapped in Europe, the United States, and even in the Soviet Union, with a particular emphasis on the area around Kiev. The phone in Ivriya's apartment never stopped ringing; using her impressive connections, Dr. Mendelssohn even managed to get several lines installed, which in itself was considered to be a remarkable feat in the State of Israel. All sorts of people telephoned, from those who were seemingly reporting serious sightings—which, of course, were followed through but to no avail—to those who called merely to commiserate or to unburden themselves of their own griefs, to those who were manifestly crooks, bounty hunters, and finaglers, to the religious zealots, the cruel and the nasty, the psychics, and the simple crackpots. "I'm afraid your God didn't choose so well," Dr. Frieda Mendelssohn observed to her paralyzed daughter. "There are a lot of weird Jews out there!"

Again and again Frieda Mendelssohn forced Ivriya to review the events leading up to Akiva's disappearance. Each time she heard the story of the burn, Dr. Mendelssohn repeated the same words with utter sadness and incredulity: "The poor, poor baby! Iodine? Iodine on a burn? Only a sadist could think of that!" She reproached Ivriya for not taking proper emergency action at once, she, the daughter of a doctor, who should have known better! See how religion twists and perverts basic common sense so that even a mother who loves her child passionately will send him forth to be sacrificed. Not that she was accusing Ivriya of being the cause of what had happened. Still, we must face the facts: the mother was not entirely innocent. All right—Akiva ran to her claiming he had seen that monster, that so-called father of his, on the top of the mountain. Had anyone else seen the bastard? "You mean to say that Golda and Sora actually climbed the mountain with their eyes closed? But why am I so surprised, anyway? When had they ever had their eyes open? And the men were rendered senseless by prayer? And the iodine sadist was so busy taking pictures he couldn't see a thing? Ivriya, my dear, I'm sorry to tell you this, but the people you've been associating with, they're not exactly normal. And that old goat, that Nissim, he just dropped you, you say, and ran up the mountain? Could it have been that lousy Shmuel up there after all? The stinker! And we thought we had buried him once and for all—if not in person, at least in effigy. But no, not Shmuel Himmelhoch, oh no—how I curse the hour you met him; no, our revolting Shmuel just won't stay down; he's like a vile dinner, he keeps on rising, keeps on returning, like a nightmare, like a ghost. Ivriya, my foolish daughter, you should have learned from your mother's example; you should have taken advantage of your child's accident to keep him forever tethered to your side. Because you, Ivriya, can never, ever live alone again. You will always need someone to take care of you, preferably your mother. Who, by the way, has been helping you out until I came?"

Before her mother's arrival, Shifra-Puah the old Bokharan midwife and Tikva Unger had taken turns visiting Ivriya morning and evening, to assist her with her needs and to relieve her external solitude. The solitude within, where she was bereft of the child, accepted no relief. Ivriya absolutely refused to admit into her presence anyone at all who had participated in the ill-fated excursion to Sinai. For Golda or Sora to appear before her would have been excruciating pain; the mere thought of seeing them again revived the sensation of the ground giving way catastrophically beneath her, as it had seemed to do that black instant when she realized her child was lost.

Even the formal visit from the Rebbetzin Bruriah Lurie made her dizzy with grief, but Ivriya felt obliged to endure it for the sake of propriety. Bruriah came to Ivriya bearing a message of consolation from her husband, Reb Lev. "We now have a computer at Uman House, *baruch Hashem*, thank God," Bruriah Lurie announced. She was pregnant again, and she came to Ivriya's silent house with four young children in tow. "Do you mind?" Bruriah asked, as her children pounced on Akiva's deserted toys. Ivriya shook her head mournfully. After that, she never lifted her eyes from her empty lap. Bruriah proceeded to deliver her message: "My husband, Reb Lev, may his candle shed light, has asked me to bring you the good news that Akiva will be returned to you, as the beloved son Joseph was returned to his inconsolable father, Jacob. This was revealed to Reb Lev one night by his computer. For the numerical value of *Shmuel chai*, 'Shmuel lives,' is three hundred and ninety-five, which is exactly the same as *yashuv le'imo*, 'he will return to his mother.' Now, since Shmuel's mother is no longer on this earth, the Shmuel who lives and will return cannot refer to your husband, who has no mother to return to, and who is, in any case, himself gone to his world, may his memory be a blessing; this 'Shmuel' can only refer to your son, Akiva, for it's not at all uncommon for the father's name to be used cryptically when the son's is intended. Furthermore, the sum of *Shmuel chai* and *yashuv le'imo*, three hundred and ninety-five plus three hundred and ninety-five, is equal to seven hundred and ninety, which is numerically equivalent to *nishmat. Nishmat* is the first word of the prayer *Nishmat kol chai tevarech et shimha*, 'The soul of every living being will bless Your name.' In this hymn that we sing on Sabbath morning, we praise God, who 'redeems and saves, ransoms and rescues, sustains and shows mercy in all times of woe and stress.' This is a clear and incontrovertible sign to you, Ivriya, that your sorrows will come to an end, and that you will soon have reason to express your gratitude to the Creator of the Universe. All this was revealed to my husband, Reb Lev Lurie, may he live many long and good days, by his new personal computer, a Commodore CBM, although he would have much preferred an IBM."

Shifra-Puah the Bokharan midwife had aged strikingly since the previous winter, when she had delivered the baby Moriah at Uman House. As frail and as brittle as a scroll of ancient parchment, she was clearly declining, well past that point where, through a stunning effort of will on her part, she might have reversed her course. There was very little that she could do for Ivriya. Even to read Ivriya's tea leaves was nearly beyond her powers. With a limp cigarette between her dry lips, Shifra-Puah gazed at the residue at the bottom of Ivriya's glass. "My own destiny is so close that it films my eyes, my radish," Shifra-Puah said sadly, "and it prevents me from seeing yours." "It's because I have no future," said Ivriya. "Ah, but look here, my onion," Shifra-Puah said, tilting the glass, as was her wont, to permit Ivriya to read for herself. "Here I am in a place—and can you see who that is standing at my side, my garlic? It is Abba Nissim of Safad. There he is, himself in his glory. We are in another world, he and I, in a place reserved for kidnappers. For I kidnap babies from their mothers' wombs, and he is a kidnapper of souls." "Is Akiva there, too?" Ivriya asked halfheartedly. "No, my scallion, Akiva is not there at all. That is why Abba Nissim is weeping. Akiva has been kidnapped from the kidnapper. And I, too, my turnip, am weeping. I am weeping over all the babies of the future whom others will pull from the womb, the exquisite babies yet to be born who have been kidnapped away from me."

Tikva Unger, on the other hand, was able to perform a good many useful services for her friend Ivriya Himmelhoch, whom she loved as a sister. She would burst into the apartment like a startling whiff of fresh bread baking. *"Baruch Hashem!"* she would exclaim. Then she would sink into a chair, unbuttoning her blouse and drawing out a broad-nippled, vein-taut breast for the baby to suck. "Ah!" she would sigh with relief. When Moriah was safely dispatched into a deep sleep, Tikva would rise, stow the baby in the carriage, roll up her sleeves, and set to work. Tikva knew exactly what to do. She cleaned the apartment, put up a good soup with the vegetables she had brought in her string bag, took care of the laundry, bathed Ivriya, conveyed her to the toilet, exercised her limbs, brushed her teeth, arranged her hair, knotted the kerchief on her head, polished her eyeglasses, and supervised the entry into her beloved friend's mouth of one spoonful of soup after another. Most of these were tasks that Ivriya could carry out very well for herself, and Tikva knew this, but she also understood Ivriya's present weakness, and she felt her need. Ivriya's state of external invalidism was now as nothing compared with how she had been heart-crippled. If Tikva would not do for Ivriya, Ivriya would have no spirit or interest to do for herself. Tikva chattered away as she worked, and she sensed exactly how deeply it was permissible to penetrate with her words; she was never guilty of trespassing. Her talk constituted a background buzz in Ivriya's ears that muted, temporarily, the rawness and savagery of her desolation.

"My Einstein is going to be the end of me, just you wait and see, Ivriya." (Tikva talking.) "You'll never believe what ideas Reb Lev has been putting into the boy's head lately! Just listen to this. They're now planning to have Einstein's bar mitzvah on the top of Mount Moriah, right on the grounds of the Temple Mount! Can you believe that? Shyke, naturally, is quivering with excitement about it—the demented old outlaw! He just came down from Safad, where he's been searching high and low for Abba Nissim. No luck, I'm sorry to say. You know, I think Shyke's brain is made of soft plastic, because now that

Abba Nissim is out of the picture and all talk of going to Uman has abruptly ended, Shyke is leaping head first into the Temple Mount movement, silly with enthusiasm. As a matter of fact, it looks as if a lot of people are going in that direction. Even Shmuel, if he were alive, may he rest in peace and in honor—even Shmuel, I'll bet, would have traded in the Uman thing for the Temple Mount. That's where it's at nowadays, baby. But a bar mitzvah on top of the Temple Mount? What about some minor technicalities, such as the fact that it's illegal and we could all be shot to death or blown to pieces by the Arabs or the Israelis—take your choice? And what are we supposed to do up there anyway—go blithely about our business while ignoring those two huge mosques and those thousands of prostrate Moslems with their behinds in the air? But do you think such reasonable objections faze our brave men at all? Not a bit! Even Roman—sensible Roman! When it comes to Reb Lev, my poor Roman is like a faithful puppy with his tongue hanging out, being led around in circles by his wet nose. And what is the opinion of the esteemed Rebbetzin Bruriah Lurie about this brilliant idea? 'God will help,' says she, as if nothing extraordinary is happening, and she calmly goes about her everyday activities, teaching her classes in childbirth and lactation and in how to clear your baby's stuffed nose the natural way, by sucking out the snot.

"So—what was I saying? Oh yes, Einstein's bar mitzvah on the Temple Mount. Now, the only obstacle that stands in the way of this noble scheme, as far as our men are concerned, is that they do not want to tread on the spot where the Holy of Holies was once located, God forbid! That, as you know, is strictly prohibited. But listen to this, Ivriya! Reb Lev Lurie is now the proud possessor of this computer thing, and, thanks to this miraculous contraption, he was able to figure out the exact boundaries of the Holy of Holies down to the last millimeter. So now, as far as our courageous defenders are concerned, there's nothing standing in their way. The bar mitzvah will take place on the Temple Mount. All we need now is to hire a caterer and send out the invitations. We have the computer to thank for that.

"Ah, the computer! That, my dear, is a story in itself. Bruriah's mother smuggled it into the country in a case of paper diapers. Did you know that? But Reb Lev was really disappointed when he opened the carton. He had had his heart set on an IBM. Ivriya, you'll never guess who it was that donated the computer in the first place! It was none other than Sora Katz's first Jewish father-in-law—Beryl Katz's father, Shneour Zalman's grandfather. Isn't that funny? It's a small world, believe me. Turns out that this Katz is a very well-to-do dealer in real estate in Boro Park in Brooklyn; he's already been supporting Reb Lev and Uman House for a couple of years now. He's been the chief sponsor; isn't that amazing? Sora didn't recognize a good thing when she had it. A *goyisheh kop!* What can you do? Even if you convert a thousand times, you can't alter your basic brain cells. Anyhow, so what does Reb Lev do as soon as he tears open the package, tosses the diapers all over the place, and uncovers this cheap, not-IBM computer? Immediately, he puts in a collect call to old man Katz in Boro Park and complains. This shrewdie Katz, he just listens very politely at the other end of the wire seven thousand miles away, and then he says, 'If you wanted an IBM, you should have schnorred from the Syrian Jews on Ocean Parkway. They, *takeh,* are loaded!' So that was the end of that.

"Meanwhile, this Katz has been putting a lot of pressure on

Sora and Shneour Zalman to come home to America. It seems that his son, Beryl, has gone off and married a real *shiksa* this time—not one like Sora, who always had a yen to be a Jew, but the genuine article, one hundred percent prime pork. As far as old man Katz is concerned, his Beryl—who calls himself Buck, by the way, he got the idea from Sora's original last name; Buck Katz, can you believe?—in the old man's eyes, Beryl-Buck is dead and buried. So old man Katz now wants to raise his Jewish grandson, he wants to try and do it right this time, he wants a proper Kaddish for the salvation of his soul. Believe me, Sora is really torn about all this. She doesn't know what to do. Especially because it looks as if Rami is going to give her a divorce, since that's what Goldie wants, and Reb Lev has advised him exactly as God advised Abraham when Sarah wanted Hagar and Ishmael kicked out: 'Whatever Goldie tells you to do, listen to her voice.' I don't know, Ivriya, I'll just never figure Goldie out. They say she has a high IQ, but I just can't see it. She doesn't have a bit of common sense, even though they like to claim that God gave ugly girls a lot of common sense as compensation. But now that Goldie has given up the dangerous secular learning that leads to pride and heresy, and has made a permanent commitment to Rami, whatever that means, she simply can't tolerate sharing him with another wife. It's driving her crazy, she says. So good-bye, Sora, it was nice knowing you. I tell you, Ivriya, at Uman House there's never a dull moment. Personally, speaking for myself alone, I could use one or two dull moments now and then."

But of all the acts of loving-kindness that Tikva Unger performed for her friend, what Ivriya appreciated most, insofar as she could, from her abyss, desire or appreciate anything, was the expeditions to the bustling shopping district of the nearby

223

Geula neighborhood. Tikva would insert the baby Moriah into a pouch on her chest, firmly grasp the handlebars of the wheelchair, and push Ivriya down David Street, up the steep hill of Yehezkel Street to Sabbath Square, and then right on Malhei Yisrael Street, where the frenetic shopping never entirely ceased, except on the Sabbath. If God had created the Sabbath solely to bring this mad shopping to a halt, it would have been enough. From early morning to late at night they pushed and jostled in the packed streets—men in long black coats and black fedora hats; women in loose-fitting dresses and covered heads framing scrubbed faces; young matrons in stylish wigs and high heels, decked out in the latest fashion but absolutely within the constraints of modesty; girls with thick braids, heavy stockings, eyes passionately religious; wild, untamed young boys, white-shirted, with long sidelocks and black velvet yarmulkes. They thronged the streets, buying frantically, intensely, as if they were stocking away provisions for the promised apocalypse that was expected at any moment.

It was a hot summer, and pushing Ivriya's wheelchair was heavy labor for Tikva. Up the hill of Yehezkel Street was particularly arduous; Tikva's body pitched forward as she pushed, her legs stretched out behind her, very much like Golda's and Sora's had been when they pushed Ivriya up Mount Sinai. Maneuvering through the viscous crowd on Malhei Yisrael Street was sheer strain and toil. In front of the bank, Ivriya spotted the beggar who ended at the waist, Yisrael Gamzu, propped up in his wheelbarrow with his palm held out. This was the match that Bruriah Lurie had once casually contemplated for her! Tikva quickly pushed her past, for she could sense Ivriya's mortification at forming a tableau of misfortune for the pitying eye of any smug beholder.

What Ivriya desired most of all, and what her friend Tikva granted, no matter how onerous or embarrassing, was to be steered into and out of the shops. It was the sight of people going about their daily business that drew her, the chatting, the joking, the gossiping, the selecting, browsing, buying, the handling, the fists rooting in pockets, the fingers rummaging in purses, the haggling, the paying—all exactly as it had always been, in no measure different. This ordinary sight had the power to penetrate and unseal her despair. The heartless indifference of everyday life, how it continued impassively despite the calamity that had changed her life ultimately, struck Ivriya as the final blow, and it released her pent-up tears. Right inside the stores, Ivriya Himmelhoch would open her mouth wide, and she would cry inconsolably. It was an inexpressible relief to cry out loud. Ivriya cried in every single store up and down Malhei Yisrael Street; her friend Tikva Unger, with a baby on her breast, steered her in and out. At first, alarmed proprietors, clerks, and customers gathered around the two tragic women, dispensing compassion and solicitude. But after a while, as Ivriya returned to the shops again and again to expel her grief, they recognized her and turned their backs, drawing spirals alongside their temples by way of explanation to those who were witnessing this spectacle for the first time.

These excursions for the purpose of disposing of her tears continued even after Ivriya's mother moved in and turned the apartment into the command post for the search, but when Ivriya's loud weeping in the shops of Malhei Yisrael Street finally reached the ears of Dr. Frieda Mendelssohn, she was thoroughly appalled. With her hands on her hips, her foot tapping rhythmically, she waited for Tikva to deliver Ivriya from one of these forays. As soon as they stepped through the door, Frieda Mendelssohn let out a full blast that woke the baby on Tikva's breast with a start. "What do you mean, taking my daughter around in this way and turning her into a laughingstock all over town?"

"She needs to cry, Dr. Mendelssohn!" Tikva patted Moriah's rump vigorously.

"Oh, for goodness' sake, don't give me that softheaded junk! She can cry perfectly well in the privacy of her own home. Everyone who sees her thinks she's deranged!"

"I'm sorry, but with all due respect, Dr. Mendelssohn, you're completely wrong. No one thinks she's crazy. They all view her as a tragic figure. She's like Rachel weeping over her children, and she will not be comforted."

"A tragic figure!" Frieda Mendelssohn repeated with contempt. "That's exactly it! You people aspire to becoming tragic figures, and you're even willing to incur the most hideous suffering to earn the right to assume that pose. Or ecstatic figures, or mystic figures—whatever the role, it's nothing more than aesthetics. What does it have to do with faith? Not that you wouldn't like to believe. You wish for it ardently, you long for it, you strain for it, but for the most part you just don't have it in you. So you settle for the counterfeit of faith, for the style, the externals, the costume, which appeal to you so much aesthetically. And what aesthetics boils down to in the end— you'll excuse me, but I'm a woman who speaks her mind— what it boils down to is nothing less than *avodah zarah*, idol worship. Mother Rachel indeed! Oh, I'm so sick and tired of having proverbs and passages and words of the sages thrown at me all the time, I just can't tell you. Simply cite the verse about Rachel weeping over her children, and there's all the excuse you need for your wretched passivity! All you people ever do is fold your hands, wipe away a righteous tear, and meekly call on God to help. Do you suppose for a minute that my poor girl's scandalous crying in public is going to bring Akiva back? Tell me that! You haven't taken a single constructive step toward solving the problem. Look at all I've done!" And Frieda Mendelssohn gestured forcefully toward the clutter that reflected her enterprise.

"I want to tell you something, Dr. Mendelssohn," Tikva said. "Whatever you've done, you've done for your own sake alone." Tikva spoke slowly now, as if it were her painful duty to confront an innocent with the unfair realities of life. Dr. Mendelssohn should not delude herself into thinking that by the sheer force of her energy she could alter events, Tikva explained with cool deliberateness. Indeed, nothing Dr. Mendelssohn could do would yield results. Not the newspaper and television and radio ads, not the flyers, not the private detectives, not the police network, not the fancy contacts with men in high places, none of it. Because the child had been spirited away to a place somewhere at the very center of the religious world, and this world was impenetrable to Dr. Frieda Mendelssohn and to anyone she could possibly know, no matter how powerful or influential. In this world, they were certain that they were right and that everyone else was wrong. In this world they didn't care about the likes of Frieda Mendelssohn, M.D. They considered her inferior, benighted, damned, not worth the trouble of a shrug, and nothing she might say or think or do or write mattered to them at all, it couldn't affect them in the least, it could do them no harm. "Where Akiva is now," Tikva said to the bereaved grandmother, "is a closed, exclusive world, and even we, the penitents, we who have returned, we who struggle every day to achieve a level of pure faith, no matter what you think of us—even we are only permitted to loiter on the margins and fringes of this sealed world, for we have been tainted by other lives and shall forever be suspect. So if you want to continue your therapeutic exercise to give yourself the illusion that you're doing something, Dr. Mendelssohn, of course you're perfectly free to do so, but I'm telling you now that it's all futile and hopeless and a pathetic waste of time."

That was how Tikva Unger expressed it to Frieda Mendelssohn. Naturally, the good doctor did not believe a word. Nevertheless, on the remote possibility that there was a speck of truth in what Tikva said, Frieda Mendelssohn set about penetrating, in her own style, the impenetrable heart of the religious world. On those long evenings of the summer of her daughter's sorrow, she, like Tikva, pushed Ivriya's wheelchair up the slope of Yehezkel Street to Sabbath Square. There she parked and confidently awaited the nightly display. She was always rewarded, on certain evenings more handsomely than on others. Even on a relatively quiet night, she could always count on a small band of scraggly-bearded yeshiva youths roaming the streets, looking for action. Suddenly they would draw fistfuls of rocks out of the capacious pockets of their black jackets, hurl them at a secular-looking object or person, or, if luck was with them, at a passing soldier or policeman. "Nazis! Nazis!" they would scream. Then they would bolt into flight, through the winding alleyways, into the sanctuaries of their study halls. Even such minor outbursts provided useful viewing for Frieda Mendelssohn. Occasionally a group of very young boys would try to stir up some excitement in this fashion, too, crying "Nazis! Nazis! Gestapo!" in their poignant, high-pitched trebles. These children Dr. Mendelssohn scrutinized with particular attention.

But the most potentially rewarding nights of all were those on which the organized demonstrations were held, drawing thousands upon thousands of black-garbed men and boys into the center of Sabbath Square, while, on the shadowy sidelines, their women clustered in support. What they were protesting so searingly did not make any difference at all to Frieda Mendelssohn, whether it was abortions or autopsies, public pools in which men and women splashed around side by side, Sabbath desecrations, archaeological excavations that threatened to tamper with Jewish graves, or whatever. None of this mattered now to Frieda Mendelssohn, even the issue of autopsies, which had once been her own fiery cause. For Dr. Frieda Mendelssohn, these mammoth gatherings represented golden opportunities to find the child. Here were all the suspects, all the specimens, in a single place at a single time. It was like a gross magnification of a police lineup for her benefit; the criminal was surely there, and it was up to her to point the finger. They had all come out of their holes for her sake alone, she was convinced; he, her child's innocent child, had to be there among them. Pushing Ivriya in the wheelchair in front of her, Dr. Frieda Mendelssohn plowed through the dark throng. "Make way, fanatics!" she cried. Miraculously, the men and boys pressed against one another, giving a wide berth to the two possessed women. Perhaps it was the authority in Frieda Mendelssohn's demeanor, the imperiousness of her voice as she cried "Fanatics, make way!" Perhaps it was the emaciated crippled woman in the wheelchair calling "Akiva! Akiva! Akiva! Akiva!" In any case, the only curse word flung at them was an occasional "Women! Women!," and only seldom would the two seekers be struck by a spray of pebbles—and these, as it happened, would invariably be cast by the youngest children, who were always the greatest extremists. Frieda Mendelssohn would stare at these children with great interest. Perhaps Akiva was struggling, in such a clumsy way, to make contact.

Only a very rare person could have split this black sea and passed through unmolested as Frieda Mendelssohn did night after night, calling "Fanatics, make way!" and accurately piloting her crippled, Akiva-wailing daughter. For Frieda Mendelssohn was a woman of extraordinary will and determination. Even Samuel Himmelhoch, in his day, had grudgingly conceded this: "If only her power were harnessed to heaven," Himmelhoch used to say, *"gevalt,* what a force she could be!" But on that night when pandemonium broke loose, when stones crossed one another in the sky and tear-gas canisters burst open, even the mighty Frieda Mendelssohn was almost swept away. Had she not been close to the edge of the mob when the violence erupted, she, and especially her low-seated daughter, would certainly have been trampled and crushed to death. As it was, she lost a shoe while scrambling for shelter, and the glasses Ivriya was wearing, which actually belonged to Tikva Unger, were knocked off by a winged elbow and smashed by a stampeding boot. "Pogrom!" blared the local newspapers of the ultra-Orthodox community the next morning. And their pages were filled with photographs of "righteous" women, their faces blanked out for modesty's sake, their stolid bodies being ruthlessly beaten by the clubs of the "Gestapo" Zionist police. But on the front page of every secular daily across the land, the report of the confrontation between the zealots and the Israeli police was accompanied by a single photograph: It was Sora Katz Marom—she, too, had been there, after all—her head swathed in her black shawl, her pale eyes staring directly into the lens of the camera. In the middle of her forehead was a perfectly circular wound about the size of a nail head. From this wound blood was dripping in fat drops—you could clearly make out the distinct drops. The separate drops of blood were dripping in a straight row down the center of her face, and were collecting in her right palm, which she held outstretched from her chin, like a dish to receive them. In the caption Sora Katz Marom was quoted: "This is not blood," were the inscrutable words attributed to Sora Marom; "this is not blood," she said. "It is scented oil."

After that night, Dr. Frieda Mendelssohn and her invalid daughter never appeared again at a demonstration. It had been a foolish idea after all, uncharacteristically optimistic for a woman who, in her daily work as a pathologist, rummaged in vain among human organs for the empty pocket out of which a soul might have slipped, a woman who every day witnessed at first hand life's paltriness and lack of consequence. How ingenuous it had been of her to expect to find Akiva in these black crowds, even when they numbered one hundred thousand. "And pretty soon, God willing, the whole land will be filled with people who look like us," she had heard a flamboyantly bearded protester complacently declare, "with a few secular ghettos scattered about here and there." How had these lambs suddenly turned so militant? But only against their fellow Jews did they dare to raise their fiery fists, these ashen, effete religious maniacs, pouring venom and the curses of heaven, to which they presumed they had a direct line, heaping rancor upon the uncovered heads of their robust Israeli brothers

231

who risked life and limb to defend the dim study halls. And they, these pallid yeshiva boys, these parasites, were just too holy, just too, too precious to serve! During that summer of sorrow, while she lived with her daughter in streets packed with driven Jews rushing about like black bugs, Frieda Mendelssohn found it necessary, again and again, to check the loathing that welled up inside of her, for she felt herself becoming, in her heart, an exterminator, a Nazi, in grim fulfillment of the shocking epithet the zealots had hurled at the Zionists.

In the month of Elul, Ivriya Himmelhoch entered into a fast of speech, letting no utterance except prayer out of her mouth. She sat in her darkened room and wasted away in silence and prayer. From Frieda Mendelssohn's point of view, the sole peculiar advantage of this new development was that Ivriya could make no protest. Whatever Dr. Mendelssohn put into her daughter's mouth, she swallowed. Passively she allowed herself to be tended, to be washed, to be dressed, to be taken out for a walk in the fresh air. Then one day Ivriya handed her mother a note in which she requested to be brought to the Western Wall. This was only the second time since Frieda Mendelssohn's arrival that Ivriya had expressed a desire of any sort. The other time was when she had asked her mother to leave.

They went to the Western Wall every day at dusk, except Fridays and Saturdays. For the grand Dr. Frieda Mendelssohn, the wide gates leading to the stone plaza were thrown open by the military guards, and she drove through in her scarlet Mercedes, coming to a halt between the palm tree and the washbasin. There they were always greeted by the outstretched hand of the beggar Frum-Frumie in her ragged green dress. Ivriya tugged at her mother's skirt. Frieda Mendelssohn snapped open her pocketbook, took out some coins and some crumpled bills, and gave them to the beggar. For this they were rewarded with a shrill blast from Frum-Frumie's shofar. "One day that loony will puncture my eardrum," said Dr. Mendelssohn, "but if my little girl wants me to give, I give. Wanting is a sign of life." Then Ivriya separated from her mother and rolled her chair directly up to the Wall. There she remained until dark, her forehead pressed against the throbbing stones. In the cool night, she never noticed when her mother drew near to lay a shawl across her haggard shoulders.

One evening Ivriya Himmelhoch brought along a pencil and a piece of paper. She leaned on the arm of her wheelchair and wrote her petition. Then she folded it until it was very small and stuffed it into a crevice between the great stones, among thousands of similar bits of paper. She wrote: "Into this cranny Ivriya bat Frieda inserts herself. From the straits she cries out to You. She begs You to answer her, in the breadth of Your generosity. Ivriya bat Frieda is asking for pity: pity her, pity her. Oh, pity me!"

Two days later she received the following message by the regular post:

To the Widow, Ivriya bat Frieda, Greetings!

This is in response to your letter of 25 Elul, which was forwarded to me. Regarding your appeal from the "straits," I regret to observe that you have failed to keep in mind the noble words of the holy Rav Nahman, that the entire world is an exceedingly narrow bridge, and the essential thing is not to be afraid. Nevertheless, your request for pity is hereby granted. Try to put it to good use.

Be comforted, Mother Ivriya! The child Akiva ben Shmuel has been to the sacred grave in Uman, where correction was administered, and he has returned. The image of his mother was always before his eyes, for Penance is called Mother. I'm sorry to report that the holy grave of Rav Nahman in Uman is a painful sight to behold, God spare us, for it has been neglected, desecrated, and defiled: it has become, you should excuse me, the repository of human and animal wastes—in short, a toilet. But whereas this spectacle of desolation evoked my uncontrollable weeping, the boy Akiva ben Shmuel laughed; moreover, he opened his trousers and contributed his donation to the facilities. Just as I was about to punish him for what I perceived as his irreverence, I was struck by the similarity between Akiva ben Shmuel's laughter, and the laughter of his namesake, the matchless Rabbi Akiva, when he walked among the ruins of the Temple Mount and viewed foxes emerging from the Holy of Holies. His companions, Rabban Gamaliel, Rabbi Eleazer ben Azariah, and Rabbi Joshua, wept at the sight, just as I wept at Uman, but Rabbi Akiva was merry, for in the destruction he was witnessing he recognized the fulfillment of the first stage of the prophecy, and this, in turn, signified the imminent realization of the second phase, the rebuilding of the holy city of Jerusalem. And just as the rabbis said then to Rabbi Akiva of old, 'Akiva, you have comforted us,' so, too, did I say, to the young Akiva ben Shmuel, 'My son, you have comforted me.'

And I say to you, Ivriya bat Frieda, that the Uman period is over. The time for weeping and mourning, for crying out for pity in every shop in town, is passed. Now is the hour for deep and genuine laughter. Now is the time to turn our eyes to the mountaintop, to restore our holy places, to rebuild our altar, once again to offer up our fragrant sacrifices upon it. The utter debasement of Uman signifies the coming elevation of the Temple upon Mount Moriah. By adding to that debasement, the child Akiva ben Shmuel was hastening the redemption, for which we must all do more than yearn—we must toil, we must fight! So cease your weeping, Mother Rachel, let your tears flow no more. Your hopes will be fulfilled. Your children will return.

It happened before sunrise in the month of Tishrei, on the second day of the New Year. A man and a boy walked in the Moslem graveyard to the east of the Old City of Jerusalem, alongside the sealed Golden Gate, barred until the coming of the Messiah. In the semidarkness that preceded the dawn, it was impossible to make out their faces. The man was wearing a tall hat and a long robe of some shadowy color, not white. A darker, apronlike garment was placed on top of this robe; suspended across his breast was a rectangular object fashioned of a stiffer substance. In the stillness of that hour the tinkling of little bells could be heard as the man walked among the gravestones beside the boy. The boy was dressed in a striped robe of a glossy material, and a full skullcap was on his head. Strapped to the boy's back was a great bundle of sticks. The man was carrying a torch that now and then cast a flickering light across the wide blade of a knife, which he was also carrying. At one point, as they trampled through the cemetery, the man could be observed inclining his head to listen to the boy, who pointed to the torch in the man's hand and to the bundle of wood on his own back, and then made a questioning gesture by lifting his shoulders and spreading his hands out, palms upward, looking around in several directions as if he were searching for something. The man replied by raising his head to the dark-gray sky and beckoning heavenward with his hand, uttering words that could not be heard from afar.

The man and the boy continued to walk in a southerly direction along the eastern expanse of the wall. They stopped a short distance from the southeastern corner. The man plunged the knife he was carrying into the belt of his robe, whose color, in the intensifying light from the east, could now be discerned as blue. He pulled a rope out from under his apronlike garment, and flung it upward against the wall until it caught onto a sturdy protruding shrub. He tugged down on the rope to check its fastness. Then the man passed the torch to the boy and squatted down. The boy mounted the man's back. His legs gripped the man tightly around the waist; his right arm hung down over the man's shoulder, the fingers digging into the flesh under the hard, glittering object that was suspended across the man's breast. The boy's left arm, in which he carried the lighted torch, was extended outward like a wing, away from the man, away from himself, far from the bundle of dry sticks on his back. Dexterously, with the boy clinging to his back, the man scaled the rough stones of the eastern wall, using the rope to assist him in the ascent. The man and the boy descended upon the plateau of the Temple Mount, in a landscaped area of trees and gardens.

The man drew up the rope and reclaimed the torch from the boy's hand. Once again they walked, the man gathering stones as they advanced. Here and there unarmed Moslem guards slept, their mouths open. If they were being observed, this man and this boy, it could only be from above. They climbed the steps toward the Dome of the Rock. The man tried the main door of the mosque with a gesture that indicated his sense of the futility of the attempt. Naturally, the door was locked. The man set down the torch. Within this lavish, golden-capped structure was housed the Rock of the Foundation, upon which Arauna the Jebusite had had his threshing floor, which King David purchased for fifty shekels of silver to build there an altar to God. Therefore, the rock belonged to David's people. It was bitter, indeed, to be prevented by strangers from approaching this rock, lawfully acquired in commerce on the open market. Nevertheless, the man set to work as close as possible to the mosque containing the rock, heaping up the stones he had collected, gathering more until he was satisfied, erecting a mound of suitable proportions. He removed the bundle of wood from the boy's back and arranged the sticks on top of the stone mound he had constructed. Then he bound the boy with the rope he had used to scale the wall. He placed the boy on the mound of stones, over the bed of sticks. The man thrust his hand under his outer garment and drew the knife from his belt. He raised the knife to slaughter the boy. Beams of sunlight from the east illuminated the knife's broad steel blade.

Crying words—"Don't lay a hand on that boy! Don't do a thing to him!"—two Israeli soldiers pulled the man down from behind, loosening his grip on the slaughter knife, which rattled to the ground. Scores of soldiers pressed around the imprisoned man and the bound boy, forming a multitiered phalanx, pointing weapons at the Arabs now stirring in a restless fury on the perimeter. "God sees!" the pinioned man was heard to call out. "Now I see that God sees!" From the direction of the Western Wall, below the mosque compound, came a series of long and

237

sustained shofar blasts. "And there's the ram!" the man cried rapturously. His face was so radiant with ecstasy, it was nearly too bright to gaze upon. The sun had risen fully. In her nearby hovel, Frum-Frumie, the beggar from the Wall, had been awakened by the commotion atop the Temple Mount. She awoke with the clear certainty of impending joy. Quickly she dressed herself completely in white, in the white dress she had been saving for this day, and she dressed the beggar Yisrael Gamzu in a long white shirt, too. She set the bottomless beggar Yisrael Gamzu into his wheelbarrow and rolled him down to the Western Wall, skipping, dancing, running all the way. Yisrael Gamzu sang and waved a bottle of brandy. As they drew closer to the Wall, closer to becoming the very first to greet the inexpressible joy, the noise from the top of the Temple Mount became louder, sharper, more and more unmistakable. Frum-Frumie raised her shofar to her lips and blew one jubilant blast after another. The message from Mount Moriah was clear: the Messiah had finally come.

Why is the account of the binding of Isaac followed in the Bible by the report of Sarah's death? That question is asked by Rashi, the lucid and diligent medieval commentator. Rashi answers that when the messenger hastened to Sarah's side with the story that her son was about to be slaughtered, the mother's soul burst out of her and she perished. Her soul did not tarry to hear the end—that the boy had been spared. And, really, had the boy been spared after all? Of the four matriarchs, Sarah alone is counted among the seven female prophets of Israel. In the flash of vision, she saw that, though the boy might have survived, he surely had not been spared. And, earlier, when a

238

laugh burst out of her at the revelation that she, a woman of ninety, would bear a child, it was not from intellectual arrogance or common skepticism that she had laughed; riding the keen edge of prophecy, she had seen that the child she would bear would not be hers at all; no, as soon as this child was weaned, the moment she released the child, he would be claimed by his father, by his faith-driven father, Abraham, who, with dazzling alacrity—without even the hesitation he would display when it was time for the concubine's son, Ishmael, to be driven out—without wavering for an instant, her Abraham would heed the voice of his God and set out to the land of the Moriah with the boy at his side, to offer him up, his son, his only one, his beloved, in sacrifice.

The child that was returned to Ivriya Himmelhoch was not the same as the one she had lost, nor was she the same woman who had lost the child. That child had been sacrificed, and that woman's soul had burst out of her and surrendered.

Ivriya, like Sarah the prophetess, had once scarcely believed that she, a woman as heavy and as inert as stone from her waist down, would ever give birth to a child. Then, for nearly three full years, she had nursed him at the breast. Afterward, without hesitation, she had sacrificed him to his father, to be shaven and prepared at the tomb in Meron. In a chamber at Meron this father had begun the journal that now rested ignominiously among the rubble and debris of what had once been Uman House, flattened by army bulldozers following the near disaster on top of the Temple Mount. When the boy was given over to his father, he was three years old; his upper lip was still stamped with the teardrop indentation, the mark of a sucking child. With her milk his mother had branded him.

Now, every Monday night, Ivriya Himmelhoch transported

herself to the narrow, winding alleyway they call the Street of the Righteous, where she sat in her wheelchair with her pitcher in her lap and waited for the milk truck to come down from Ramot. She waited in a corner, an emphatic distance from a small cluster of men, women, and children who were also waiting; these were the representatives of the purest and most aristocratic families of Mea Shearim, and they shunned her as a penitent defiled by other worlds, visibly cursed for her sins. At ten o'clock every Monday night the milk truck arrived. The driver was an old man with a majestic beard, like Abba Nissim's. Up in Ramot, by the tomb of Nebi Samwil, he listened attentively to the melody of each blade of grass that went into his cows, and the milk he gently drew out of them at the proper time was the sweet song, the combination of all the individual melodies. From two great metal cans he ladled this milk into the pitchers that were held out to be filled, first into the vessels of the men, then those of the women, the children, the damaged, and the tainted.

At home Ivriya boiled the milk and covered it with a clean square of white muslin. In the morning she poured some of the milk into a glass and placed it on the table in front of the child. She cut a thick slice of bread and spread it with translucent honey. She rolled her wheelchair up to the table, set her elbows on top, and rested her chin in the sling of her palms. Not for one second did she take her eyes off the child as he ate the bread and the honey and drank the milk. This was mother food. Each time the child drew the mother food away from his face, the down above his upper lip was filmed in white, and his breath dripped sweetness. Flowing with milk and with honey. For the sake of this milk and this honey, you must speak no ill of the land, and of its inhabitants say no unkind word.

Temple Israel

Minneapolis, Minnesota

IN HONOR OF THE BIRTHDAY OF
NANCY SHILLER
BY
DEBORAH COOK